Advance Praise for *Be*

"Tristan is a hottie, tattooed man w̶̶̶̶̶̶̶̶ ̶̶̶̶̶̶̶̶ ̶̶̶̶ ̶̶̶̶get
any better than that?!" —*Girls with Books*

"I never expected this book to grab a piece of my heart and not let
go! I am still going through each of the characters and reliving
this book over and over in my mind. Season Vining has found a
fan in me!" —*StarAngels' Reviews*

"Unique, gritty, and heartbreaking . . . you will not be disappointed. It was a fabulous read that kept me on the edge of my
seat, and left me in tears." —*Allison J's Book Blog*

"Sure to get your pulse racing . . . one hell of a ride."
—*Just Romantic Suspense*

"Dark, twisted, and full of surprises. It's completely engrossing.
This is a fantastic debut from Season Vining and I'm very much
looking forward to what she comes up with next."
—*Sinfully Sexy Book Reviews*

"I loved the dark, intense tone and the suspenseful plot. It stands
out in its uniqueness and I applaud Season for doing something
different." —*Lilybloombooks*

"Oh my gosh, oh my gosh! All I can say is oh my gosh!!! *Beautiful
Addictions* blew me the hell away. This is a love story that will
take your breath away." —*Nicole's Sizzling Page*

"An entertaining read in which the characters' development and
the arc of the story are deftly blended to create a wonderful unity.

Without a doubt I will be scouring the shelves for more works by Season Vining."   —*New Adult Addiction*

"Both sweet and sensual, a new adult romance with a backdrop of darkness and heartbreak."
                                        —*The Window Seat on a Rainy Day*

"This book completely sucked me in. I can't wait to see what this author has in store for her next book."   —*Swoon Worthy Books*

"An amazing debut novel. I'll be watching Season Vining closely from now on."   —MCG *Reviews and Rants*

BEAUTIFUL
Addictions

SEASON VINING

ST. MARTIN'S GRIFFIN ⚓ NEW YORK

BEAUTIFUL ADDICTIONS. Copyright © 2014 by Season Vining. All rights reserved. Printed in the United States of America. For information, address St. Martin's Press, 175 Fifth Avenue, New York, N.Y. 10010.

www.stmartins.com

Designed by Anna Gorovoy

Library of Congress Cataloging-in-Publication Data

Vining, Season.
   Beautiful addictions / Season Vining.
      pages cm
  ISBN 978-1-250-04878-3 (trade paperback)
  ISBN 978-1-4668-4985-3 (e-book)
  1. Addicts—Fiction. 2. Abused women—Fiction. 3. First loves—Fiction. 4. Organized crime—Fiction. 5. Attempted murder—Fiction. 6. San Diego (Calif.)—Fiction. I. Title.
  PS3622.I57B43 2014
  813'.6—dc23

                         2014000135

Previously published in e-book format by St. Martin's Griffin in January 2014.

St. Martin's Griffin books may be purchased for educational, business, or promotional use. For information on bulk purchases, please contact Macmillan Corporate and Premium Sales Department at 1-800-221-7945, extension 5442, or write specialmarkets@macmillan.com.

First St. Martin's Griffin Paperback Edition: June 2014

10 9 8 7 6 5 4 3 2

FOR DANIELLE,
MY BIGGEST CHEERLEADER,
WHO TALKS ME OFF LEDGES AND TABLETOPS,
INDULGES MY OBSESSION WITH TATTOOED BOYS,
AND KILLS ALL THE BUGS

ACKNOWLEDGMENTS

Thank you to Danielle and Chap, who endured many evenings listening to the click-clack melody of a MacBook keyboard. Thanks to Becca, who, through three different colored fonts in a shared Google document, helped with the mapping of this wild ride. To the readers, especially Bridget and Ricky, who endured the first, second, and third drafts of this manuscript, I apologize and thank you. From coast to coast, much love to my Fuckery Book Club girls—defenders, motivators, and pimps extraordinaire. Gracias to Jerry, my official Spanish Mexican Slang Consultant. To the watchers of the Internet, thanks for not putting me on a high-profile list somewhere for the things I research.

A special thank-you to the two ladies that I met in the swamp, where we toasted a beautiful sunset and drank wine off the library's reference cart. Rose, who fell in love with this story from the very first page, and whose enthusiasm and editing eye made it better with each pencil mark. And Rachel, my cape-wearing, fine-print-reading, top-notch-negotiating, corgi-loving, voice of reason and pusher of all things me.

Lastly, I'd like to recognize all artists, whether they express themselves through the written word, enamel paints, or inked skin; anyone fighting the demons of addiction, who had the strength and will to overcome; and those who were once victims, but refuse to wear that label, you are all an inspiration.

EVERYONE IS A MOON AND HAS A DARK SIDE
WHICH HE NEVER SHOWS TO ANYBODY.

—MARK TWAIN

1. CONJUNCTION
TWO PLANETS IN CLOSE PROXIMITY
TO EACH OTHER IN THE SKY.

"Hey, babe, hand me my smokes."

"I'm not your babe," Josie replied.

"Fine. Hey, bitch, hand me my smokes."

She laughed darkly and complied with his request. One-night stands were not afforded the privileges of pet names. Contrarily, the neatly arranged rails of white powder on the tray across the room meant he could call her anything he damn well pleased.

As the stranger lit a cigarette, Josie sat up and stretched her arms over her head. The air reeked of sweat, sex, and tobacco. The humming fan that helped lull her to sleep a few hours ago now got on her last sober nerve.

Spotting her underwear across the room, Josie slid from between the sheets and retrieved it. She slipped on each article of clothing as she found it, eventually donning her outfit from the previous night. The young man's eyes followed her around, seeming amused by her hunt-and-gather technique.

"You were amazing," he said.

His voice rasped like he had cotton and sawdust in his throat. The way his slate blue eyes shined, she could see all his lust. She had no interest in dwelling there.

Josie ignored him and leaned over the tray, holding the rolled-up dollar bill to her nose. She closed her eyes and smiled as she inhaled the drug, knowing that numbing bliss would soon find her. With a final sniff, she stood and let the chemical absorb into her blood. It was soft feathers across her skin, drifting down from the sky and landing around her toes. Her body tensed and prickled with the warmth of a prolonged orgasm. In this high, she had no name, no past, and no future. All she had was now. And now was amazing.

"Can I get your number? Sam Bradley is playing the Casbah on Wednesday. My boy could get us in for free."

His words punched holes in her buzz. Irritated, she slung her bag across her body and pasted on a smile. The morning light peeked through the vertical blinds, casting stripes of gold across his body. He smiled and she could feel his desire for her again. To Josie, he was just a guy—a guy with a warm bed, pleasurable hands, and a large supply of coke.

"It was fun. Let's just leave it at that."

She spun on her heel and headed for the door.

"Yeah, whatever. I'll see you around," he shouted.

"Not likely," she answered, stepping out into the blinding light of another morning after.

☾

Josie sat back in the dark corner of the familiar bar. Graffiti-riddled walls and empty chairs were her only company. A journal lay open in her lap while her charcoal-stained fingers clutched the pencil hovering above the page. Hundreds of words flashed through her mind, yet she did not possess the will to choose one and write it down. The first word of a sentence, the precipice of an idea, usually held all the power as far as she was concerned. This is why, most nights, she kept to sketching—the curved lines and shading smudges were easier to commit to.

Most bar patrons took no notice of her. They were too busy, focused on their immediate goals of sex and intoxication. Josie's intentions were the same as every other night spent in this establishment. She'd come to see about a boy.

Routine was not something she was accustomed to, though lately she'd been devoted to him. She always arrived an hour before his shift started and slipped out when he took his last break. She'd convinced herself that her obsession was normal.

With glossy eyes, she glanced up from her blank paper, awaiting the arrival of her muse. She sighed and blew her bangs from her eyes, wishing she'd smoked a bowl before coming here, something to take off the razor-sharp edge.

Since she was fourteen years old, Josie Banks had existed this way. She floated on whatever high she could get, reluctant to touch down, afraid reality might never let her go again. There wasn't a physical addiction to the drugs. She never used one long enough to develop a taste for it. The addiction was solely to the state it provided, a numbing blissful high of indifference. Her savior wasn't always drugs or sex with strangers. Sometimes her pencils, along with fresh paper and a silent room, could deliver the much-needed feeling of ecstasy. The rough scratch of charcoal or the shake and rattle of paint cans calmed her in a way that no therapist ever had.

"Hello."

Josie looked up to find a stranger staring down at her. He seemed to stand at the edge of her personal space while wearing a brittle smile. She did not respond but impatiently waited for his next line. It was delivered like a rehearsed speech.

"You're too pretty to sit alone. Can I join you?"

Her silence answered. The man turned swiftly and retreated to where he came from. Josie didn't watch him go. In any other place, at any other time, she would have entertained the idea. He was tall and handsome and she loved how nervous she made him. But not here.

Plenty of charmers had told her that she was attractive, but she always dismissed their words as a systematic technique to get into her pants. If only they'd known she didn't need to be seduced. She gave it up freely and often. Shame did not exist in her bank of emotional labels; it had no place in the life she led. Fucking was always enjoyable. Even bad sex was still sex. Ever since she'd lost her virginity, she'd felt empowered by her feminine allure. No man or woman, no matter how attractive, had ever held her attention for longer than it had taken to get off.

Until him.

She leaned back in her seat, curling her fingers around the nearly empty glass, and thought back to their first and only encounter.

Clouds stretched across the moon, stealing her natural light. Josie settled herself on the fire escape, drawing by the glow from her apartment window. Dirt and dust on the glass cast a freckled pattern over her. Haunting eyes stared up from the page as she tried to recall a connection to them.

A hooded figure stormed into the alley below, catching her attention. The lead of her pencil ceased in its track, its intended path abandoned. His dark garments blended into the shadows as if she could smudge him out of one of her drawings.

"Fool!" he shouted. His voice rolled up the alley walls until being freed into the sky like thunder.

He pushed the hood back, his nails scraping through dirty hair. It wove through his fingers, staying upturned in a veritable crown of thorns. Heavy footsteps counted off his rhythm as Josie watched him rage.

"Unforgivable," he said. He tried it again, repeating the quiet chant over and over until it mirrored the beat of Josie's pulse.

She gasped as he ripped off his hooded sweatshirt and threw it to the ground. Brilliant inked images covered his arms, interrupted only by the white beater that molded to his body. He slammed his forehead into the wall and then landed punch after punch. His blood painted the bricks and Josie knew a part of him would die here this night.

She sat stone-faced, her gaze fixed on the raging figure below. She was envious of such a physical kind of anger. She had never unleashed her fury that way and wondered if it would do any good. His chest heaved in a quick cadence, and Josie fought hard to keep her own breath even.

In that moment, the moon broke through the clouds and cast a blanket of silvery light over the alley. He froze, mesmerized by the grid-pattern shadows created by the fire escape. His eyes traveled up the shadow as if navigating a labyrinth, until a small, solid shape obstructed the path. He looked up, catching her.

The pencil slipped from Josie's grip, rolling and falling over the edge. As connected as she felt to the lead and wood, she did not watch it drop. Instead, she stared down into the face of something so familiar—heartache. She'd never seen such a beautiful, broken expression, and it took her breath away. Somewhere in the back of her mind, she registered the soft *tap, tap, tap* of the pencil hitting the ground.

Josie felt bound to him in that moment. They were two souls

snared by chance and circumstance. Though they did not feel like strangers.

She wanted more, but she didn't know what. It tugged at her like the undeniable pull of the moon. She couldn't name it, but she craved it like her drugs and her art.

A siren wailed from somewhere down the block and they both blinked, released from each other in a defeated kind of way. He turned away slowly. Josie leaned forward against the railing as he disappeared back into the dotted path of streetlamps.

When he was gone, she raced down the steps of her building and retrieved his abandoned hoodie from the alley. Josie wrapped herself in the black cotton and, for the first time in years, slept through the night. Almost every day since, she'd worn the over-size article, growing attached to it as if it were a long-lost friend.

"You need another drink?" the waitress asked. Josie made eye contact with the girl and nodded. "Another rum and Coke and no conversation. Coming right up, hon."

She smirked when the waitress left to fetch her drink. Alone again, Josie began sketching a couple making out against the bar. The woman was standing, squeezed between the man's thighs, while his hand gripped her waist. Their faces pressed together in heated kisses and whispered words. Their display garnered the attention of everyone in the place before the waitress tapped the bar and told them to take it elsewhere. Josie couldn't care less. Her boy had arrived.

He took his place behind the bar after a smile and a wave to the waitress. He looked good there, backlit by mirrors, lavender lights, and half-empty bottles. Gone was her tortured boy from the alley. This version was sexy and confident.

It was pure luck that she'd found him here, tending bar at this yuppie establishment. Josie had come in one night, looking for a release of any kind, when she'd spotted him. She recognized his tattoos, and when he turned, she remembered his flawless face as well, even after six months. The images had been burned into her memory on a cellular level. It hadn't taken long to learn his schedule, and soon she saw him four nights a week. But he never saw her.

Josie wanted him. The one-night stands that left her feeling coveted but isolated were no longer satisfying. She wanted to taste his lips and trace the patterns on his skin. She wanted to live in his clothes and feel the weight of his body on hers. Their relationship was complicated, existing only through one-way glass and never shared. Josie liked it this way. She felt anchored to him but not possessed.

Tristan Fallbrook was complicated and just barely a man. At the ripe old age of twenty-two, he'd suffered heartache, seen his fair share of violence, and thrived as a professional criminal. His life could rival that of a drafted wartime soldier, including battle scars and haunting memories.

None of this was planned. His life should be different. Yet here he was, living in a new place, facing a new direction that still felt faulty. All of his knowledge, through personal experience and countless books, could not help him. Tristan was alone and trapped in the foreign city, with only a 9mm and an addiction to literature to save him. Night after night, he tucked away his one-hundred-thirty-seven-point IQ and stood behind the bar, wearing his inked armor and crooked smile.

"Looks like Bundy is back," Erin said, sliding her tray onto the bar. "Same as always, rum and Coke."

"You got it," Tristan answered. "Why do you guys call her that?"

"Because she's really pretty and really weird, in a serial killer kind of way. She never comes in here with anyone. She never leaves with anyone. She just sits in that corner, sipping her drink and scribbling in her notebook. Sometimes she draws pictures on the napkins. I feel like she's leaving them for me on purpose. Like it's some kind of clue I'm supposed to decipher."

Tristan placed the drink on the tray and shrugged.

"Maybe she's just shy, Nancy Drew. Did you know Picasso and Warhol both had the habit of sketching on napkins?"

"So what are you saying? I should be saving them? She'll be famous and I'll be rich?"

"Maybe. What's she drawing, anyway?"

"Usually faces of people in the bar. There's a sketch of me on the wall in booth twelve. Some of her finest work, I'd say." Tristan smiled, amused at Erin's confidence. "Whatever she is, she definitely needs some wardrobe help. You should see the ratty old sweatshirt she wears all the time. My bet is serial killer. That pretty face could lure you chumps in, no problem."

Reaching his quota for small talk, Tristan gave her a grin and sent her on her way. He rested against the shelf of smartly lined bottles and considered the behavior of Bundy. He didn't see anything wrong with someone wanting to be alone with her poison and her thoughts. He wasn't so sure what solidified her status as a freak. Many nights, Tristan had found himself half deep into a fifth of whiskey while venting frustrations to strangers. Vagrants, fellow employees, even customers had been subjected to drunken rants of pipe dreams. Some offered advice, some only listened. He soon learned that talking about it never mattered. His life's course seemed to be fixed.

Tristan watched Erin deliver the drink. He forced himself to focus on Bundy, his curiosity piqued. She was shrouded in shadows and he could make out nothing but a faint silhouette. He recognized the intent of her posture and placement. Her hiding was intentional.

Josie did not look up as her new drink was dropped off, her mind preoccupied by the presence of him. The smell of the waitress's flowery perfume brought forth an angry memory she quickly expelled. Then she wondered what he would smell like. His scent and her memory of it had faded from the hooded sweatshirt.

Would he smell of heavy colognes and aftershaves or just a simple combination of soap and cigarettes? She scolded herself, knowing that her fascination with this man was unreasonable. She had no right to want him the way she did.

Josie knew the name the bar staff had branded her with: Bundy. She'd overheard two of the waitresses talking on their break. They hadn't seen Josie there as they chatted about her weirdness and state of dress. She hadn't been the subject of their conversation for long, though, easily dismissed as in every other aspect of her life. Her eagerness to simply be in his presence outweighed any humiliation she'd had to endure.

Suddenly, Josie felt a burning fire on her face, a pull from across the room. She glanced up to see his eyes on her. He was looking, really looking. Even though she knew he couldn't see much, she felt as though she were being dissected in front of a crowd of spectators.

After weeks of her veiled presence, he'd finally taken notice. His muscled forearms leaned on the bar and his gaze stayed fixed. Sure, she wanted him, but on her terms. She wasn't ready. He wasn't another man to be conquered and forgotten. He was different. Josie felt smothered with the need to escape.

Spying no movement from her corner, Tristan finally dropped his eyes back to the bar, liberating his subject. He knew she was a creature of habit and wouldn't be leaving anytime soon. He would wait her out.

An hour passed, steady and unhurried, neither one of the players giving up on the waiting game. By midnight, Tristan couldn't take it anymore and needed to step out for a smoke. He let his coworker know and headed out the side door. The alley welcomed him with quiet darkness.

When he was out of sight, Josie threw a few bills down, including a generous tip, and packed away her notebook. She slid from the booth, hastily making her way outside. When the rubber soles of her shoes hit the sidewalk, she breathed a little easier. Out here, she could disappear again. Out here, she was anonymous.

Josie turned to make her way home but was met by a familiar form leaning against the building. She sucked in the crisp air, almost choking, as his eyes worked themselves up from her feet. Even after all this time, he recognized her.

"You," he whispered, curls of smoke escaping through his lips.

Tristan dropped his cigarette, crushing it under the toe of his shoe, before shoving his hands deep into his pockets. Before him stood a girl full of secrets and history, and he knew that she was alone in the world. He took two steps toward her, expecting she would retreat. He was wrong.

Josie trembled with some feeling that she didn't recognize. Her head felt light and her legs became shaky under the weight of this moment. He moved closer, his beautiful face contorted in caution. She wasn't afraid. Their long-awaited reunion outweighed any unease. Without thought, Josie lifted her hand toward him, wanting to make sure he was real. She had no doubt that her mind could invent his presence just to mess with her. She slid her fingers along his jaw. It felt like warmed stones and sandpaper. Eventually, Josie rested her palm against his face, and he let her.

Tristan leaned into her touch. Their eyes held firm, locked on each other in a battle for understanding. This bond, this connection was undefined yet all-consuming. In the familiar moonlight, their breathing had become synchronized and the rest of the world fell away. Tristan needed to say something but feared that it would end the fragile moment. He took the chance anyway.

"I'm Tristan."

"Josie," she replied.

A long, silent moment stretched between them. It remained comfortable and reminiscent of reunited lovers. Tristan's brows dipped in confusion as her face morphed into a younger one in his mind, a smiling one. He considered the familiar eyes, measuring them against the dark and guarded ones before him now. Like a forceful blow knocking the breath from his lungs, he connected Josie to the girl who had haunted his memory for the past eight years.

"You look just like a girl I used to know. McKenzi Delaune," Tristan said. "But that's impossible."

Josie, not having heard that name for so long, dropped her hand and looked down at the sidewalk. She didn't associate with that girl anymore, she hadn't for years. Fear clawed at her chest as she wondered how much she should say. Something pulled the confession from her.

"I used to be her," she answered.

"I thought you were dead."

2. OPPOSITION

TWO CELESTIAL BODIES OPPOSITE
EACH OTHER IN THE SKY.

This was Josie's secret, the only truth that anchored her to a forgotten past. Her safety and her sanity deemed that she keep it
locked away. Josie found herself ensnared by his statement: *I
thought you were dead.* She almost laughed at his half-truth. Cat-
egorically, she'd felt dead for years. She'd survived the tedious
clockwork of day-to-day living, physical pain, and emotional
woundings. So many times, especially when she was alone in the
quiet darkness of her existence, Josie had begged to abandon this
life. She wasn't sure if those prayers had gone unheard or simply
unanswered. It no longer mattered, since she'd lost her faith long

ago. These days Josie believed only in things she could see and touch. At this moment, she believed in Tristan.

"I know you," he whispered.

Recognizing her face, not only from months ago, but from years ago, Tristan continued to gape. Her touch was gone now, but his skin prickled with warmth where her hand had been. His brain felt overwhelmed and burdened by the connection. Quickly firing synapses struggled to keep up with his recollection of this woman as a child. So many questions formed lumps in his throat, choking the ability for even one to escape.

"You don't know shit."

Unable to handle the heaviness of the moment any longer, Josie turned to flee. She was too sober to deal with confessions right now. She knew it was cowardly; still, she clutched her messenger bag close as her feet shuffled away. Her retreat was silent. Long ago she'd perfected the art of carrying her bag in such a way that the paint cans didn't rattle. She shifted her eyes down to the sidewalk, divided by lightninglike cracks in its surface. She wished they would swell open and devour her.

"McKenzi! Josie!" Tristan called out. Josie's name, the word she'd been so desperate to hear from his lips, was now tainted by her cowardice.

☾

After McKenzi left him stunned on the sidewalk, Tristan raced inside and hid himself in the restroom. Barraged with conflicting emotions, Tristan gripped the edge of the sink just to stay upright. Sweat formed along his hairline while his pulse thundered in his ears. He felt nauseated and betrayed and relieved all at the same time. Facing his reflection in the mirror, he barely recognized the man staring back. His skin was pallid, drained of heat and blood. His eyes were dilated and unable to focus on one single spot for long. They burned with unshed tears as he bit down on his lips to keep them from trembling. He looked like a sickly version of himself, a stranger. He looked like he'd seen a ghost.

"Hey, man, you okay?" a man asked from behind him. "You don't look so good."

Tristan met the man's eyes in the mirror and tried to focus on his face.

"That's because I'm trying to fight the effects of psychological shock. My blood pressure has dropped, making me feel dizzy. Also"—Tristan stopped and tried to take a deep breath—"my shallow breathing is leaving my body with a lack of oxygen."

The man cocked his head to the side like a dog trying to understand human speech. His eyes became slits as though that would help him comprehend. Tristan dropped his gaze back down to the sink.

"Uh, okay. Well, I'm just going to . . ."

By the time Tristan looked up again, the man was gone. As smart as he was, Tristan's brain was not always successful in navigating social situations.

He was an intellectual conundrum beneath his tough-as-nails veneer, a medical falsehood. His father had called the condition eidetic memory. Remembering had always come easy. There was no effort in regurgitating every detail of a photograph or every word of a novel. Grocery lists, dates and times, even names and faces just seemed to stick with him. It wasn't a skill that he'd mastered after years of training or retaining information using mnemonic devices. It was something he'd been born with. It was part of his genetic makeup, like eye color or curly hair.

When he was old enough, Tristan had researched the term, trying to understand why his brain worked this way. With his nose buried deep in his father's medical journals, he learned that his ability was swarming with controversy; some even regarded it as myth.

"A myth?" he'd cried.

Huddled on his father's lap in the leather office chair, he'd begged to be normal like the other kids.

"Tristan, what you have is not a defect. It is a special ability. You've been blessed. Think of it as being bulletproof or having X-ray vision."

"Like Superman?" he'd asked, wiping the tears from his cheeks.

Dr. Fallbrook smiled down at his son and nodded. In the amber-lit room, lined with shelves of books and family portraits, seven-year-old Tristan beamed as he pictured himself in tights and a billowing cape of recollection.

Eventually, Tristan resumed his post behind the bar, greeted with nothing more than an annoyed glance from his coworker. He used a clean towel to dry the whiskey tumblers, a thoughtless action built into his bartender automation. Tristan poured drinks and opened bottles, but his thoughts were set on McKenzi. From her painted black eyes down to her curves and endless legs, there was no doubt the girl he once knew had become all woman.

"Tristan?" He turned to find Erin staring at him. "I *said* I need a Blue Moon, a vodka tonic, a million dollars, and Ryan Gosling's phone number."

"Sorry," he said. "Coming right up. I can't help with Ryan. But why stop at one million? If you had more money, you'd probably have a better chance of getting that phone number yourself."

"I'd hate to be greedy," Erin answered, winking at him. "But I like how you think."

He smiled and set the drinks on her tray. Once she was gone, Tristan's thoughts returned to Josie.

Tristan combed through every detail, starting with the first time he'd seen her up until the first time he'd seen her again. That night in the dark alley, she'd silently looked on as he raged. She'd watched him bleed and sweat and give himself over to despair. When their eyes had met, he'd felt the familiar force drawing them together but had dismissed it so easily. He understood that pull now and he wondered if she felt it too.

He needed answers. He remembered that she lived in the forty-one hundred block of Iowa Street in an off-white stucco building with green awnings. If he wanted to, he could bang down her door to confront her. But she seemed too skittish for that approach, too scared of her own history.

Tristan sighed and scrubbed at his face with the palms of his hands. He decided not to agonize anymore tonight, as if he could just release himself from her hold. He felt that she would seek him out again, and he would give her anything she wanted.

☾

Dean Moloney sat in the back of the parked car, running his index finger along the stitched seam of the seat. The soft, cool leather slid beneath his touch until the edge of the seat fell away. A teenager flew by on his skateboard, a punk with spiked hair. He reminded Moloney of Terry Sanders in grade school. This kid would endlessly tease him. He would chant "Moloney Boloney" and get all the kids to join in. That was, until Moloney smashed his face with a brick from the schoolyard. Blood ran into Terry's blond spiky hair. It was Moloney's first taste of victory.

The skateboarder's eyes tried to penetrate the dark tint of the car, and Moloney sneered at him through the glass. He knew he couldn't be seen, but it was instinctual. Hate lived inside of him. It circulated through his body and infected every piece of his being. His stare followed the boy as he jumped the loading dock ramp before disappearing down Tchoupitoulas Street.

The building outside Moloney's window looked harmless with uneven patchwork of new and old brick. Its cracked lines and rusted vents told nothing of its ominous innards. This was one of many buildings used to house goods.

His offshore drilling venture was a great cover for importing and exporting through the Gulf of Mexico. Half of his inventory consisted of illegal weapons and drugs, while the other half represented a legit business. This building had been his first acquisition when he took over the organization. It was special to him. Among the cargo boxes and palettes inside sat the most important men of his enterprise. Having them all in one place was risky but, under these circumstances, necessary.

His man, Frank, sat behind the wheel checking the status of employees in attendance.

"Sir, everyone is inside."

Moloney nodded and exited the car alongside his driver. Frank walked two steps behind him, always a villain's shadow. They entered the warehouse and approached the group of men. Moloney took his place at the head of the table and all conversation ceased. He leaned back in his chair and scratched at his neatly trimmed beard. He soaked in the blind admiration of his employees. The feeling of complete control over these men's lives pleased him. The thrill of power supplied the breath in his lungs and the blood-metal taste in his mouth. Moloney would never give this up.

"The Italians are moving in on my ground."

He was a man of short statements and simple ideas. He paused here to emphasize the seriousness of this announcement, letting his glacier blue eyes rake over each man.

Since the beginning of his career, Dean Moloney had been considered small-time. Being raised in an Irish, middle-class suburban home had certainly left him wanting. He had always longed for bigger adventures, wealth, and power. Greed had rooted itself in his heart, and no matter how much he acquired, he always wanted more. In the last decade, he'd been expanding his business and apparently gained the attention of larger operators.

"Gino Gallo is enemy number one," Moloney announced.

The men broke into murmured conversations, their words melded together into anxious white noise.

"They can't come in here and take over!" one man shouted.

"The Italians? Over my dead body!"

"I believe that's the point," Barry said calmly. The older gentleman stood from his seat next to Moloney and buttoned his suit jacket. "Hotheaded threats will not solve anything. We've got to outsmart them and make sure all loose ends are tied up. Leave nothing they could use against us."

Moloney nodded, supporting the underboss's instructions.

"Agreed," he said. "See that all debts are collected, all inventory accounted for."

"Keep an eye open for rats. Gallo will try to steal our business, recruit our men. If you find anyone leaking information, he will be dealt with," Barry said.

"In fact, we've already learned that someone has been feeding Gallo information," Moloney said. "Do any of you have anything to confess?" he asked.

The men looked at each other. Each innocent and accusatory glance between them fueled Moloney's rage. He would not tolerate treason.

"No?" he asked with a finality that felt like one foot in the grave.

In a flash, Barry raised his pistol and shot Kevin Landry in the forehead. The loud bang bounced off the walls of the building and created a wild drumbeat to match every man's pulse. Kevin, though instantly dead, remained upright as if still in attendance.

Moloney sneered. He felt himself grow stronger from their fear.

His muscles flexed, pulling the fabric around his arms tighter as he adjusted his tented crotch. The power of taking someone's life was the strongest aphrodisiac he'd ever known. His girl was in for it tonight.

With a flip of his hand, Moloney dismissed them. Only Barry and Frank remained. Moloney knew he was lucky to have the allegiance of such men. Frank kept him safe. He had been brought into the business as a teenager to repay a debt. He had stayed because he loved the rewards of his position. Barry, however, was a lifer. He'd worked for the previous boss, and when Moloney took over, Barry had pledged his loyalty. He was Moloney's right hand, his trigger finger, his voice of reason.

"Any news on the girl?" Moloney asked. "Do we know if she's still alive?"

Barry tented his fingers on top of the wood table and squared his large shoulders. Although he wasn't responsible for the messy situation, he felt obligated to fix it.

"Mort is using his most persuasive techniques to retrieve information."

Moloney nodded, satisfied for now. Gino Gallo would be able to use any neglected problems against him, so it was imperative that the girl be eliminated. Finally, these aggravations could be put to rest and he could move on with destroying the Italians.

Josie sat cross-legged on the floor of her apartment among the dust bunnies. Sheets of paper pulled free from their binding lay scattered around her like fallen leaves. She repeated Tristan's name over and over, as if the sound of it would jar her memory into revealing their past. He knew her. He knew her in her former life, the one that had chewed her up and spit her out. She was conflicted as she recognized both the urge to forget him completely and the one to reacquaint herself with everything he was.

A rhombus of light slanted across her floor from the window, blazing yellow-gold. Dust particles floated in and out of the beam, and when Josie moved, they swirled frantically, like a shaken snow globe. She found herself entranced by them, jealous of their carefree and aimless existence.

Tristan, her mind repeated again. She now had a name to go with the seraph's face. She smirked, realizing that the things she wanted to do to him were quite devilish. Josie wanted to explore and conquer that man, like no one before him. She wanted to mark his skin and exchange breaths while whispering sexual promises. Before letting the fantasy run freely, she focused her attention back on her sketch.

There was more now, more than a carnal desire for the taste of his flesh. Josie wanted to memorize him, inside and out. She wanted to dissect the memories he possessed and reenact each one to make them concrete. She wanted to give herself over to Tristan and ask him to mold her into something better than she was. But when had she ever gotten what she wanted?

A pounding sounded against her door. She ignored it. Instead, Josie focused on recreating the needle-made art of Tristan's left shoulder. She glanced at the clear plastic grab bag of pills sitting on her table. They seemed to be calling to her. *Eat me. Feel good. Forget everything.* She sketched the shapes of Tristan's tattoo, filling them with gray. What a disservice to the original art, she thought. They should be red and violet and deep-water blue. She hadn't used color on paper in years. She didn't even own the tools to do so.

The pummeling sounded again, startling her from her drawing. Josie looked at her rattling door, the secured chain swinging from the force. As much as she loved her isolation, she knew she'd have to answer.

Freeing the chain and twisting two dead bolts, Josie swung the door open to find a smiling Alex, dimples on display. His hulking form dwarfed her as he beamed his most charming smile and waited to be invited in. She moved aside and secured the door behind him.

"You know you don't have to lock that when I'm here, Jo. I got you." He winked and flexed his huge arms in her direction.

Josie was not impressed.

Alexander Hernandez was a beast of a man, a giant in reputation and size. He'd been raised in the roughest part of the city, tainted with crime and violence, and he'd never left. This metropolis and its pollutants flowed through his veins, more important to survival than his Hispanic blood. He was a sinner and a mortal, and he knew in the end that meant he'd smolder in the fiery pits of hell. He was okay with that. Acceptance was apparently the key to inner peace.

Alex knew misdeeds and narcotics and only one way of life. He had been in and out of juvenile detention as a teenager, eventually landing in jail for an eight-month stint. There had been no deprogramming and no reform behind those bars. He'd emerged ten times worse than when he'd went in, only his allegiances had changed.

As a young man, he'd held no authority there. However, his loyalty and willingness to do dirty work quickly earned him respect in the ranks. His incarceration was more of a training exercise than a punishment. Lessons that could be taught only by experience were now ingrained. Never trust anyone, never turn your back on the enemy, and never share personal information. One newbie had let his girl's name slip from his lips in casual conversation in the yard. Six weeks later, she was dead. That's the thing about jail, your enemies inside were your enemies outside. A security fence and state-mandated freedom changed nothing.

When Josie moved into the dilapidated building, he'd been surprised that she lived alone. He'd tried to hit on her when they passed in the hall, but his efforts always fell short.

"Hey, *mamacita*. You're new so I'mma help you out. I'm Alex."

"Josie."

"You need anything, come see me."

"Anything?"

He smiled and grabbed onto the door frame above his head, flexing his biceps. His eyes shined with victory.

"Anything."

"Nah. I'm good, thanks," Josie had replied as she retreated to her apartment.

"I bet you are," Alex answered.

Six weeks later, things changed. He'd come straight home after having to teach one of his lackeys a lesson. The man's blood stained his clothes in a speckled pattern and Alex knew his message had been delivered. A few beers later, he'd come down from his adrenaline high. While he was showering, the power had gone out. It wasn't five minutes later that Josie came knocking. Her face, while trying to portray sexual prowess, showed nothing but fear.

"I knew you couldn't resist."

"Shut up," she'd demanded before pushing him inside the apartment.

Shrouded in darkness, he took Josie bent over his kitchen table and again in his bed, never questioning her sudden change of heart. He realized later that she'd done it only to have company during the blackest of nights. She was a girl too afraid to admit fear, opting for security in the arms of a stranger.

Since then, he kept an eye on her as best he could. He installed three locks on her door and insisted that she use them. He brought her food a few times a week; otherwise she'd forget to eat. Recognizing her need for companionship and protection, Alex began to take a more platonic interest in Josie. All the other neighbors insisted that she was bizarre, but he knew better. She was defensive and hurting and completely alone. Perhaps Josie could be his one good deed. Not that she could ever redeem him from a lifetime of wrongdoing. Alex was damned regardless.

Before taking a seat, Alex slid the pistol from his waistband and laid it on the table in front of him. He tossed the paper bag to Josie and assumed his usual position on the sofa, relaxed with legs splayed like a sexual lure. His large form took up her entire couch, but she never minded, keeping to her favorite spot on the floor. He brought her food and stayed until she ate. There was little dialogue, sometimes none at all. It wasn't because she was shy or rude, just uninterested in forced conversation. Though, through all of their time spent together she had told him her story, shared just enough pieces for Alex to fill in the gaps.

"Eat, Josie," he demanded when she sat staring into the blinding light of the open window.

"I'll eat if you bring me some more of that coke. The good stuff. Not the crap you sell."

"I told you I'm not supplying you anymore. Eat. And stop buying this shit."

He gave her a threatening look that said everything in the arch of his eyebrow and purse of his lips. He held up the bag of pills that were so varied in color and shape they looked like candy. She didn't answer or acknowledge his request, insisting that she was an adult and could take care of herself. She'd been doing it for so long now.

Josie knew she'd never win this contest of wills. He would stay until she ate, no matter how long that took. She refocused her attention on the paper, shading the petals of each flower just so.

She liked that Alex didn't feel the need to ask about her well-being. She didn't want to lie to him, but she knew that if asked, she'd give him what he wanted to hear. She'd tell the lie she'd told a thousand times: "I'm fine." Alex looked after her; she didn't understand why. If she had just an ounce of self-preservation, she would thank him.

From what he could gather, Josie's story sounded like one of the tragic mystery programs Alex's mother favored on late afternoons. While she drank her Café Bustelo and prepared dinner, she'd watch the tiny black-and-white television mounted to the kitchen counter. Even through the static, she clung desperately to the sordid lives of the unfortunate men and women. Many days, Alex had come home from school to find his mother cursing in Spanish at the blurry picture. At dinner, she would warn him and his brothers about whatever danger had befallen that day's victims.

"Mrs. Thompson's cat escaped again. Meowed outside my door for two hours. Fucking beast don't know what floor he lives on. *Pendejo*," Alex grumbled.

"I think she trained him to annoy you," Josie said, giving a slight laugh.

Alex had come from a large family, but being the youngest of six boys, he'd never had to play caretaker to anyone or anything. No matter all his pleading, he never had a dog or a cat or even a goldfish. His mother would always say there were enough mouths to feed without adding an ungrateful beast to the mix.

He watched as Josie finally lay down her pencil, retrieved the bag of food, and ate quietly. Alex spun his pistol on the tabletop, a habit that helped him focus. He planned his day, making a list of deliveries to schedule and overdue debts to be collected. Today was going to be either a very profitable day or a very messy day. Alex wasn't sure which one he'd prefer.

"Do you have to do that?" Josie asked, her cheeks swollen with food.

"What?"

Josie pointed to the gun, still spinning after a recent nudge from Alex.

"You know I hate that thing."

Alex rolled his eyes and slammed his hand down over the rotating pistol, abruptly halting its movement. He picked it up, released the clip, and placed it on the table. He waved his hands over the disassembled firearm, wordlessly asking if she was satisfied.

"Whatever," she answered before taking another bite.

Tossing the empty weapon from hand to hand, he smiled.

"Where were you on Wednesday?"

"I went to see him," Josie mumbled.

Alex thought for a second before realizing whom she was referring to.

"You see him all the time, stalker."

"I'm not a stalker, just an interested observer. Besides, this time he saw me too."

Alex turned, checking her face for seriousness.

"You talk to him?"

"His name is Tristan. He remembers me."

"I guess so. Some *metiche* watching him lose his shit in the alley."

"No. He remembers me from New Orleans."

Alex dropped the pistol, letting it clatter to the floor.

"What?"

"Yep," Josie confirmed.

"You gonna see him again?"

Josie nodded, pushing the last of the noodles into her mouth. She knew she didn't have a choice.

"Be careful, Jo."

She nodded again as Alex stood and headed out.

"Lock the door."

Josie followed his instructions, threw away the empty food car-
ton, and resumed her position on the floor, completely ignoring
the plastic bag of pills.

3. MACULA
A DARK SPOT OR POSSIBLE IRREGULARITY.

When he'd taken this job, Mort figured it would be an easy case. Eight years after her disappearance, there had been a rumor that the boys in New York screwed up and McKenzi Delaune was alive. All he had to do was go there and prove that she wasn't. Seemed easy enough at the time.

Mort always found himself in these positions. In the business, he was what's known as a cleaner. He cleaned up other people's messes. No matter what kind of failed objective or botched operation, Mort always came through. Entering the situation objectively, assessing the missteps, and calculating a solution came naturally to him. Whatever was needed, from the simplest task to the downright heinous, he was the man for the job. He always succeeded and did so with a heartless resolve.

Chasing paper trails, bribing officials, and navigating his way through her disappearance had been a great deal of work. Moloney's associates in New York had been useless, cowering behind excuses and fading memories. After learning nothing new, he'd dispatched them quickly, moving on to the next clue. Interrogations of federal agents in dark secluded rooms yielded cries of pain and eventually results.

"You'll tell me what I want to know or you'll die," Mort told the agent.

The man struggled against the ropes that bound his wrists, but it was no use.

"I'll die anyway," he said.

"Yes. One way you die fast, the other . . . well, I've got days."

Mort turned and grabbed a hammer from the nearby table. He inspected the metal head and ran his fingers over the clean and shiny surface. He approached the agent and displayed the weapon of choice.

"Where shall we start?"

The agent flinched but did not answer.

"If you don't tell me what I want to know," Mort said, circling the agent, "when I'm finished with you, I'll pay a visit to your little brownstone in Brooklyn Heights."

The agent's eyes widened and he struggled against his bonds.

"You stay away from there!"

"Tell me," Mort answered.

The agent was silent again, his chest heaving with angry breaths.

"The girl wasn't dead. We knew her father was working with us to nail an organized crime leader in New Orleans. So we faked her death, changed her name, and she was put into witness protection."

Tears fell from the man's eyes now. He felt relief and shame for giving up this girl to save his own family.

"The name? And where did she go?" Mort asked.

"I don't know," the agent answered. "The file was sealed."

Mort swung the hammer hard, landing it on the man's knee-cap. His screams of pain echoed through the empty building, startling a group of pigeons that'd been nesting there.

"I know you worked the case."

"I work a lot of cases. I can't remember every detail," the agent screamed.

"Your wife Bonnie sure is a beautiful woman. I bet she's a fighter. Is she a fighter, Agent Townsend?"

"Josie! Josie Banks is her name! She was placed in state custody in San Diego!"

Mort smiled, pulled his pistol from its holster, and shot the man in the forehead.

He dialed Moloney as he exited the building. The cool night air welcomed him and he grinned victoriously up at the moon.

"What have you found?" Moloney asked.

"She was alive. They changed her name and sent her to California."

"Interesting."

"I'll follow up and get back to you," Mort promised.

"See that you do."

☾

Tristan stood in front of his bathroom mirror, raking his nails over the scruff covering his jaw. He didn't feel like shaving today. Connie, his cougar of a manager, always said that he looked like a hobo when he didn't shave, but his tips never proved that. Tristan assumed it was her personal preference and had nothing to do with image. Connie had a way of feigning interest in people's lives, making them think that she only wanted what was best. All she cared about was the bar's bottom line. That, and discovering what the young male employees were willing to offer in exchange for a raise.

Once a week she would call Tristan into her office and make him stand at attention while she sat filing her acrylic nails. Today was his day. The leathered skin of her chest was sprinkled with freckles that seemed to cascade into the deep valley created by her silicone breasts. She pressed them together and leaned over her desk.

"How's it going, Tristan? You still happy with our arrangement?" Connie asked, her voice raspy with tequila and menthol cigarettes.

Tristan huffed, annoyed at her ability to make every conversation sound like a sexual invitation.

"Yes, ma'am. I love my schedule."

"Ugh, don't call me ma'am. You make me out to be some old church lady. I'm not your mother. Am I, sweetheart?"

"No." Tristan squashed his desire to add "ma'am." "You certainly are not."

It was the same song and dance each time and Tristan had mastered the steps. Connie searched for conversation, anything to keep him in her eyesight longer. He felt her try to stay professional, but it never lasted long.

"Is there anything that you need, Tristan? Anything I can give you? To help you better perform your job, of course."

"I'm capable of stocking the bar, checking IDs, and mixing over twenty-two thousand drink combinations. I think I've got a handle on it."

Privy to her internal battle, Tristan smiled and toyed with her, playing his part. Though deep down he hated the way she regarded him solely as a pretty boy moneymaker.

"So it seems," she answered and dismissed him. "Make sure to send Lee up here when he gets in."

With a salute, he left her office feeling relieved and disgusted for playing her game.

Three hours into his shift, Tristan was struggling to remain focused. His eyes darted to that dark corner every few seconds, willing McKenzi to materialize out of thin air. He had no idea what he would say to her, everything in his head sounded childlike and flimsy. All he knew was seeing her had rekindled a fire inside his gut, a fire that he loved.

Last night, his dreams had been awash with the face and voice of twelve-year-old McKenzi Delaune. It all meshed together in a photomontage of sorts. The way his brain filed each image chronologically made it easy to relive his past. Tristan saw her adolescent face smiling down at him while he climbed his way up their tree. He heard her giggle as he chased her around his room with a frog croaking its displeasure. His visions morphed into their first awkward dance in junior high, to the first time he'd seen her in a bikini, and eventually to their first kiss.

He wasn't sure who she'd become now. Tristan was selfish and didn't know if he wanted to mar his idealistic memories with this new, darker version of McKenzi. She seemed so severe and troubled, like she'd been through a lifetime of hurt. Something drew him in, like a kamikaze moth to a flame. He had no choice in the matter. Thinking back, he never had.

His eyes checked the corner again. Nothing. He watched as Erin made her way to each table before sauntering up to the bar, smiling widely.

"Thank God!" she said dramatically. "I don't have to wait on Bundy tonight." She grabbed four bottled beers and turned to leave again. "She's all yours."

Tristan's brows furrowed. He checked the corner again, still empty. Finally, his eyes slid down the bar and found her there, scribbling. He took a deep breath and stepped over to face her. He did not miss the drawing of his anchor tattoo now decorating the bar's surface.

"I may have to call the San Diego Graffiti Control Program and report you for that."

"What's stopping you?" Josie asked, one eyebrow raised in challenge.

"Well, that particular image," he said, pointing to the defaced bar, "is directly related to me. I could be implicated. There's paperwork, a long form that you have to fill out. Then you have to take it downtown to file the complaint, waiting in lines and spending far too much time bathed in fluorescent lighting and breathing government air."

"Government air?" Josie asked.

"Yes. The exhaled breaths and sighs of people working for an uneducated supervisor whose cousin got him the job. They bring paper bag lunches and drink diluted coffee, both of which fill the air with stink and dissatisfaction. On their lunch breaks, they sit in a room that hasn't been dusted since the first Bush administration and brag about a home life that is less fulfilling than their monotonous job. All those feelings, words, dust, fumes, and tastes combine into the stench of regret for a life never lived and dreams long forgotten. Government air."

Josie just stared at him, wondering if she could make sense of this rant. After a few seconds of inner debate, she decided to move on.

"Why don't you just fill out the form online?"

"I prefer face-to-face interaction."

"Even in government air?" she asked.

"Even then."

"Thanks for not reporting me, I guess."

"No problem. What can I get you, Mac?"

"Mac?"

"That's what I called you when we were kids," Tristan said, his eyes shining with memories.

"My name is Josie," she corrected.

"Okay, Josie," he said, raising his hands in surrender. "Rum and Coke?"

"Yes."

Tristan made her drink and set it before her carefully as though it represented more of a peace offering than a simple beverage. He watched as she capped her marker and slid it into a pocket on her bag. She sipped her drink, the stretch of silence between them becoming unbearable.

"What happened to you?" he asked, his mouth acting before his brain had worked out a more subtle approach.

"Last night?" she asked.

"No, the summer after we turned fourteen."

"Oh. Not here," she pleaded, shaking her head.

"When? Where?" Tristan begged.

"You get off at midnight, right?"

"Yes," he said.

"Meet me at City Deli."

Tristan noticed this was not a question. He nodded.

Josie drained her drink in one swallow and left cash on the bar. She slung her bag across her body and exited onto the street, leaving the sole connection to her past behind. She had three hours to kill before meeting him and wondered what kind of trouble she could get into before then.

Josie stocked up at Trader Joe's and headed down Sixth Avenue toward the park. The quiet of the street was strange for this time of night. There was a couple out walking their dog, patiently waiting as he sniffed every inch of sidewalk. A block later she spotted two queens in four-inch heels trying to hail a cab. They weren't having much luck. A group of teenagers flew past, the recognizable sound of their skateboards approaching like a roaring train. They challenged each other to kickflips and ollies before coasting down the hill.

Josie turned into the park, ignoring the sidewalks for the plush feel of grass beneath her feet. The city's nighttime shine filtered down through the trees, cloaking her in a lacy pattern of light. She loved the smell of the plants. It made her nostalgic for something she couldn't quite remember.

"Hey, Gavin. What's up?" Josie called out as she approached the familiar bench. It was the only one in the park with her trademark graffiti.

"Stems! Long time no see. You two-timing me?"

The woman gave Josie a flirty smile, displaying a set of teeth that reminded her of mismatched furniture. Gavin's expression was easy, but the coldness in her eyes always told her truths. The streets had an artful way of taking life from you when you were busy just trying to survive. The way she leaned back on the bench with her arm resting across the top made her look like a woman who felt at home here. When you didn't have a physical address to belong to, you could feel at home anywhere.

"Stems?" Josie asked while taking a seat on the opposite end of the bench. "What's that about?"

"Your legs, baby girl. They go on for days. Your stems," she answered, shrugging as though it was the most logical explanation in the world.

"Well, I guess that's better than the last one."

"What? You didn't like Perdy?"

Josie made a face, squishing up her features and shaking her head. "No! That sounds like some redneck in overalls who butchers people."

Gavin laughed, a full belly chuckle that momentarily hid her sharpness and made her appear young again.

"Well, when you put it that way."

"I got a new piece up downtown. On Fifth. Took me two hours."

"I'll have to check it out. I know you got mad skills."

"You hungry?" Josie asked, holding out a granola bar.

"Thanks," Gavin said, ripping open the paper and humming in delight at the taste of chocolate.

"Here's the rest," Josie said, handing over the four bags filled with food. "You'll give it to the kids down in the plaza?"

"I always do."

"Good. Keep what you want, but make sure Sarah gets the gummy worms. She loves those."

"Yeah."

"Anything new? Those asshole cops still bothering you?" Josie asked.

"Nah. Shorty was arrested for bathing in the fountain again. Gregory sends his love, as always. Kim and Kim moved down by the 163. And Logan . . ."

"Out with it, Gavin."

"Logan's gone. Haven't seen him in weeks."

Josie blew out a breath, frustrated she couldn't keep up with the kids better. Since her time on the streets, she'd become attached to them. They represented the only family she'd ever known.

"Well, if you see him, let me know. How's your girl?"

"Who knows, Stems. I heard she's headed up to L.A. with her new boyfriend."

"Sorry. I thought you two were going to make it."

"Sure felt like it. That's what I get for messing with a bi girl.

They never know what the hell they want." Gavin sighed. "Maybe she didn't like her nickname."

"Well, I like Stems," Josie said. "Maybe I'll have to give you one too."

"What's wrong with Gavin?"

"I've never met a chick named Gavin before."

Gavin closed her eyes and tilted her face away from Josie, her shoulders tense.

"It's just a way to stay anonymous on the streets, you know? It was my brother's name," she admitted.

Josie didn't press her for more information. She knew what it was like to have a past that you'd rather not relive or retell. Both had been discarded by society. The difference was Josie had felt empowered by the freedom of unregulated days and nights. They had shared a common ground, a common sleeping hole, and a common need to burn their pain away. An easy silence fell between them as they waited for their miracle man, the deliverer of coping aids and pharmaceutical highs.

4. EJECTA
THE MATERIAL THROWN OUT OF AN IMPACT CRATER
BY THE SHOCK PRESSURES GENERATED.

"Hello, hello. What can I get for you this evening?"

Josie eyed the greasy man suspiciously.

"Where's Nigel?" she asked.

"He's busy tonight, but didn't want to leave you fine ladies hangin'. He sent me to take care of you."

"How do we know you're not a cop?" Gavin asked.

The man laughed and tugged on the brim of his hat.

"Shit, I ain't no cop. Hate them bastards. Just got out of lockup a few weeks ago."

"Likely story," Gavin said.

"Show your tits," Josie demanded.

"What?" he asked.

"You heard her."

The man shook his head but followed instructions. He lifted his shirt up under his armpits. Josie made a twirling motion with her index finger and he turned in a circle. The girls eyed him skeptically, but each nodded, confirming she was satisfied.

"See? No wire. No cop."

Gavin reached into her bag and pulled out an envelope of money, counting out a stack for him. She folded the envelope and shoved it deep into the bottom of her bag. The man watched her carefully, averting his eyes just in time.

Josie pulled out her fold of ready bills and handed it over in exchange for a new bag of pills. She smiled at the comfort they represented.

When Gavin finished her purchase, the man stood there, lingering. Josie didn't like the hunger in his eyes. He seemed to be wavering, waiting for something. Suddenly, he reached down, grabbed Gavin's bag, and took off running.

"Hey!" Gavin screamed.

Josie jumped from the bench and took off after him. She caught up in no time. When she reached him, she threw herself onto his back. They both tumbled to the ground, rolling down a small hill. On the way, Josie took an elbow to the eye. When they stopped, she was on top with the bag firmly in her grip.

"Drop it!" she yelled.

"Make me," he spat.

She shrugged and stood up, feigning defeat.

"Ha. That's right." He gloated.

Josie swung around, raised her foot, and slammed it down between his legs. He let out an awful howl and rolled onto his side, releasing the bag. Josie put it over her shoulder and walked away.

"You bitch!"

"They call me Bundy!" Josie yelled victoriously.

☾

Tristan took a seat in a corner booth at City Deli. The waitress, in standard uniform and orthopedic shoes, smacked her gum and asked for his order.

"I'll just have coffee for now. I'm waiting for someone."

"Sure," she answered, rolling her eyes before shuffling off to fetch his brew.

He pulled a paperback book from his back pocket and opened it to the dog-eared page. He read the words, but by the end of the page he had no idea what they were. It was an odd feeling for him. So he reread them, this time absorbing each one permanently. Every time the door opened, Tristan craned his neck to look for Josie. Each time it wasn't her, he would return his attention to the book, concentrating on Amis's words about John Self's wild and glutinous life. Soon he was wondering if she'd even show up.

His coffee appeared in front of him as if mentally summoned, and the waitress took off for her next table. He poured copious amounts of sugar into the black drink, stirring until the clinking of the spoon against ceramic annoyed him.

Josie threw herself through the door of the diner like she was being chased. The sight of Tristan tucked into her favorite corner booth filled her with relief she hadn't even known she'd needed. She brushed off her clothes, as if it would somehow help her disheveled appearance. Slowly, she passed each booth, labeling patrons as she went. He's a prick, she thought, as a fat, balding man wiggled his eyebrows in her direction. Josie flipped him off and continued past the others. They're having an affair, he's in the closet, that one's an alcoholic, she might be a he. Gold digger, prostitute, and cabdriver rounded out her assessment.

Tossing her bag into the booth, she slid in after it. The sound of metal cans and ball-bearing mixers announced her arrival. Tristan's shoulders jumped in surprise and he wondered when he'd stopped checking the door. Their eyes met across one steaming cup of coffee and a Formica tabletop.

"What the hell happened to you?" Tristan asked, his face screwed up in worry.

Josie reached up and smoothed down her knotted hair. She knew she should have gone to the bathroom to check herself before sitting.

"What?" she asked casually.

"You have a huge red mark on your cheek and your eye is bruising."

"Oh, that. I got into a fight."

"What the fuck?" he replied loudly, garnering the attention of every guest in the quiet establishment.

"Calm down," she said, shushing him. "What do you have, 'roid rage or something? I'm fine. I met a friend at Balboa and this asshole tried to steal her bag. I didn't let him."

"He hit you?"

"Yeah, but I hit him back," she answered, smirking.

"What were you doing in the park at this time of night?"

"Buying drugs."

Tristan went quiet at her admission, not sure how he should react to such honesty. He thought her frankness could either mean that she was fearless or that she had indeed found the drugs.

"Are you hungry?" he asked.

"Not really. Maybe a little something," she mumbled, her voice trailing off as her eyes scanned the menu.

The waitress reappeared, her pen ready to jot down their order as she smiled her practiced smile.

"I'll have the huevos rancheros," he said.

"I want a strawberry milk shake, order of bacon, and coffee," Josie said, closing her menu and not looking up as the waitress left.

"This Canadian food company did a survey and found out that forty-three percent of people would rather have bacon than sex."

"Canadian bacon or regular bacon?" she asked.

"It didn't say."

"Well," Josie said, "it would really make a difference."

Tristan took a cautious sip of his coffee while they waited for the waitress to return with hers.

"Are you saying that standard breakfast bacon may be better than sex, but Canadian bacon is lacking?"

"That's exactly what I'm saying," Josie answered.

"Would you equate it with any kind of sexual act, or is it just not that good?"

"I might have Canadian bacon instead of giving a hand job."

"But you get no pleasure from that," he said.

"Exactly." Josie gave a shrug of her shoulders.

"Maybe the Canadians don't know what they're doing," Tristan said.

"Hardly. Their bacon-making skills are, as you put it, lacking."

Tristan nodded in agreement. When the waitress returned, Josie dumped sugar into her coffee, stirring counterclockwise. She turned to the wall and traced an outline of intricate text permanently etched there.

"More of your work?" Tristan asked.

"I'll never tell. You might report me."

"So . . ." Tristan started, for once having no plan to finish his sentence.

"So?"

"I haven't seen you in almost nine years. Why don't you remember me? Why were you reported dead? How did you end up here?"

Josie looked at the air above his head, as if the questions hung there and she was deciding which one to pluck down and begin with.

"You're from New Orleans?" she asked.

"Yes," Tristan answered.

"Look, I'm not really supposed to talk about it. Legal issues, blah blah blah. My safety, blah blah blah. What the hell do I care? I can't even give you details, because I don't have them."

He gestured for her to continue, letting his eyes roam over her face, traveling from her sepia eyes down the gentle slope of her nose and finally resting on her lips. When she began to speak, Tristan found himself captivated by her story.

"My father and I left Louisiana when he took a new job in Brooklyn. We moved into an apartment. We only lived there for about six weeks. No one knows what went down, but it was a few days before the landlady noticed we were missing. Three days later, my father's body turned up in the harbor. A few days after that, a witness saw me stumble into a subway station, where I collapsed. I woke up in a hospital two days later, surrounded by FBI agents, with no memory of who I was or where I'd been."

Tristan noticed that she wasn't telling a story; she was simply reciting the words. They were void of emotion, as if she'd memorized an official report of the happenings.

"You had amnesia."

The waitress appeared, refilling their coffee cups and moving on, clearly uninterested in the conversation.

"Have. I have amnesia. Retrograde dissociative amnesia," she clarified, repeating the clinical term she'd heard so many times before. "I have no idea what happened in New York or anything before that. Doctors say I probably never will."

Tristan dissected the words in his head, working out her diagnosis.

"So 'retrograde' meaning all preexisting memories are lost, but you're able to remember everything since." Josie nodded. "'Dissociative' means it was likely caused by psychological events, as opposed to injury."

She shrugged, suddenly avoiding his gaze. They both reached for the sugar, their fingers intertwining around the glass container. Tristan pulled back, gesturing for her to go first. Josie poured her sugar before sliding it over to him.

"Are you some kind of doctor pretending to be a bartender?" Josie asked.

"No. I read a lot," he answered, realizing that statement explained nothing. "I happen to remember everything I read. I have a really good memory."

"Huh," she said, shrugging. "We're like opposites."

He nodded, saddened by the defeated nature of her statement. Tristan had a feeling that the amnesia was her mind's way of dealing with something terrible, some kind of horrific event that refused to be processed. She had no memories from their shared childhood. She couldn't recall the happiest time of her life, her family, her friends, not even him. Meanwhile, he remembered everything, with agonizing clarity.

"'August 25,'" Tristan began. Josie's eyes snapped up to his when he spoke the words as if they were right in front of him. "'A body found in the Hudson River near Weehawken, New Jersey, has been identified as Earl Delaune, 41, a recent transplant from New Orleans to Brooklyn. Delaune was reported missing three days ago by his landlord. State Police say a fisherman found the body in the river, but the location of Delaune's death has yet to be determined. The victim's daughter, McKenzi Delaune, 14, remains missing.

"'August 31, New York City Police identified the body of a fourteen-year-old girl found dead in the Jay Street subway station yesterday morning. Authorities are withholding the identity of the Brooklyn girl, but it is suspected to be McKenzi Delaune, a teen reported missing nine days ago. NYPD said they were having difficulty locating any of the girl's remaining family. There were no obvious signs of trauma and, for now, police aren't commenting on suspects or motive.'"

Josie blinked rapidly, suddenly realizing that she'd been holding her breath, her attention seized by Tristan's words.

"The local paper reported both of you had been murdered but didn't give any details. You didn't have family there, so the school held a memorial service. We took turns telling stories about you and had your picture hung in the hall," Tristan finished.

Josie spied the waitress coming and was relieved by the distraction. Unfolding her napkin, she scrubbed at the black on her stained fingers, silently cursing the charcoal and lead. No matter how hard she tried, the dark dust clung to the beds and underneath each nail, making her look like she'd been playing in dirt. Never mind the slash of green paint across her forearm that would have to be removed later. The plates slid in front of them before the waitress disappeared again, promptly returning with Josie's milk shake.

"I hated that fucking picture," Tristan said.

"Why?"

"They used your freshman yearbook photo."

"And?" she asked, frustrated.

"We got into a fight right before photos that day. You weren't even smiling. It was like having this sad ghost haunting me every time I walked past the office."

Josie bit into the bacon and moaned in delight. She may have been a little overenthusiastic as a result of their earlier conversation.

"What were we fighting about?" she asked.

Tristan smiled at her, a smile so genuine she wanted to return it. He set his fork back down and sipped his coffee.

"I was mad because I found a drawing in your room of another guy."

"So, you were jealous?"

Tristan nodded.

"I ripped it up," he said.

"Oh, I bet I got pissed."

"Yeah. That's an understatement. You didn't talk to me for three days, a record for us."

"Damn, guess I cut you off too?" she asked.

"We weren't having sex at fourteen, Josie."

"Nothing?" she asked.

"Nothing past second base."

Josie shook her head and wondered if she had been a prude or if he had been the one trying to protect their virtue. Tristan, with all his memories, made her nervous. He looked at her as if trying to crack a code, break her down and understand her. She'd never wanted someone the way she wanted him. Josie couldn't risk his finding out how damaged she was.

Trying to fool herself into thinking that it was a purely physical desire, she closed her eyes, imagining him crushed in a grip between her thighs. Quickly, her mind was lost to a fantasy of touching and tasting his flesh.

Tristan cleared his throat, startling Josie and reminding her that there was a conversation taking place. Feeling as though she'd been caught with those visions in her head, Josie dropped her eyes down to her plate. She scrambled to divert his attention.

"The FBI changed my name. Shipped me cross-country. They said it was for my own protection," Josie finished, rolling her eyes at the thought of being protected.

A broad silence stretched between them. Josie busied herself with eating as Tristan sat dumbfounded.

"Then?" Tristan asked.

"Then what?"

"That was eight years ago," he said.

"I won't bore you with the tales of living in foster homes, Tristan. Imagine the worst, multiply that by ten. It's nothing a few decades of drugs and alcohol won't cure."

Josie shoved a piece of bacon into her mouth. She chewed thoroughly before swallowing and making eye contact with Tristan. He sat frozen, suspended over his food.

"I had no idea. None of us did."

"That's kind of how witness protection works."

Josie continued to eat while Tristan sat watching. He felt sick to his stomach. It seemed as though a black cloud had settled over their table.

"Josie! Where you been all my life, girl?"

The pair looked up to find a young black boy leaning on their table. His denim jacket covered a dirty T-shirt, and braids stuck out from his hat. He smiled at Josie and gave her a wink.

"Gregory, what's up, little man?"

"Ah, you know. This and that. How you doin'? Ain't seen you around in a while. We gettin' your deliveries all the time, though."

"I'm good."

Josie ducked her head and sucked on her straw. She felt exposed having this conversation with Tristan present.

"Yeah, looks like you real busy."

Gregory turned to Tristan and gave him a once-over, tilting his head and sliding his lips sideways in disapproval.

"Where's your sister?" Josie asked.

"Stop trying to change the subject, hottie. You know I'm tryin' to holla at you."

Josie shook her head and put down her milk shake.

"When I'm into fourteen-year-olds, you'll be the first to know."

"I may be fourteen, but I got game. Better than this . . ." Gregory said, motioning to Tristan.

"Tristan, this is Gregory. Gregory, Tristan," Josie offered, waving back and forth between the two. Tristan wiped his hands on a napkin and held one out toward the boy.

"Nice to meet you, Greg."

"Oh, shit," Josie whispered.

"Greg? Did you say Greg? Did this sexy woman right here say my name was Greg? No. She said Gregory. Three syllables. Big effort for a lazy fool like you, but work it out, white boy."

Josie giggled, pressing the palm of her hand over her lips.

"Gre-gore-ree," Gregory pronounced, unhinged by Tristan's gall. "Where did you find this clown?" he asked Josie.

"My apologies, Gregory," Tristan spoke up, saving Josie from answering. "I'm sorry."

"Yes, you are."

"Nice jacket. Gavin give you that?" Josie asked.

"Yeah, you know. I guess she grew out of it or whatever. It's a little old and a lot country, but I ain't gonna complain."

"It's actually vintage Levi's. It's got the single-stitch at the bottom of the button placard and only has breast pockets, so it's pre-1971."

"Are you speakin' English? It's just a jacket, man," Gregory moaned. "Seriously, Jo? You could do better. I mean, why not me?"

"Because curfew law says you're not allowed outside of the home between ten P.M. and six A.M. on weekdays," Tristan stated, pleased with himself.

"Guess that don't matter when you don't have a home," Gregory answered.

With that, he rolled his eyes, gave Josie a quick wave, and was gone.

"Wow," Tristan said smiling. "He was . . . colorful."

"Is that a racist joke?"

"What? No! Josie, I would never," he said, dropping his fork to the table.

"Yeah, I know. It was funny watching you freak out, though."

Josie winked and ate the last piece of bacon.

"He's homeless?"

"Gregory uses the phrase 'residentially challenged.'"

Tristan nodded.

"Are all your friends residentially challenged?"

"He's not a friend, just a kid I know."

Tristan noticed that her demeanor changed instantly and he felt the warning in her posture. Subject closed.

"So, you saw me that night in the alley."

Josie unconsciously smoothed down the hooded sweatshirt and nodded.

"Is that mine?" he asked, recognizing the red stitching on the sleeve.

"Yeah. You left it in the alley."

Tristan weighed his options and contemplated which questions he could get away with asking. After coming up clueless, he decided to be satisfied with what he'd already learned. That alone would take time to process.

He wasn't someone who believed in fate or destiny. There was always a scientific, mathematical, or coincidental explanation for anything. The fact that little McKenzi Delaune sat before him munching on bacon was blowing his mind.

Tristan lay in bed after their midnight meeting, trying to piece together the broken girl he'd just learned existed. There used to be this ache, this burning pain in his chest. It held all the love and loss for a girl named McKenzi. Before the punishment of ink etched into his skin, there had been McKenzi. Back when he knew who he was and what he wanted, when life was full of possibilities and everyone expected the best, there had been McKenzi.

She had lost everyone and everything. Tristan knew that she would guard herself from more pain. The girl was beautiful, full of sex appeal and mystery. While he knew he couldn't pick up where they left off, he longed to seize her. He turned off the light and stared up at a gray shadowed ceiling, wondering how on earth he'd found her.

Twenty-two blocks away, Josie paused to tag a stop sign in purple marker. The squeak and slide of the felt tip against metal comforted her. So did having representations of herself all over the city. Even though she felt like nothing, these markings would prove that she was here. Just to see what it would look like, she wrote Tristan's name too. Stepping back and admiring the way their stacked names connected, she smiled and headed toward home. That night she fell asleep wrapped in the hoodie that belonged to a boy who'd once loved her.

In the sixty-nine hundred block of Levant Street, Mort snuck into the San Diego Child Welfare Services office. He quickly hacked into the computer system, not slowed down by the archaic password protection screen. Gathering all the necessary information to do this remotely next time, he began his hunt.

He had grown tired of this chase. If he had been any other idiot, he would have crossed his fingers and said a prayer that this would give him a clue, some sort of direction. That was for superstitious idiots who had more faith in a higher power than in themselves.

Mort had been on this job for so long that when he lay in bed at night it was the only thing on his mind. It ruled his brain every waking minute and even in his sleep. What he wouldn't give to be free of this troublesome girl.

He had not yet alerted Moloney to his whereabouts. He didn't want to get the man's hopes up before he'd discovered anything concrete. Finding out the girl was still alive had been a matter of luck. Finding out where she had been sent had been a matter of painful and bloody coercion.

After maneuvering through the complicated filing system, he was finally able to type in his search. Clicking in the waiting box, the cursor blinked at him. Mort's fingers moved swiftly over the keyboard, pecking out the name that had come at such a high price. He was so close he could taste it.

He hit Enter and smiled as the screen displayed JOSIE BANKS: ONE RESULT FOUND.

5. SATELLITE
ANY OBJECT THAT ORBITS ANOTHER CELESTIAL BODY.

Monica Templeton, all five feet nothing of her, approached the dilapidated redbrick building without hesitation. Though she didn't live in the neighborhood, she was here often. Being a social worker took her to every nook and cranny of this city. There were no boundaries set by race, religion, or social status. Her job included everyone. It's what brought her into the field in the first place. Monica truly believed that everyone deserved a fair chance at a happy and healthy life.

Home visits were usually unpleasant, but they were a necessary part of the job. It was imperative to visit the children in their homes, making sure they were taken care of and provided for. In her many years on the job, and through trials that tested her moral strength, she had learned to take nothing for granted. Monica became an expert at seeing things that were not meant to be seen, at assessing visual clues and behaviors. In short, she'd learned a great deal from her mistakes.

She smiled at three girls jumping rope on the sidewalk, their plastic snap barrettes dancing at the ends of their braids. Together their sweet voices serenaded the street corner.

"Cinderella dressed in yella went upstairs to kiss her fella. Made a mistake and kissed a snake. How many doctors did it take? 1, 2, 3, 4, 5—awwww!"

The girls laughed as they tripped on the rope. In seconds, they were set up to try again. Two women watched from a balcony on the second floor, smoking their cigarettes and talking animatedly with their hands. Though engrossed in their conversation, one of them always had an eye on the girls. On the stoop sat four large men, looking comfortable and uninterested in Monica's arrival.

"Excuse me," she said, looking each one of them in the eye. No one moved. "I said excuse me," she repeated a bit louder, popping her gum to get their attention.

One man stood, his ribbed shirt clinging to his muscles. He wore three gold chains and pristine sneakers. Monica knew his type.

"Yeah, we heard you," he answered, stepping closer, towering over the tiny woman. "What you want here?"

"That is my business. I suggest that you and your friends move aside. While I appreciate the whole thug look you've got going on here," Monica said, waving her hand across his body like a game show host, "I don't have time for it. Take your disrespectful attitude, mooching off of some hardworking single mom, deadbeat ass out of my way before I perforate your skull with the heel of my imitation Jimmy Choos."

A chorus of "oohs" rang out from his friends as he glared at her. Monica refused to back down, her neck aching from returning his gaze.

"I got shit to do anyway," he said.

A few seconds later, he stepped away and let her pass. So did the others.

A light tapping at Josie's door pulled her inside from her place on the fire escape. She knew, just from the patience of the knock, that it wasn't Alex. She approached the door and spoke through the solid wood.

"Who is it?"

"Your friend Monica," her high-spirited voice sang.

Josie rolled her eyes, unlocked the door, and motioned for her to come inside. She suddenly wished for a strong drink and a joint, some sort of chemical buffer between them. Monica immediately took a seat at the small kitchen table. She blew a bubble of her pink gum and sucked it back in. Josie didn't like how Monica looked in her apartment, a perfect little package among motley furniture and chipping paint. If it weren't for manners, she knew Monica might be tempted to clean her chair with an antibacterial wipe before sitting. Josie was almost positive the woman had them in her purse.

"I don't have any friends," Josie reminded her, taking a seat in the opposite chair and crossing her arms defensively.

Josie considered herself a solitary soul, always avoiding relationships and the human race in general. The interaction, attention, and conversation it took to maintain relationships required too much exertion. Most often, people's true intentions were buried beneath fake smiles and how-are-you handshakes. Josie was unhappy that her worth was determined by the number of friends she had—or, in this case, didn't have. Friendship was a commodity to be bought and sold, and she was not interested.

"You may not be my friend, but I'm yours. You have Alex too."

Josie hated the way Monica always looked at her with pity and self-loathing guilt. The woman's face, though usually smiling, always held this contrite intensity. Josie wondered if she always had that look or if it appeared only when they were within six feet of each other. They sat in a customary standoff, each trying to guess the intention of the other. Monica knew this visit wouldn't end well; she could feel the hostility rolling off of Josie in battering waves. She could practically see the confrontation written across the girl's face.

Josie stared out the window, hoping that when she turned back, Monica would be gone. No such luck. She could see all the pity that fueled her own anger. Monica's face was masked in casual interest, but Josie saw right through it.

"Did you need something?" Josie finally asked.

"I was in the neighborhood."

"I'm fine," Josie answered.

"Well, I had a cancellation and thought I'd check in on you. These people have no consideration. I drove all the way over here for our prearranged appointment time only to find out they are in Anaheim for the day. I mean, really."

"Sorry you had to slum it for nothing. You better run along before someone steals your car."

While Josie didn't have ill feelings toward Monica, she wasn't exactly a fan. As a state-appointed social worker, Monica had been free and clear of her obligation to Josie for four years now. Josie had always assumed that Monica's feelings of failure would eventually wane and the woman would disappear from her life like everyone else. Yet here she was, still keeping watch over Josie.

"You always say you are fine. How are you really? Are you working? Going to school?"

"No and no."

Monica leaned back in the rickety chair and crossed her legs. The toe of her shoe tapped anxiously against the table leg while she pondered how far to push today.

"Josie, you really should consider getting a job or at least decide what to do with the rest of your life. It's great that you sit around drawing pictures and getting high all day. Hell, if it were up to me, I'd spend my time reading romance novels in front of the Home Shopping Network while munching on Oreos. But I live in the real world. It's just not possible."

Josie stood and grabbed a glass from her kitchen counter. She filled it with tap water and swallowed the whole lot down at once. She felt smothered by Monica, held down and accountable. But she wasn't quite sure what she should be accountable for. The water didn't cool her insides like she'd hoped, so she turned and faced Monica.

"Why isn't it possible? If that's what you want to do, I say do it! Your ass would be the size of a house, but you'd be happy. Go buy some stretch pants and Oreos. Dare to dream."

Josie again turned her back on Monica. She focused on the pristine empty space of tile behind her sink. She pictured ink and paint in lines of fury covering the surface and seeping into the old grout.

"I know you have plenty of money from your inheritance, but one cannot live on sex and drugs alone. It's going to kill you one day," Monica said, ignoring Josie's rant.

"I'm counting on it."

"You don't mean that," Monica insisted. Josie sighed at Monica calling her out. "And I don't understand why you live in this place when you can afford more. Get out and do something. Be productive. You should start contributing to society."

Josie spun around and threw her arms in the air.

"Like they contributed to me?"

Her words seemed dipped in a guilty poison that would certainly hit their mark. Monica flinched at the verbal jab while trying to hide the sympathy that Josie detested. She could still remember their introduction. Monica was all smiles and hugs while shy Josie wrapped her arms around her middle protectively. Her eyes had stayed fixed on the speckled linoleum floor when they spoke. She was soft-spoken and placid back then.

"Hi, Josie. I'm Monica. I've been assigned your case. I'm so glad to be working with you," Monica had said to the mute girl. Josie looked around the office and back to the floor. "Let's see, your file says you lost your mother a year ago and recently your father passed away too?"

Josie looked up at her and shrugged. "If that's what it says," she'd answered.

"Wow. I'm so sorry, honey. I know we could never replace them, but I promise I'll try my hardest to get you into a nice foster home soon. Okay?"

"Okay."

"What can you tell me about yourself?"

"My name is Josie Banks," she said, as if she'd been practicing.

"And do you have any hobbies? What kind of music do you listen to? How about boys? Any celebrity crushes? I just love Matthew Fox from the show *Lost*."

"I don't know."

"Well, Josie Banks." Monica flipped through some papers and smiled up at Josie. "You'll be placed in an all-girls home until we find somewhere more permanent for you. There you'll have access to grief counselors and lots of people who can help if you need anything. Maybe they can get you to open up and talk about your past a bit. It won't hurt. I promise."

The sweet, confused girl that Monica met eight years ago had grown into this cynical woman. While it saddened her, it wasn't a surprise in the least. With the horrific things Josie had endured, Monica couldn't fault her for any of it. Still, in the depths of her heart, hope hadn't died for Monica Templeton. She still held firm to the belief that good things could happen for Josie.

Monica dug through her bag and placed a stack of papers on the table.

"Here," she said. "I brought you some art school applications. It's worth looking into, Josie. You're so talented. You deserve to see where it could take you. Of course, you'd have to sober up first."

Josie took the applications but did not look at them.

"I don't think I'm cut out for formal education. I've been told I have a problem with authority."

"Well, that's true. If you keep tagging the entire city with graffiti, that could land you in jail. Now that is *real* authority and tacky orange jumpsuits." Monica shuddered at the thought. "Did you have anything to do with that piece up on Fifth Avenue?"

Josie smiled.

"It's beautiful, Josie. But that's illegal. If they can nail you for enough damage, it becomes a felony."

"I know."

"Then why don't you take that energy and dedicate it to something legit?"

"What I do *is* fucking legit," Josie growled, stomping across the small space and curling up into a ball on the end of her sofa.

The silence that followed was uncomfortable. Her loud declaration followed by nothing left an enormous weight of silence pressing down on them. It was a burden Josie would gladly endure. Monica, however, could not.

"How about the support group down at the community center? Have you been there lately? I hear the director's quite a dreamboat. Oh, and he's an art major at SDSU. I bet you two would have a lot in common."

"No, Monica, I haven't been down to the community center. I don't want to listen to people talk about their terrible child-hoods and compare them to mine. I don't want their looks of pity. I get enough of that from you. And who the fuck uses the word 'dreamboat' anymore?" Josie said.

"Also, I don't eat three meals a day. I get high whenever pos-sible. I have sex with strangers, many strangers. I don't exercise and I pick fights with drug dealers." She paused, catching her breath before delivering the final blow. "Don't you have an abused kid somewhere to save?"

Monica averted her watery eyes, picked up her purse, and left without waiting for an apology. She knew not to expect feelings of regret from the stone-cold girl. The words were wounding and her buttons were pressed. As much as she had tried to atone for her mistakes, Monica always suffered at the hands of Josie. She took it because she deserved it. Holding back tears as she ran down the steps, Monica fled from the first and last kid she had ever let down.

After such a long and gruesome day on the job, Monica found herself parked on a barstool, sipping a strong vodka tonic. Mel-low music drifted through the room, adding to the ambient noise of conversation and clinking glass. The whole place was deep mahogany, as if it had grown out of the earth or had been carved out of one giant tree. With the wall sconces and pendant light-ing, the top of the room glowed a rich, golden honey before fad-ing into a chocolate floor. Monica felt warmed and at ease here.

She blew out a breath and pushed the negative energy from her lungs. For once, she was glad to be alone. She enjoyed the feeling of alcohol seeping into her blood, creating detachment from her job. It was days like this that had begun to wear on her positive attitude. No form of meditation could prepare or repair the angst she faced in Josie Banks. Josie had a way of draining the fight from Monica. Monica had a way of letting her.

A prickling chill ran down her spine as she felt another's gaze upon her. In the stagnant air of the room, it felt as though a breeze had drifted across her skin, rousing her defeated spirit. Monica looked up from her melting ice cubes and found two stunning blue eyes looking back.

He was handsome with his wavy blond hair and broad shoulders. His tanned skin seemed to glow beneath the lights. His jeans looked soft and worn, in a natural way. In a prowling and unapologetic stride, he approached her, taking a seat on the next stool.

"Hi," Monica said.

"Hello. Looks like you need another drink."

His declarative statement and deep voice stirred a flutter in her stomach.

"Well, I don't usually accept drinks from strangers."

"My name's Robin Nettles, but my friends call me Rob."

"I'm Monica."

"Well, darlin', it seems we're no longer strangers."

Monica smiled and shook her head. His charming introduction and smooth Southern drawl left her feeling like an inexperienced schoolgirl with a crush. They fell into conversation easily, discussing sports allegiances and Rob's recent move to the city, but never work. It was refreshing.

"Recap," Rob said.

It was a game Monica had started to make sure he'd been listening to her rambling. She'd gone out with so many men who had perfected the smile-and-nod technique to deal with her incessant talking. Not one of them had ever really listened to her. After so much information, she would call for a recap. It was declared a test of attention spans and soberness. Rob passed every time and even took to testing her.

"You don't know who Michael Kors is, you've never heard of sexting, and your favorite movie is *The Getaway*. Not the remake, the original 1972 film with Steve McQueen."

"You've been paying attention."

"Of course I have. I'm a woman. We are amazing multitaskers. I'm probably better at it than most. It may even be in my job description. Your turn."

"Okay, let's see. You've never been to Mississippi," he said, frowning as he placed a hand over his heart as if wounded by the idea. "You love the smell of fingernail polish, your mother is an accountant, and your favorite place in the city is a tie between Sunset Cliffs and the Horton Plaza Mall."

"I do declare, sir, you are correct," Monica said using her best Southern accent.

"Well, ma'am, it's a good thing you're beautiful, because that accent was terrible."

"What? It couldn't be that bad. I've seen *Gone with the Wind* like a hundred times."

"I believe the entire Confederate infantry just turned over in their graves."

Monica laughed before emptying her glass. It felt amazing to have the attention of such a handsome man, and she wondered how she'd gotten so lucky. She flirted as best she could, touching his forearm to keep his attention and adjusting her cleavage discreetly. She'd been out of the dating game for a while, swearing off awkward meetings and cheap bastards for the past year. Somehow she knew coming out of retirement for this man would be worth it.

When he excused himself to use the restroom, she pulled out her compact and reapplied her vanilla-flavored gloss. She barely recognized her tired eyes as they stared back. While she still felt youthful, the tiny lines around her mouth and at the corners of her eyes gave her away. Perhaps if she didn't worry so much, Monica thought, pulling taut the soft skin to smooth it out.

"Want to get out of here, darlin'?" he whispered from behind her, while his hands came to rest on her hips.

Monica could feel his body against her back, his warm breath sliding down her neck and settling over her skin. Every touch felt undeniably right.

Without another word, she nodded and signaled to the bartender to close her tab. There was no uncomfortable air as they shared a cab in silence. Within the confines of her modest yet impeccably decorated apartment, they discussed her passion for changing the world and his passion for burning it.

Monica delighted in Rob's daredevil approach to life and his lilting drawl. Among hours of conversation, they kissed until breathless and held each other tight. By the time the morning sun's rays filtered through her curtains, Monica Templeton had fallen in love. She never knew it would be so easy.

On the other side of the city, Tristan stirred from his sleep. He rolled over and found a book pressed into his back. He reached beneath him, pulled it out, and marked the page. He wondered if its sharp dialogue and methodical plot had spurred the fantastic dreams of sexual banter and foreplay in a sleek limousine with Josie. He could still picture her straddling his lap with her hands braced on the roof. Soft lighting highlighted her face while the black windows blocked out the bustling world. He could almost hear her voice chanting his name in pleasure. Tristan groaned at the memory and willed away his morning wood.

He worked the early shift today, and that meant that he'd see Josie soon. He ran his fingers through his hair, a nervous habit developed years ago, but his hair was gone. A couple weeks ago, he'd needed a change, so he'd shaved it off. While liberating, it had left him with nothing to calm his anxiety. His hand passed over the fuzz, but it didn't have the same effect.

Tristan's theory was that this new coif would make him less recognizable to his former associates. Those people were tainted by Fiona and her father's manipulations, not to mention they held all his secrets. When he left the business, Tristan assumed they would come for him, but apparently he'd overestimated his worth. Still, he slept with his cold steel piece tucked safely beneath his pillow each night.

Smirking up at his ceiling, Tristan considered what his pompous father's reaction would be to the black oxide Desert Eagle pistol that had saved his life too many times to count. He pictured rolling up to the Fallbrook estate in his 1967 Impala and mowing down a few of the perfectly manicured hedges. Parading his branded skin, he would shove bars through his flesh, filling each pierced hole just for the reunion. His poor, docile mother would have a stroke and his father would call the authorities before he even recognized his own son. Tristan laughed at the absurdity of it all.

Some days, he missed them. He missed his mother's hugs and the way she sang church hymns as she cooked that evening's dinner. Even though he'd read them all, he missed his father's library and their afternoons of "man time" spent fishing or watching football. The country singer Kinky Friedman had said, "A happy childhood is the worst possible preparation for life." Tristan couldn't agree more. He hadn't been prepared for any of this.

He found his nerves frayed and he was anxious for Josie again. His chest seemed to vibrate with the need to see her, touch her.

Soon, the need to move, to fly took over, and he flung himself from the bed.

Tristan threw on some shorts and a T-shirt while trying not to glimpse his pathetic face in the mirror. He laced his running shoes and stretched his hands toward the ceiling before heading outside. Mornings on the California coast were so different from back home. The air was cool and welcoming. His steps sounded off left, then right, left, right. He emptied his head and pushed himself harder, sprinting up every hill until his lungs screamed for more air.

Every piece of graffiti caught his eye. Every colorful scene, every line of illegible text brought him back to her. He wondered if any of them had been done by Josie. By the time he made it back to his block, he was exhausted. He felt emptied and exorcised.

A young couple passed him on the sidewalk. Their joined hands swinging between them as if love could not nail them down. They barely noticed Tristan there, huffing and puffing.

It was easy to imagine a different life, playing out in an alternate universe. He would be graduating from college about now, then moving on to law school. Nothing but pride would reflect back at him from his family.

Dreams were something his parents encouraged. For a long time, Tristan had dreamed of McKenzi. In all the times he'd imagined a bright, shining future, he'd pictured her by his side.

Tristan had always been the most accomplished student, the shining example. He'd won science fair ribbons, academic awards, and scholarships to the nation's most prestigious universities. Through all his accomplishments, Tristan never disclosed, not to his jealous classmates or his adoring teachers, the secret behind his success. It was his ace in the hole, the one thing that guaranteed a future. However, when it had come time to cash in his chips, he'd thrown it all away for the love of a girl. Perhaps if

McKenzi hadn't left him with an expansive pit of sadness and hurt, he would have never sought out the company of Fiona Moloney. He wouldn't have been dragged into Fiona's world and her crooked family. He wouldn't be a shadow of his former self.

Though he may have been misguided and misled, he'd made every bad decision on his own. He didn't blame McKenzi or her father, Earl. Tristan understood now what he never could as a child. McKenzi was taken from him by a father who wanted only to provide a new beginning for his little girl. After suffering the loss of his wife, he was hurting and wrecked and needed to distance himself from everything familiar. He doomed them by trying to save them.

Tristan took the stairs to his apartment two at a time. He thought of a cold shower, then falling back into bed and more dreams of Josie. But the thought of seeing her in the flesh kept him motivated. Today, he'd be a half hour early for his shift.

☾

Josie approached the Darkroom knowing that Tristan would already be a couple of hours into his shift. She walked down the sidewalk, flitting between other pedestrians. She slid down the urban hill, watching the sun disappear into the bay. The orange hues looked like flames on the water. Soon the night would come, that purple-blue polka-dotted sky that embraced her like nothing else. Josie turned the corner and sighed at what she found there.

Tristan was leaning against the brick, smoking a cigarette like it was his last before execution. She watched as his eyes squinted when he inhaled and the long fingers of his free hand tapped against his thigh. When finished, he threw the cigarette into the street, letting it roll downhill and out of sight. She stepped closer, finally gaining his attention.

His lips volleyed between a half smile and a nervous frown as he took in her appearance. Every curve of her body called to him, every nerve ending felt frayed and drawn to her. Free from the oversize hoodie, she looked amazing, and he instantly felt the familiar stirring of lust.

Silently, Josie made her way over, grabbing his hand to tow him along. She didn't shy away from his shocked expression. They ducked into the alley and she pushed him against the wall. Her small, frenzied hands ran from his belt buckle, up the hard planes of his chest, and around his neck. His eyes flicked back and forth between her mouth and her cleavage, while he denied the temptation to return her touch.

Her slight pucker hovered just below his, her heels giving her the perfect height to reach him. Their ragged breaths washed over each other while the heat radiating between their bodies created an almost visual aura of need. She had always taken her conquests with no apologies, but with Tristan it was different. More than she wanted him, she wanted him to want her too. Josie hung there, just out of reach, waiting to make sure he would not reject her. She wasn't sure if he gave in or gave up, but she moved forward when his eyes fluttered closed.

Josie crushed her mouth to his, finding purchase on his delicious bottom lip. He moaned against her mouth, only fueling the hunger that grew inside.

Unable to resist any longer, Tristan pulled her flush against his body. The way she molded to him, a perfect puzzle piece, told him this was right. They were a mess of roaming hands and lips, a dance of lust and claim-staking kisses. They were reunited after what seemed like a lifetime of purgatory, though the moment would be short-lived.

Tristan reluctantly pulled himself from her lips, willing his physical and emotional need to dissipate. Josie attempted to pull him closer, but he found the strength to resist.

"What's wrong?" she asked, annoyed with his resistance.

"I mourned you," he said.

"I'm not dead."

"I didn't believe you were dead at first. I begged my mom to take me to New York so that I could look for you. Well, until I found out there are eight million people there."

"You were a kid."

Tristan shook his head.

"I was pissed at your dad. So mad that he took you away from me just for a better job. Now I wonder if that's really why you left, if there wasn't more to it. You broke my heart, McKenzi, and here you are. It's just too much."

She didn't correct her name. Instead, Josie was silent as she tried to work out his declaration. Was she too much? She'd never been too much for anyone. She'd never even been enough.

"I loved you from the first time I saw you," he whispered, placing a soft kiss against her neck. "We were seven years old. Your hair was in braids. You were new to school and had nowhere to sit at lunch. You marched over and offered me your pudding if I'd let you sit down."

Josie blinked, trying to visualize the scene through his words. She'd never wished for her memory to come back, scared to tap into the darkness locked away. Now that she knew there was more than pain, she wished for the ability to reminisce.

"Did you let me sit down?" she asked.

"Hell, yes. It was chocolate pudding."

He smiled at Josie, his green eyes bright as he tried to push the images from his head into hers. She started to return his smile before she caught herself and corrected it. Was this guy for real?

"No one falls in love when they're seven," she stated, dropping her hands from his body and taking a step away.

"'The magic of first love is our ignorance that it can ever end,'" Tristan quoted. "Of all the things I've ever been unsure of, my feelings for you were never questioned. It wasn't puppy love or teenage infatuation, it was real. You loved me too, Mac."

"My name is Josie."

She took another step back, fearing the sudden shift in direction. She crossed her arms over her chest and glared at him. Lust, greed, hurt, pain, fear—these things she knew. She knew nothing of love.

Tristan had romantically loved only two people in all of his twenty-two years, and each of them had broken him in her own way. McKenzi had provided him an innocent beginning, paving the way for many of his firsts. Their relationship had been exciting and fun, built around a solid friendship. With her gone, he'd lost so much more than just a girlfriend. Fiona had destroyed him to the very core, crippling his trust and his future. Every rational fiber screamed at him to use caution, remain distant. Still, here he was professing his faith in love, surprising even himself.

Josie thought about what a contradiction Tristan was. His exterior was industrial-strength steel, designed to keep intruders out, but beneath that lay a kind and honest soul. She squeezed her arms tighter around her body, wondering if he could save her. Did she want to be saved?

"I'm not McKenzi. She's dead."

Josie needed to make this clear. She felt his curiosity, his adoration, for who she used to be. McKenzi once had him. Josie would never deserve him.

Tristan stepped toward her, cautiously closing the distance between them. He felt the warning in her words. He understood the significance of her arms wrapped tightly around herself, her fingers clawing at her ribs.

"But Josie's not dead." He spoke softly, placing his large palm over the left side of her chest. "Every second, your heart valves push blood through here and snap shut, creating a thump, thump."

He paused. "Thump, thump. You can hear it. It's proof that you're still alive."

Josie sucked in a deep breath, her brain reeling from his words. Her eyes looked everywhere but at his face. She knew his sympathetic gaze would unravel every bit of her protective housing. After a few breaths of silence, she looked anyway.

The blue neon light from the bar's sign reflected down the alley and across his face. His embellished skin glowed sapphire every other second, the blinking rhythm casting him as a saint, then a sinner. He was a beautiful stranger, fucking up her world.

"I can't do this," she said firmly, stepping back so that Tristan's hand fell away. "My past is not even mine. I don't want it."

"That's not true," he challenged. "You sought me out, Josie. You found me. You followed me and watched me. You're drawn to me just like I am to you. That's why you're here."

She winced, feeling his words cut her with truth.

"No, I'm here because I want to fuck you."

Tristan felt the weight of her audacious statement sitting heavy on his chest. If he had been a lesser man, she would have crushed him with those words. He recognized a defensive maneuver when he saw one.

He remained silent as she left him in the alley, alone with his thoughts, a littering of cigarette butts, and the fading click of her heels.

☾

Josie capped the marker and leaned over to blow on the drawing. She watched closely as the ink soaked into the wood wall and dried to a matte finish. These things always gave her a sense of worth. They were the opposite of her, permanent and immortal.

She finished the last of her drink, waiting for the alcohol to deliver what she needed. It had been a mistake staying sober tonight. She had wanted to do it for Tristan, and to prove to herself that she could. But now she needed the pain washed away.

"Hey there, can I buy you a drink?" a man asked from the table next to hers.

Josie smiled and looked him over. He was moderately attractive, middle-aged, and married. The distinct tan line on his left hand was a dead giveaway. She didn't care, though. He was the lucky guy tonight, his win concreted by the absence of tattoos and all-knowing green eyes.

"Hell, yeah, you can," Josie answered, waving him over.

"You here alone?" he asked, taking a seat next to her.

She almost rolled her eyes at his clichéd pickup lines. This guy had been out of the game a very long time.

"Not anymore."

Josie's drink arrived and she downed it in one long swallow. The burn of the alcohol stoked her furious need to erase Tristan for good.

"So, what do you do for a living?" he asked.

"Look, this is not an interview. My name is Josie and I'm a sure thing. You want to see me naked or not?"

A few minutes later, the waitress returned, only to find two empty chairs.

☾

"Whaddya mean you're not gonna to see him again?" Alex yelled, his voice three octaves higher than usual.

He tossed the bag of burgers and fries to her and sat on the edge of the sofa.

"Jo, he knew you back in New Orleans. Which means he knew your family, *mami*. You don't gotta be best friends, but you gotta get some info. Then kick him to the curb."

Alex knew he'd have to approach this carefully. He just didn't understand her willingness to let go of this person who held so many answers.

"My past is better left in the past, Alex."

Josie pulled the greasy food from the paper bag and threw a few fries into her mouth. She wanted to avoid this conversation altogether, but Alex had this inexplicable ability to pull information from her.

"That's bullshit, and you know it."

"Do you remember everything in your past?" she asked.

"Shit, yes."

"How much of it do you wish you didn't?"

He shrugged, not wanting to further prove her point.

"Still, I'd wanna know what he knows," Alex said.

"You know what they say about curiosity?"

Josie smirked, knowing she'd gained the upper hand. He shook his head and headed for the door.

"You're not a cat, more like a stubborn burro," he said, the *r*'s rolling off his tongue in annoyance.

She felt relieved when Alex was gone, not having to keep her façade in place any longer. Josie wanted to believe her own lies. She wanted to own them and plant them firmly into her resolve. In all honesty, she wasn't sure how long determination alone could keep her from seeking out Tristan again.

6. GRAVITY
THE ATTRACTIVE FORCE THAT GOVERNS
THE MOTION OF CELESTIAL BODIES.

Ever since Josie walked away from him, Tristan had felt that aching pain return to his chest. Although reminiscent of the first time he lost her, it felt deeper and more excruciating, knowing that this time it had been her choice. Having never been convinced of God's existence, he didn't have a higher power to plead to, though most nights he found himself begging an empty room to return her. He wasn't eating enough, and as much as he knew it would numb his pain, he ignored the alcohol leering at him from behind the bar. For sixteen days Tristan had survived on gas-station dinners and Marlboro cigarettes.

Now he stood behind the familiar bar and filled drink orders with no attention to anything else. Erin was still training the new hire, Brandie, so she was not hanging around for her usual chitchats. Tristan was thankful.

For the past two days, Brandie had been flirting with him, and it was starting to wear on his nerves. Lee had told him that the girl gave great head, and just to feel some kind of release, Tristan considered finding out for himself. She was attractive, though her beauty was marred by her shallow personality. None of that mattered since his mind and body craved no one but Josie.

When Brandie's shift ended, she sat at the bar wearing her practiced smile.

"I'd like a margarita, no salt," she requested, placing her hand over his on the bar.

Her eyes violated Tristan as he moved behind the bar, mixing and shaking, before pouring the concoction over ice. She seemed mesmerized as she watched the colorful images twist and stretch over the muscles of his forearms. Tristan set the drink in front of her dismissively. Upon tasting the drink, she licked her lips and purred with approval.

Throughout the evening, he continued making her drinks, and she continued to brazenly flirt. It took every last bit of bred-in manners to not lose his cool. Each flutter of her eyelashes, every overenthusiastic laugh infuriated Tristan further. He tried to control his anger; it wasn't her fault she wasn't Josie. Finally freed on his smoke break, Tristan hurried outside into the shadow of the alley. He sucked on a cigarette and kicked at a loose brick in the base of the wall.

"I wondered where you went," Brandie said, appearing out of nowhere.

Two more buttons on her shirt had come undone and there was an exaggerated sway to her hips as she wobbled toward him.

Within seconds she had her tight little body pressed up against his with her hands on his waist.

"What are you doing?" he asked.

Tristan tried to make his voice light, but it came out strained. She mistook that for mutual lust.

"I want this," she said, grinning up at him and palming his crotch.

Tristan jumped and pushed her away.

"Fuck, Brandie," he complained.

"Exactly," she answered.

"You're a beautiful girl, but I don't want you like that."

Tristan ran both hands over his nonexistent hair and darted back inside. He let Lee know that he was cutting out early. Only one destination entered his mind. He would not fight it any longer.

☾

In theory, sixteen days doesn't seem like a long time. In the grand scheme of man's historical existence, it is less than nothing. Yet during these sixteen days, Josie had endured the greatest test to her willpower.

It had been just over two weeks since she'd seen Tristan, and she felt as though she was fading inside. The bit of light he had ignited, the spark of hope that had emanated from her very soul, was all but extinguished. She could never go back to the time before he'd come along because now she knew he was out there, calling to her.

She hated rejection. To kill the hurt, she found a man to fuck her senseless. When that didn't work, she got so high she couldn't remember who she was or why she hurt. When that had worn off, she felt even worse. She snuck through the nighttime streets, searching out white walls to deface. When she found them, she'd get her piece thrown up and find somewhere to sit and inspect it. Perfectly formed letters filled with blues and oranges made words that defined her. *Alone. Want. Need.* Though they looked like single-word declarations to everyone else, they were so much more.

Josie spent the rest of her time pacing the floors of her apartment. Like a caged animal, she wanted to beat and scratch at the walls that held her captive. Though her confinement was self-imposed, she knew that venturing out again would be too tempting. She missed the nights spent in the Darkroom, nights when drunken strangers and a familiar staff left her feeling like she wasn't so alone.

In her earliest memories, Josie could recall what it felt like to be frightened by the unknown. Because of her amnesia, everyone had been a stranger. She remembered the police telling her that her father was dead. She remembered feeling crushed by the news, not because of his death but because she could not recall his face or voice. They had given her no information about her mother or any other family, just a vague report of who she was and where she was going. She felt cheated that she wasn't allowed to retrieve any personal items from their apartment, all of it becoming state's evidence. With no mementos of her former life, Josie had been left to fly blind.

That seemed like three lifetimes ago. Josie felt old and weathered now, a seasoned veteran to the ways of the world. She was not the naïve little girl they found in the subway. She was wary and untrusting of people's intentions. Her emotions were severed from her heart, leaving only her jaded mind to make decisions.

The past sixteen days had proved her to be a coward. Josie could not openly admit that she needed anyone or anything. Her usual drugs seemed to leave her in more pain. She'd thrown out the rest, only to buy more pills the next day. She didn't even take them. They sat untouched in the plastic bag tucked into a kitchen drawer intended for utensils. Knowing they were there was enough to get her through.

She didn't understand why she felt defenseless in Tristan's presence, the way his touch set her on fire, or how Earth seemed to tilt on its axis just to bring them together. She felt weakened by the unfamiliar heartache of wanting him. Lying on her floor, Josie pressed her cheek against the wood planks as her hand sketched mindlessly. She didn't know what time it was or what day it was, only that she'd seen too many sunsets since she'd last seen his face.

She closed her eyes and imagined running her fingernails along his scalp, through that short bit of hair. Josie just knew it would feel like the soft fuzz of a velvet toy against her fingers. Mentally, she traced every permanent line of ink on his skin, memorizing the curve of each design and the meaning behind it. She envisioned flattening her tongue and sliding it over the scruff of his jaw, eventually biting down for a better taste. Even more curious, she imagined herself wrapped in his arms with no sexual connotations, while he whispered secrets of their past against her skin.

Frustrated, Josie pulled herself from the floor and plodded to the bathroom. She showered and dressed and awaited Alex's arrival. As she sat and stared at the blank paper, her leg bounced nervously. She glanced at the kitchen drawer holding her escape and back to her sketchpad. She decided she would power through this on her own.

She almost ignored the pounding at the door, delighted at the idea of messing with Alex. When the sound shot through her apartment again, she decided that she'd better put him out of his misery before he destroyed the door completely. Josie unlocked and opened the door, only to find Tristan standing there, fist poised to knock again. She whimpered, her pencil clattering to the floor. Relief flooded her body along with an inclination to attach herself to him and never let go.

"Josie, please," he whispered, his voice scratchy and thick.

He wasn't sure what he was begging for. He only knew that whatever it was lay within her. Nodding, she took his hand and pulled him inside, closing the door behind them. Silently, reverently, she sat him down on her sofa and crawled into his lap. Tristan's arms embraced her and crushed her to his body, molding them into one form. Her head lay tucked on his shoulder. She'd never felt so safe.

In the quiet space of the apartment, Tristan simply held Josie. He surrounded her with himself, creating a shield between the evil outside world and the beautiful wounded girl. He concentrated on the bare skin of her arms beneath his fingertips, inhaling deeply just to breathe her in. This moment, imagined so many times, had been lacking in power compared to reality. Without even trying, without any conditions, this girl owned him.

Just after midnight, Alex found the couple curled into each other in the corner of Josie's couch. Even as they slept, their possessive fingers dug into the other's flesh. He'd been angry when he found her door unlocked again and was about to scold her as if she were a forgetful child, but when he spotted the sight before him, he understood.

Alex had never seen Josie so peaceful, so free from the darkness that permanently loomed over her. Even without an introduction, he recognized Tristan. He knew no one else could invade Josie's space like that. He left the pizza box on her table and locked the door behind him.

As he kicked Mrs. Thompson's brainless cat from his door, he couldn't help but feel a tinge of sadness. With Tristan around, he feared that Josie wouldn't need him anymore. He had served his purpose and he'd be dismissed like one of her crumpled drawings. Perhaps, one day, someone would unfold him, smooth out his wrinkles, and hang him up anyway.

Tristan woke in the early hours of the morning, his legs and arms aching from the position he'd slept in. He looked at Josie's sleeping face and was reminded of the young innocence that was McKenzi's. It was easier to see now that she was unconscious and defenseless. Needing the bathroom, he shifted over and left her to finish her rest.

He stretched his arms high above his head, bending and twisting to bring circulation back to his limbs. He relieved himself and threw some water on his face. The liquid dotted his skin with crystal-like drops. It clung to his eyelashes, matting them together, and dripped from the scruff of his chin, taking with it the grunge from the night before. The circles beneath his eyes were nearly invisible. He looked refreshed in a way that made him feel like a fool for staying away. With Josie cradled in his arms, he'd slept better than he had in years. They'd both waved their white flags and given in to the gravity pulling them together.

It had always been this way for them. Even in grade school, they would argue over something silly, swearing off their friendship forever. By recess, they'd be huddled together beneath the monkey bars, whispering apologies. McKenzi had been more stubborn than Tristan, but she always came back to him.

Tristan used the bottom of his T-shirt to pat his face dry. He looked for an extra toothbrush, but all he found were tampons, charcoal pencils, and paint markers in her medicine cabinet. He pushed the toothpaste around with his finger as best he could and rinsed.

There was only one door besides the bathroom, and as Tristan let himself inside, he had no idea what he'd find. At first it was too dark to see anything, but his eyes quickly adjusted to the dim light coming through the curtain. There was a mattress on the floor, tucked into the farthest corner of the room. No bedding or pillows topped it. Haphazard stacks of spray-paint cans lined the perimeter of the room, along with sketchpads and a few articles of clothing.

He walked to the window and pulled back the curtain, flooding the room with daylight. Tristan gasped. Pencil and charcoal sketches covered every inch of wall from ceiling to floor. He turned, scanning the rest of the room and finding each wall plastered in the same way.

"Holy shit," Tristan whispered.

A familiar face drew him in as he stepped to the wall for closer inspection. A young boy of eleven or twelve stared back at him, his smile a bit higher on one side. Tristan ran his index finger over the lines of his baby face, reflecting the crooked grin.

"Tristan?" Josie's voiced called out. He spun to find her displaying a defensive posture, leaning against the door frame. "What are you doing in here?"

"Just looking," he answered.

"These are private."

He nodded, leaving a beat of silence in case she wanted to continue. She didn't.

"You drew these?"

Josie nodded.

"You don't know who they are, do you?" he asked.

Her scowl disappeared as she shifted from foot to foot. She refused to meet his eyes.

"No, but I dream about them. I see nothing else when I sleep. Just these faces," she answered, pressing her palm to her forehead.

Tristan walked to her and pulled her inside the room. He placed Josie in front of his body, facing the middle of the largest wall.

"This," he said, pointing to the wild-haired boy, "is me." Josie gasped, her hand flying to cover her mouth. "Your shading is amazing, you even included my eyebrow scar." Tristan took a step sideways and brought Josie with him. "This one here is your mom. She was always laughing like that. The one above her is your dad. He was the chief of police in Gretna."

Tristan glanced over her shoulder to see her trembling fingers still covering her mouth and her other arm wrapped around her waist. He slid his hands around her, holding Josie to his chest for support. Even though she had no conscious recollection of her childhood, she'd always had these faces with her. After a minute of silence and stuttered breaths, she finally spoke.

"She was beautiful," Josie said, running her fingers over her mother's face.

"Yes, she was."

"I can't believe my dad had that beard," she said finally, smiling as her eyes scanned the drawings. "I look like him."

Tristan squeezed her tighter in confirmation. Josie took a step closer to Tristan's sketch now, scrutinizing the curve of his chin and the weight of his smile.

"I should have seen it sooner. Your smile is just the same," she whispered.

Tristan kissed the side of her neck and she hummed in satisfaction. Josie spun in his arms and kissed his lips. She lacked the verbal ability to thank him otherwise, so she stuck to what she was good at, pouring all of herself into that kiss.

It had never felt like this for either of them, and somehow they knew that it never would again. When the intensity became overwhelming, they pulled away.

"Tell me about the rest of them," she said.

He nodded and pointed her toward the wall again.

An hour later, after each drawing had been identified, they

emerged. Josie felt lighter, like her shoulders could stand a little taller now. These faces had haunted her for so long she'd begun to resent them. But not anymore. Now she knew these were the people who had been most important to her. These had been the ones to love her, to mold her and, in Tristan's case, eventually to mourn her. It had always felt like Josie versus the world, but in reality she'd never been alone.

They huddled around the room-temperature pizza and ate until they were satisfied. Josie led Tristan back to the couch, where she curled her knees up to her chest and tucked her toes beneath his thigh.

"This is a first, you know," Josie said.

"What?"

"Having someone sleep at my place, and," she paused, feeling a bit embarrassed by her lifestyle for the first time, "waking up with someone I didn't have sex with."

"Well, I've read that cuddling is more important than the act of sex. It's more intimate and relaxing, opening people up for more honest bonding."

"Huh."

"Yeah, I don't buy it either," Tristan said, smiling at her.

"We could change that, you know," she suggested.

She ran her hand up his thigh with a feather-light touch. Scratching her nails up the seam of his zipper, Josie was pleased with the deep moan Tristan let out.

"Josie."

"I want you, Tristan," she purred.

His hand clamped over hers when she reached for his belt buckle. Tristan surprised himself with the amount of restraint he possessed.

"I want you too. I do. But not until you're ready."

Josie frowned at him.

"Oh, I'm ready. I'm always ready."

"That's the problem," he said. "I'm not going to let you use sex to distract from what is really happening here."

"What exactly is happening here?"

Tristan didn't answer her with words. He simply smiled and laced his fingers through hers. He knew she couldn't handle any big declarations or stark truths.

Josie released his hand and scraped around her cuticles, trying to remove the charcoal dust. She ignored the paint flecks dotting her nails.

"Tell me something that only I would know," she demanded.

Tristan knew exactly what she meant. He looked into her shining eyes and thought it over. Memories flooded his mind and he scrolled through them quickly, finding the perfect one to share.

"I saved you from drowning once."

"What?" Her eyes grew large and she gestured wildly for him to continue.

"We were at the lake behind my house, walking on the pier, when you tripped and fell in. You must have hit your head or something, because you didn't come up. I panicked and jumped in, somehow finding your arm beneath the water. It was freezing and I struggled for a few minutes to drag you out. You weren't breathing. So I started CPR. After a few forced breaths, you started choking and sputtering water. I carried you back to my house and gave you some of my clothes while I threw yours in the dryer. We never told anyone."

Josie wiggled her toes beneath the weight of his leg and smiled.

"How did you know CPR?" she asked.

"My father's a doctor. Dr. Daniel Fallbrook always liked to make me a shining example of his abilities."

"Lucky me," she said.

"Lucky me," he repeated.

Silence enveloped them as they sat in the afterglow of bygone days. Tristan loved how it was so quiet here, nothing to distract them from each other. Josie sighed and looked at the clock on her wall, wondering how much longer she could have him.

"We got into a fight the next day because you considered the CPR your first kiss and I argued that it was only a medical procedure," Tristan continued, laughing at the memory. "You were so stubborn. I shut you up."

"How?"

"I kissed you and told you that was your real first kiss. You didn't argue."

Josie ducked her head, blushing at his devilish smirk. Tristan had a way of dissolving her tough exterior, revealing glimpses of the adolescent girl inside.

She started at his wrist and traced a line up his arm until the art disappeared beneath his sleeve. She loved following the paths across his skin, wondering where she'd end up. Her fingers ghosted over traditional tattoo flash such as spiderwebs and harsh red flames before tracing the gray bark of a large oak tree.

"What is this one for?" she asked, pointing to the image on the inside of his forearm.

"It's a tree in my yard back home that you and I practically lived in. It was always where we'd go to play and hang out. Later, we would climb up there to spy on my neighbors or make out."

Josie's fingertip moved over the twisting limbs as though she could feel the scratchy bark beneath her touch.

"This was for us," Josie stated, gesturing toward the art.

"For you," Tristan corrected, picturing her laughing face covered with dots of light and shadows beneath the branches of their tree.

She lay her head down on her knees. Josie knew that she was venturing into unknown territory with Tristan. She felt the kindness in his eyes. The way he offered himself up made her want to fall apart with unworthiness. Wrapped in the cocoon of her apartment, it would be easy to get lost in his memories.

7. ECLIPSE

A PARTIAL OR TOTAL OBSCURING OF
ONE CELESTIAL BODY BY ANOTHER.

Rob pulled into a parking space and killed the engine. It was rare
to find a spot so close to home. He grabbed the four bags of groceries and walked the half block to his door. The sun was shining
and the air was cool and salty. When all was quiet, he could even
hear the waves against the shore. Beach life was good.

"Hey, man. How's it going?" his neighbor asked.

The man stood in the shade of a palm tree waving at him. He
wore board shorts and no shirt, standard dress code for these
parts. Rob's neighbors were pleasant enough, old hippies who made
a living painting murals and teaching tourists how to surf.

"Good, thanks," he answered.

He put the bags down on his front porch while fumbling with his keys. He could feel his neighbor's eyes on him.

"Groceries?" the guy asked. "Man, I'm starving."

Rob nodded and slid his key into the lock. Was he supposed to offer him some groceries or invite him over for dinner? He didn't know protocol for curing the munchies of your stoner neighbor. Once inside, he found comfort in the distance between them, no longer responsible for his side of their awkward conversation.

New to the city, and the West Coast, Rob Nettles found himself out of sorts. He had moved for work, transferred for a more advantageous position. He hadn't thought twice about leaving his former home behind.

He'd settled himself into a small beach neighborhood within the city, trying to mingle among the locals. The community was home to free spirits who supported local businesses and were sympathetic to its large vagrant population. In the four weeks he'd been there, he'd become addicted to authentic Mexican food and learned to identify the best places for imported beer. That was the extent of his adaptation.

At sunset, he walked the short block to the beach. Content to just sit in the sand and watch the sun drop into the water, Rob knew he had it good. He wondered if the people who had been here for years still felt the appreciation he did. He couldn't imagine ever taking this for granted. This city felt alive, like the thriving metropolis knew him and welcomed him.

He'd called some of the biggest cities in the country home, but this place was different. The Pacific Ocean calmed him, and the energy of the city fed him. He knew it wouldn't be long until he assumed the way of life here. With its laissez-faire attitude and persuasive charm, he'd be a fool not to.

Mississippi, the place of Rob's childhood, was an alternate

universe compared to the white sand beaches of California. Back home, the oppressive summer's heat and humidity could melt you to the sidewalk. Meanwhile, San Diego always offered a cool breeze and moderate temperatures. Rob had traded his boots for flip-flops, his hat for a messy haircut, and his bluegrass for reggae. Still, each day he returned home to the empty apartment, he felt like he hadn't exactly found where he fit in.

That was, until he'd found a woman by the name of Monica Templeton. Within a matter of minutes, she'd turned his world upside down, making him abandon all reason. He let down his guard and pulled her inside. This wasn't supposed to happen. This doesn't happen in real life, not this fast.

Twenty-four hours after their first encounter, he knew he'd never been more wrong. It happens. And it had happened to him.

After spending that first night on the couch with Josie, Tristan hadn't stepped foot outside her apartment. He'd called work, citing a family emergency, and stayed for two more days. They did nothing more than talk and sleep, and sometimes he'd watch her sketch things in her notebook while he read. Most of their time together had been spent telling stories of their past. For so long those memories had been pushed into the background of his mind. It invigorated him to relive those happy scenes, playing them out for Josie to hear.

Tristan slid his tray onto the lunchroom table and took a seat. He poked at the brown glob of chili with his spoon.

"Where's Mac?" he asked.

"She checked out in second hour," Kohen answered.

"Why? What's wrong?"

"I don't know. April told Ryan who told me. April's in that class with her."

Tristan abandoned his food and searched the rows of tables for April Landry. This girl was the mouth of the South, and if anyone knew details, she surely would. Spotting her three tables over, he approached the group.

"Why did Mac leave?" he blurted out, interrupting a conversation already in progress.

"Who?" she asked.

"McKenzi!"

"Oh, her," April said, rolling her eyes. "I don't know. One minute she was there, the next she was gone."

The afternoon was torture. Tristan's mind went over every possible scenario, each one more terrible than the one before. By the time the last bell rang, he'd convinced himself that McKenzi had suffered some sort of life-threatening injury and was lying helpless in Charity Hospital.

When the last bell rang, he ran the entire way to her house, tripping up the steps and collapsing onto the front porch. He beat on the front door, yelling for Earl to answer it and tell him that Mac was okay.

Finally, the door was thrown open and McKenzi stood staring at her exhausted boyfriend.

"What are you doing here?" she asked.

"Are you okay? Let me look at you," he almost shouted. Tristan entered her house, his hands checking the functionality of each limb, his eyes searching for signs of injury. He spun her in place, completing his thorough examination. "How's your pulse? Are you feeling faint? Seeing spots? How many fingers am I holding up?"

"Are you done?" McKenzi asked, one eyebrow quirked at his crazed behavior.

"Why did you leave school?" Tristan asked, his voice accusatory.

"None of your business."

"Tell me, Mac!"

"I don't want to."

"Fine! Just have your little secret," he yelled.

"I can't, Tristan."

"You sure the hell can. I'll go up there and rip every ★NSYNC poster from your wall!"

"Fine, you hardheaded pig! I got my period, okay? I bled all over my favorite blue jean skirt and had to come home! Are you satisfied, you nosy ass?"

Tristan scrambled backward off her porch and, without another word, took off toward his house. When he finally made it home, he begged his mother to help him make it right. He couldn't stand the idea of Mac being angry with him.

Two hours later, McKenzi answered the door to find a blue gift bag topped with a yellow bow. She looked around but found no sign of its owner. Tristan smiled from his hiding place, watching her carry the package inside. Having a doctor for a father, Tristan's thorough sex talk had involved all aspects of reproduction and the female cycle. McKenzi sat at her kitchen table and unpacked her gift, item by item, unaware of being observed through the large bay window. There was a bottle of ibuprofen, a package of chocolates, a brand-new blue jean skirt with a tiny note written in Tristan's obsessively neat cursive. McKenzi smiled, barely stifling her laughter as she read it: "I'm sorry. You'll feel better in five to seven days. Tristan."

Josie was so tickled by the story she smothered his face with kisses and insisted that he had to be the sweetest twelve-year-old in the history of the world. Tristan returned her kisses and whispered how he wished she could remember that day to tell him her own version of it.

Their relationship was a curious one—giving and taking in small doses. Josie still seemed shielded, as if she were awaiting rejection. Tristan knew no matter what he verbally promised, she'd never believe that he was here to stay. So he vowed to show her, to prove to her that he wasn't just a fleeting reminder of her past. He felt as if his roots had taken hold and wrapped themselves around Josie. He was immovable and he'd remain that way for as long as she'd allow it.

The woman who sat before him was molded from years of acts so damaging Tristan couldn't bring himself to imagine them. The fact that the people who were entrusted with her well-being had brought harm to her made him boil with anger. He didn't understand how anyone could look into those eyes and bring hurt to this girl.

Tristan had always been protective. His father taught him to love and cherish women and to keep them safe at any cost. Dr. Daniel Fallbrook was just that kind of man. He still believed in chivalry and courtship and reverence for your elders. Tristan learned early on in life that his father's word was final, his mother was never to be disrespected, and he was to put forth his very best effort on all tasks.

When Tristan lost McKenzi, he'd been devastated. He'd felt abandoned and completely cheated by her death. Everyone looked at him with sympathetic but dismissive eyes. They thought he would soon get over it. He was just a child. No one understood what Mac meant to him; they never would. Tristan had mourned her with every piece of his mind, body, and soul.

It had been one thing when she'd moved across the country. Both of them had been heartbroken. But they'd made promises to find each other again. There was solace in the fact that McKenzi still existed, however unreachable she may have been. When news of her death surfaced, Tristan hadn't believed it. He'd thought that it had been a joke of the cruelest nature and raged out at anyone who would listen.

Looking back, he recognized now that he had gone through

every Kübler-Ross stage of grief. After denial, Tristan's anger had tried to purge McKenzi from his system, and when she wouldn't go, he had begun to bargain. He'd begged and pleaded for just one more chance to see her, for just one more moment to tell her how much he needed her.

To a fourteen-year-old-boy, depression was not a familiar state. Though he knew the definition of the word and all its symptoms, Tristan was not able to recognize it in himself. Even though his grades suffered and he didn't have the will to eat, Tristan thought he had finally accepted the loss of his best friend. His mother had watched him with a worried eye and his father had grown tired of the moping.

The summer after his sixteenth birthday marked two years since McKenzi had been gone. He'd finally become social again, hanging out with friends and spending more time outside his bedroom than in it.

This particular day, a group of boys had gone down to the lake for a party. There had been loud music and kids dancing around an overgrown bonfire. Couples huddled in dark shadows, kissing and pawing at each other. Girls, wearing next to nothing in the heat, danced together, taunting the boys. Tristan was immune to all of it. The waves lapped at the shore as he sat motionless, eyeing the beer growing warm in his hand.

She'd first appeared as part of a group, though Tristan would say that Fiona stood out like a goddess among mortals. Her cheerless blue eyes had reflected his own feelings and he'd felt drawn to her sadness. That was the instant that his life shifted, the circumstance that set into motion the destruction of every dream he had ever built.

Fiona, the bottle blonde with an acidic smile, had changed who he was destined to be. The girl had redirected his life, and he'd been all too willing to let her. Tristan had left behind his family and embraced her as the only thing tethering him to happiness.

"Where were you?" Josie's voice startled Tristan, and he looked down to see her eyes fixed upon his. "Up here," she clarified, tapping at his temple. "Where were you?"

"In Wonderland," he answered absently.

"How's the Queen?"

"Which one?"

"Huh?" Josie asked. "The mean one."

"Well, there's the Queen of Hearts in *Alice's Adventures in Wonderland* and then there's the Red Queen in the sequel, *Through the Looking Glass*," Tristan answered.

"Whichever one said 'Off with their heads!' I liked her."

Tristan smiled.

"That's Disney's version. She's more of a combination of the Queen of Hearts, the Duchess, and the Red Queen. Pretty much a sadist who is easily annoyed."

"So she just goes around beheading anyone who irks her. I can get behind that," Josie said.

"If we lived in a world like that, we'd have a much smaller population. Get cut off in traffic? Bang. Cashier doesn't take your coupon? Bang. Chaos and no laws to hold people accountable for their actions."

"Can you imagine the thrill, though? Never knowing when you were going to die? Maybe you piss someone off and that's it. You're gone. I think it would force people to live the best life possible all the time. No working at jobs they hate or staying in bad relationships."

"And also people would go around fulfilling all of their selfish desires, however heinous they might be. How would you separate the general population from the guy who wants to chain women up in his basement and torture them? You couldn't. Anarchism is a philosophy that holds the government to be immoral because of its use of violence, authority, and force. Seems ironic that, with lawlessness, the citizens would be just as immoral."

"Depends on your definition of morality, I guess," Josie said.

"Conformity to the rules of right conduct. But then, what is right?"

"Exactly," she said. "Getting high and tagging pristine walls feels right."

"Psychopaths and deviants believe what they do is right. Or they just don't care."

"Kind of like me," Josie teased.

"I don't believe you don't care about your self-destructive behavior. I'd say you were more masochistic as a result of neglect and dysfunctional feelings about yourself."

Josie popped up and stomped to the kitchen. She pulled a beer from her otherwise empty fridge and twisted off the cap. As she brought the bottle to her lips and let the coolness soothe her scorching insides, she squeezed the cap tight into her fist. The metal edges cut into her palm until she released it to the floor.

She kept her back to Tristan as she finished the beer. When she slammed the empty bottle down, Josie realized her fingers were trembling.

Tristan's shadow cloaked her in darkness as he approached. Josie closed her eyes and tilted her head toward the ceiling. She exhaled slowly and deliberately before speaking.

"Not you too," she said. Tristan remained silent, but he wrapped his arms around her. His embrace was comforting and the answer to all her problems. "Don't head-shrink me. I've had enough of that. Not from you, okay?"

"I'm sorry," he whispered.

Josie spun in his arms and gave her most convincing smile.

"Do you want to get out of here?" she asked.

"Yeah, where to?"

She just pulled him toward the door.

"Do you have your car?" He nodded. "Good."

No questions asked, Tristan drove her to Trader Joe's and followed her around as she shopped. He loved how domestic and utterly normal it felt to do this with her. As they loaded the bags into his car, curiosity finally got the best of him.

"Are you cooking?" he asked.

Josie laughed, throwing her head back and placing her hand over her stomach. Tristan just watched and waited for an answer.

"Uh, no. This isn't for us."

She instructed him toward Balboa, and when they were parked, she wordlessly grabbed half the bags and started walking. Tristan carried the rest of the food and followed her through the grass.

"Stems!" Gavin shouted. She sat on their usual bench smoking a cigarette.

"Hey, Gavin. What's up?"

Tristan made it to the bench and set his paper bags down next to the others. He looked between the two women and waited for an explanation.

"Holy hell, Stems. Who's this?"

"Tristan," he answered, holding his hand out. Gavin placed her hand in his and smiled sweetly.

"Well, it's certainly nice to meet you," she said.

Josie laughed at the exchange while Tristan looked on.

"Stems?" he asked.

"It's just Gavin's nickname for me."

"Yeah, it's those legs," Gavin answered.

"Oh. Well, I can second that appreciation. Gavin's an interesting name," Tristan said. "Some people think it originated with Sir Gawain who was a knight of King Arthur's round table."

"And smart too? Don't you two make a pair. Damn," Gavin

said. Her eyes roamed up and down Tristan while she licked her lips.

"Gavin!" Josie almost shouted. "I thought you liked girls."

"I did, until about two and a half minutes ago."

The girls laughed while Tristan rubbed at the back of his neck and shifted from foot to foot.

"Anyway, make sure those get to the kids?"

"Of course, dear. She just loves to crack that whip," Gavin said, giving Tristan a wink.

"You have no idea," Tristan answered, returning the wink.

Josie stood and took Tristan's hand in hers.

"I'll see you around, Gavin."

"You're not staying for—"

"Nope. Don't need to," Josie cut her off.

Gavin smiled up at the couple as they walked away.

The ride back to Josie's was quiet but not uncomfortable.

"Did we just deliver food to homeless kids?" Tristan asked when they parked in front of her building.

"Yes," Josie said, looking out at the street.

Tristan sighed and looked at her. Every time he thought he had her figured out, something surprised him. He wondered if he'd ever truly learn all the secrets that made up Josie Banks.

"'An outlaw that dwelled apart from other men, yet beloved by the country people round about, for no one ever came to ask for help in time of need and went away again without.'"

"What is that from?" Josie asked.

"*The Merry Adventures of Robin Hood.*"

"I don't steal from the rich, though that's an interesting idea," she said.

"Let's not add to your list of illegal activities, okay?"

Josie shrugged and stared out the window.

"When I turned eighteen, I left my foster home. I just had to get away from them. I didn't have anything. So I ended up with a group of kids living near I-65 in the park."

"Couldn't anyone help you?"

"I was legally an adult. No one cared."

"I'm not sure I'm an adult yet," he said.

"After a few months Monica found me again. I had just started tagging. Throwing up pieces wherever I could. She tracked me down that way. She's a persistent woman."

"So she got you back on your feet?"

"She told me about my inheritance. Helped me get the money and a place to live. Now that I'm more fortunate, I bring them food whenever I can. It's the least I can do."

"That's how you know Gavin and Gregory," Tristan said, placing his hand over hers.

"The worst part is, most of us were better off on the streets than at home."

Josie exited the car, ending the conversation.

A couple hours later, Tristan and Josie sat together on her couch.

"I've got to go soon," Tristan said softly, running the pads of his fingertips along the back of her hand.

"What? No!" Josie protested.

"There's nothing I'd rather do than stay wrapped up with you, but I can't stand another day in these clothes, Josie. I have to work tonight."

When he said things like that, Josie felt dizzy and mindless, like a happy drifting cloud with no direction. Despite his declaration, she huffed and pushed out her bottom lip, pouting like a child.

"Okay, I'll let you go on one condition."

"You'll let me go? Am I being held hostage?"

"I guess it depends," Josie hedged.

"On what?"

"Whether you're here against your will or not."

"Touché," Tristan consented. "Well, the first phase of hostage negotiation is that you tell me your demands."

She brought his nearest hand closer to her face, inspecting the small scars across his knuckles. She kissed each one reverently.

"Tell me about that night in the alley."

Tristan frowned and curled his lips in on each other, as if locking his confession away. It occurred to him that Josie had already shared so much that he owed it to her to share this.

"Next we have the standoff. Ideally, this results in a peaceful ending," he said. "But sometimes it ends in violence."

"We wouldn't want that," Josie answered.

"Fine. I'll terminate negotiations by giving in to your demands."

"Good. I love winning."

Taking a deep breath, he prepared himself to reveal secrets never spoken aloud before.

"I met Fiona when I was sixteen. She was beautiful, in that bought-and-paid-for kind of way. She was sad like me. I found out from a friend that her twin brother had recently died. I felt connected to her. At first, she ignored me. No matter how hard I tried, she dismissed me. She told me she wasn't interested, but I never gave up."

Tristan paused and glanced at Josie, nervous about her reaction.

"So not everything comes to you so easily?" Josie asked, grinning.

"No, not everything. After a few months of friendship, something changed and suddenly Fiona wanted more. By the time we graduated high school, I was completely infatuated with her. I was valedictorian of our class, had plans to go to Harvard and then law school. Fiona accused me of abandoning her. She cried and begged me to stay. I asked her to come with me, but she said her father would never allow it."

"What did you do?" Josie asked.

"I blew off Harvard and enrolled in UNO. My parents were outraged. They said I was throwing away my future for a girl. They were right. I knew they were right, but I didn't care."

He could picture the fight in his head, his mother sobbing into her hands, his father throwing things around the house, cursing and shouting. He remembered feeling numb and unaffected by the theatrical meltdown. Tristan had only wanted to be with his girl. It was as simple as that.

"A few months after we moved in together, her father came for a visit. He was an intimidating man, loved to bully people with his money. He offered me a job. Said I'd be paid well and all I had to do was be available to deliver packages. He wasn't the kind of person you turned down. That's where it started. I didn't know it at the time, but I was delivering illegal weapons, drugs, and cash to some of the dirtiest crooks in the South. Just like that, I was sucked into a life of crime."

"Did Fiona know?"

He nodded and fiddled with the hem of his T-shirt. Of course Fiona knew, she knew everything. Tristan knew nothing.

"After a while, I dropped out of school and did her father's work exclusively. I got my first tattoo after someone tried to kill me, the Day of the Dead skull on my shoulder. I also bought my first gun that week. I dealt with the shadiest people. They all feared me, and for a moment I felt like a god. The power, the money, it all got to me. My parents begged me to come home. Instead, I cut them out of my life."

"How'd you end up here?" she asked, interlacing her fingers with his and pulling their joined hands into her lap.

"The guy in charge of the West Coast had been taken out and I was ordered to relocate. We moved four days later. When I wasn't working, I was with Fiona. I could tell she wasn't happy, not with me or our life. The more I tried, the more she resented me."

Josie just shook her head, unable to imagine not being happy with Tristan.

"One night, I was supposed to accompany a delivery from Tijuana, but it was our anniversary. I wanted to do something nice for her. I got Padre, my second-in-command, to see about the delivery while I stayed home to surprise Fiona.

"She finally came home around eleven, but she wasn't alone. From where I stood in the kitchen, I could see her kissing this guy with all the passion that she'd never given me. It was a side of her I'd never known. He fucked her, bent over our six-thousand-dollar leather sofa, and I just stood there.

"It was Fiona's voice that broke me out of my trance; her declarations of love for that man sent me over the edge. Before I knew what I was doing, I pulled my piece and placed it to the back of his head. She screamed when she saw me. She begged for his life. I wanted to see his blood on her hands. But I didn't do it. Instead, I threw everything that was important to me in a bag and left."

"I would have probably killed them both," Josie commented.

Tristan shook his head. He'd been a part of so much violence, he hadn't had the will to destroy another life.

"I emptied my bank accounts and drove down to San Diego. I got a new apartment and had no idea what to do with myself. My jealousy and hurt consumed me. I tried to drink away my anger. That only left me worse off. One night I just walked. I walked and walked until my legs hurt and my high had disappeared. I saw this graffiti on the corner of your building. This boy's face seemed familiar. I was drawn to it."

"That piece is you," she stated.

"Yeah. Maybe subconsciously I recognized that. I just lost it."

"You were so wrecked that I couldn't take my eyes off of you," Josie admitted.

"I remember your face, lit by the moon that night. When I got home I wasn't sure if I'd imagined you or not. I figured I'd made you up."

"But you didn't."

She leaned over and kissed his jaw, then his chin and eventually his lips.

"So you could say that my graffiti led us to each other."

"*You* might say that. I might say that your dangerous illegal activities captured my attention long enough to have a mental breakdown in an alley where I was more likely to be mugged than find you."

"There's nothing dangerous about what I do."

"Right. There's only being arrested, felony charges, going to prison. No big deal. Eighty percent of graffiti is gang related. That's super safe."

Suddenly, the door burst open and Alex came barreling in.

"Damn, Josie, I told you to lock this door. You want some crackhead to walk in here?"

His voice boomed through her apartment before Tristan caught his attention.

"Oh, you're still here."

Tristan stood when Alex entered the room, his eyes assessing what he thought was a high-risk threat. Immediately, his hand slid along his waistline, searching for the gun that currently sat tucked beneath the front seat of his car. He cursed to himself and practically growled. His muscles twitched, readied for confrontation. Josie marveled at the ability of Tristan to switch from geek to guardian in a matter of seconds.

"Tristan, this is my neighbor Alex," Josie said, standing between them now, not prepared for this introduction so soon. "He sort of keeps an eye on me."

Tristan's shoulders relaxed and he held out his hand. They gripped each other tightly and shook once before retreating back to their corners. As men often do, they sized each other up. A prickly air hung between them, and Josie could almost hear the snarling warnings between the two. She knew Alex relied on his size to do half the job of intimidation, but it was clear that Tristan wouldn't be intimidated by the devil himself. She felt only a small tinge of shame at being turned on by the manly display of bravado.

"I'm heading home," Tristan announced.

He stepped over to Josie and pulled her flush against his body, placing a less than chaste kiss on her lips.

"I've got to be at work in a few hours. I'll call you." Tristan nodded at Alex and headed toward the door.

"Wait, Tristan! Your book," Josie said.

She grabbed his forgotten book and waved it at him.

"Keep it. I'll be back."

He gave Alex a pointed look over her shoulder and turned to go.

Josie couldn't help the smile that swept across her face as Tristan ran down the steps, disappearing from view. She closed the door and turned to face her neighbor.

"Well, that was smooth," Josie said to Alex, rolling her eyes.

"What?"

"That whole pissing contest you two just had. I'm surprised you didn't just pull out your dicks and compare size."

"I don't wanna shame your man," he said, giving her his dimpled smile.

"He's not my man. Give me that," Josie demanded, eyeing the bag of food still clutched in his giant fist.

"So what did you guys do for two whole days?" Alex asked, wiggling his eyebrows in a suggestive manner.

"Not that. I thought about it nearly every second, though. We just talked."

"Are you gettin' up tonight? My boy said your piece on Fifth is crazy good."

Josie nodded. While she loved her art, she didn't want the notoriety that many writers did. She just wanted to be seen and heard in a way that didn't make her vulnerable.

"Tell him thanks. Oh! There's something you have to see," she insisted, leading him down the hall toward her bedroom.

"I've already seen your chichis, Jo. They're amazing."

She smacked him on the back of the head and opened her bedroom door, glancing at the papered walls of now familiar faces.

"Come on, I want to introduce you to some people."

8. TRANSIT

THE MOVEMENT OF A CELESTIAL BODY
ACROSS THE FACE OF ANOTHER.

Mort's secondhand table was blanketed in government documents. His celebration upon finding Josie Banks in the California Child Services system had been short-lived when the path ended abruptly. It had shown the date she arrived and listed the caseworker assigned, Monica Templeton. After a few months, she went into a foster home, where she remained until the age of eighteen. The foster parents' home was the last known address for her. Mort visited the home and found the only resident to be the couple's son.

"Hi, I was wondering if you could help me out?"

"Who are you?" the man had asked while leaning against the open door.

"Oh, sorry. My name's Chris. I knew Josie before she came here. I was hoping to reconnect with her."

"Josie? Haven't seen her since she put my parents in prison."

Mort feigned surprise and shifted his feet uncomfortably.

"Wow, sorry to hear that, man."

"Yeah, well, I don't know where she is. After the trial she kind of just disappeared. We only lived together for the two months before I went away to college. Everything seemed normal back then." The man closed his eyes and took a deep breath. "She's probably one of those bums living in Balboa by now, she used to like to go there."

"Well, thanks for your help."

With a convincingly appreciative smile, Mort left the middle-class home no closer to finding the girl. It was a long shot, but he'd have to check out Balboa Park. Maybe Josie had run away and disappeared into the streets like so many discarded children before her. She could be living under the freeway, begging for change, or sleeping on benches. He grimaced, knowing that it would be near impossible to find her.

He reached for his phone and dialed the familiar number.

"Speak."

"Barry, it's Mort. I think the girl is here in San Diego, but I don't have proof yet. She goes by Josie Banks now."

"I'll let Moloney know. We're on a deadline here. Gino Gallo has asked for a meeting next month."

Mort ended the call and blew out a breath. He had to be missing something. He was close now, he could feel it deep in the marrow of his bones. Like a mother sensing her lost child, he suspected that she was still here in the city. Mort knew, without question, that his life could never return to normal until hers was extinguished.

Josie sat on the floor of the apartment, familiar terrain for her. A tablet lay open in her lap while she sketched Tristan's handsome features. It was easy to see the similarity to the boy's face she'd drawn for so long—same piercing eyes, same twisted grin, same look of mischief even when at rest. He sat on the floor as well, leaning against the sofa reading the autobiography of Keith Richards. His long legs were straight and crossed at the ankles with Josie's thrown over them. It had become habit—if they were in the same room, they were touching. As if intertwined legs or joined hands sparked some kind of current that made them truly exist.

Josie craved his touch and she couldn't understand why they hadn't had sex yet, or any form of it. She wanted it; her fingers ached to touch him in places she'd only yet imagined. It was obvious that Tristan felt the same way, so she failed to make sense of his need to take things slow. She longed to feel his sweat-slicked skin against hers and inhale the scent of their bodies combined. Not ready to admit any kind of emotional connection, she desperately needed a physical one. It was the only thing she was comfortable with.

She found it curious that her dependency seemed to be shifting. No longer did she need meaningless sex or drugs to numb her. Josie wanted only to submerge herself in Tristan, to soak up everything he offered. He was her new addiction.

Tristan was in a constant state of arousal in Josie's company. Never able to completely relax, his muscles remained tense and rigid with yearning. If it had been any other girl, he would have taken her already, hard and fast, several times. But he knew that Josie used sex to avoid attachment. He didn't want to be just another mark on her therapeutically notched bedpost. To him, Josie was something new yet familiar, something he wanted to cherish. He felt like two ancient souls, separated for a lifetime, had suddenly been reunited.

Unable to contain the sexual tension clawing at her skin, Josie slid her notebook from her lap and straddled Tristan. He gave her his lopsided grin as his long fingers wrapped around her waist. Josie smiled triumphantly, thinking that she'd already won.

"What are you up to?" he asked, dipping his head so that his lips pressed ever so softly to her shoulder.

"I need to feel you, Tristan. Just touch me."

The sound of Josie's words echoed around the quiet room. She winced when they hit her ears, noting that she sounded so desperate. Never having to beg for her release before, the statement sounded foreign and troublesome. When Tristan placed another kiss at the base of her throat, she decided she didn't care. She would beg him with humbling adulation if she had to.

Losing patience with his stalling, Josie grabbed his face in both hands and brought his lips to hers. They crashed together. Tristan's hands slid to her back and pressed her to his chest. She moaned into his mouth at the feel of his hard body pushing into her soft one.

Tristan's lips sucked on hers. Her tongue was sweet, not laced with one hint of the bitterness she lived with. When Josie rocked her hips against the button fly of his jeans, he felt every ounce of control slip away. A conflict of emotions and physical need warred in his mind.

"I want you."

Those three little words left him breathless. Such a brazen statement from Josie sent his willpower into a faltering tailspin. He hummed in agreement, sliding his kisses down to her neck. Josie's arms crossed between them, where she grabbed the hem of her shirt and pulled it over her head.

Josie ran her nails along Tristan's scalp, making his eyes close in contentment. The feel of her hot body pressing down on him caused momentary insanity, totally emptying his brain of rational thought. He wanted her more than anything he'd ever wanted before. Not here, not now. There was so much more to say.

"Can I take you out?" Tristan asked, suddenly moving his hands back down to her waist and resuming a neutral position.

"That's an interesting question to ask while my fucking shirt's off," she deadpanned.

Tristan grabbed the garment and pulled it back over her shoulders. Defeated, Josie slipped her arms inside and slid back onto his thighs. She did not look up.

"There. So, can I take you out?" he repeated.

"Out of the apartment?"

"Out on a date," he clarified.

"A date?" Josie asked, her frightened voice making the words sound foreign.

"You know, an appointment for a particular time, especially with a person to whom one is sexually or romantically attached."

"Are we attached?" she asked, not really knowing what she wanted the answer to be.

"More than you know," he answered.

While it would be easy to fall into an intensely wild physical relationship with Josie, Tristan wanted more. He wanted to show her that she deserved more than this shallow life she was treading through. He wanted to lure her out of her protective shell and wrap her in his love. Yes, he knew it was love. Even after all this time, it had always been.

Josie jumped out of his lap. She had never been on a date in her life. She didn't pretend to know what people even did on dates. She'd always felt the tradition was so antiquated and pointless. It was a meeting of two strangers whose ultimate goal was to have sex. She'd always found it easiest to skip the awkward conversations and formal mealtimes.

"A date? Like in a fancy restaurant with lots of strangers?" she said while pacing back and forth in front of Tristan.

Her arms flailed about as if they kept her balanced on a tightrope of panic. She looked to the kitchen drawer that housed her drugs and back to his waiting face. Josie recognized her need to kill the anxious feelings rising inside of her. She closed her eyes and took a deep breath. She pictured a chain and lock around that drawer, forcing herself to stay present and deal with this.

"Mac."

He spoke softly as if appeasing a belligerent child.

"No! I'm not her. I don't *do* dates. I mean, what do you expect from me, Tristan?" His mouth bobbed open like his jaw was unhinged and broken. "Well?" Josie asked again.

Speechlessness was not something Tristan was used to. Though he tried to form thoughts to comfort her, to find the right words to talk her down from the ledge, he simply could not. So he fell back on things that he knew absolutely.

"'There are only two tragedies in life: one is not getting what one wants, and the other is getting it.'"

"Stop reciting shit from your perfect memory, Tristan. Tell me what you want!"

"I want you. All of you. I want to possess you. I want to love you and protect you."

His heavy words knocked Josie to her knees, their eyes now level again.

"Too much," she said, her anger dying off and being reborn into something new and delicate.

"Then I'll settle for a date," he answered. "Just us. No expectations. No requirements."

"I don't know if I can. Besides, what's in it for me?"

"Riveting conversation and a free meal," Tristan said.

"You can do better than that," she hedged, running her fingers down his chest and tugging on his belt buckle.

"Are you proposing sexual favors in exchange for going on a date with me?"

"Tit for tat."

Tristan chuckled, a dark kind of laugh that drove her crazy.

"Sex bartering is usually reserved for long-time married couples. She wants some ice cream, but she wants him to go get it. She offers something easy first. If the weather is nice and the store is close, the husband might agree."

"But if there's a snowstorm and he has to walk barefoot, uphill, both ways, he will want to negotiate for something better," Josie says, playing along.

"Right. There's negotiation and analysis involved. Are both parties getting something they want?"

"You want a date. I want to see your O-face. Sounds reasonable to me," Josie answered.

Tristan took a deep breath and reminded himself of the reasons to hold out on their physical relationship. It was for the best. It would prove to Josie that he wanted her on every level. It would prove that she was more than a pretty face and a willing partner. While these things were true, staring into her pleading eyes made him want to abandon reason.

After a long moment, he nodded his consent.

"Okay," she said, "I'll go on a date with you."

He smiled cautiously and reached for her hand. Tristan knew that he already belonged to Josie. He had since he was seven years old. But he understood that the woman in front him was not the same girl she used to be. There was so much more to learn.

"Tomorrow night," he said. "I'll pick you up at seven."

She nodded and chewed her bottom lip uneasily. Sex she could do. Seduction, conquering, abandoning were her trademarks. Josie figured that she could teach a class on how to remain emotionally unattached and still get what you want. But a date would test her.

Tristan's thumb slid across her mouth, freeing her lip from its confines. He placed a gentle kiss there before heading off to work.

☾

As Tristan took his place behind the bar, he found Erin, Brandie, and Lee talking. With only a few customers to serve, they were happy to sit idly and gossip about the big tippers or the latest episode of a reality television show. He stood a few feet away as Brandie glared at him, not yet over his rejection.

"Haven't seen Bundy in a while," Erin muttered while inspecting her new nail polish.

"Who's Bundy?" Brandie asked.

"This freaky girl who used to come in here all the time," Lee answered. "Erin thinks she may be a serial killer."

Tristan cringed at those words, so careless and cold.

"Yeah," Erin said. "Maybe one of her victims fought back and took her down."

"I sure hope not. That bitch was hot," Lee chimed in.

"What did she look like?" Brandie asked.

"Sort of like Wednesday Addams meets Audrey Hepburn," Erin answered.

"I bet she was crazy in the sack too. I'd like to bang the freaky right out of her."

"You're a pig!" Erin chastised.

When the words left Lee's mouth, Tristan found himself in motion. In three short steps he was there, twisting Lee's arm behind his back and slamming his face into the bar. The surge of adrenaline pumping through his veins made him feel like he could crush the man's skull into the countertop. Tristan leaned down so that his angry breaths were heavy in Lee's ear.

"Don't you ever talk about her like that. In fact, don't ever speak about her again or I'll fucking kill you."

Tristan released him and stomped his way outside for a breath of fresh air. He slid down the wall, squatting in place, his hands in his nonexistent hair again. He wasn't sorry for what he did, he was only sorry that he'd lost his cool at work. Surely this incident would get back to his boss and he'd be job hunting again.

"Hey," a soft voice called to him. Tristan raised his eyes to find Erin watching him with a worried expression. "Are you okay?"

"Shouldn't you be asking Lee that question?" he growled at her.

Tristan stood and lit a cigarette, offering one to Erin. She declined and leaned against the wall beside him, watching his calm demeanor return.

"Nah, screw that asshole. He had it coming."

They both chuckled and felt most of the tension slip away.

"So you and Bundy, huh?" she asked.

"Her name is Josie," Tristan replied with a bit of hostility.

"Okay, Josie," she replied, holding up her hands in apologetic surrender. "How'd that even happen? She never talks to anyone."

Tristan took a deep drag and blew it out above their heads.

"I knew her when we were kids. She's an old friend."

"Well, she seems like an interesting girl. I hope that works out for you. Lord knows it's hard to find anyone decent in this city. I seem to only attract guys who are more muscle than brain or still live with their parents."

"They can't all be bad," Tristan said. "If there hadn't been women we'd still be squatting in a cave eating raw meat. We made civilization in order to impress our girlfriends."

Erin laughed and smiled at him.
"That's clever," she said.
"It's not mine. Orson Welles said it. But it's true."
"Well, the last man who impressed me was my daddy."
Erin patted his forearm and stepped back inside.

Monica stood before Josie, her arms crossed, eyes scanning in
inspection mode. Josie suppressed the urge to roll her eyes at
the tiny woman's appraisal because she didn't want to offend her.
Not this time. She watched Monica's eyes rake over her body
and immediately wondered what the woman saw there. Pain and
pleasure weren't etched into her skin like they were on Tristan's.
Josie wore her scars inside.

Normal girls had friends to call for backup, friends who would
dress you and tease your hair and tell you what gloss to wear. Josie
didn't have any such friends, so she figured Monica would do.
Once summoned, Monica Templeton eagerly came running. Josie
didn't know if it was customary for your social worker to keep in
touch long after her legal obligation had ended, but there Monica
was, an immovable pillar. She never blamed Monica for what had
happened to her in those homes, everyone had played their roles so
convincingly. She simply enjoyed toying with the woman's sensi-
bilities. She loved being in control of something for once. Punish-
ing Monica by withholding her forgiveness was the one thing Josie
had.

The fact that Josie and Tristan already knew each other did
nothing to appease her anxiety. Their lopsided relationship was
emotionally difficult to navigate. Though Josie couldn't recall
their beginnings, she felt in her bones that what they had was
concrete. She had fought with herself all day, almost canceling

on him two hours ago, but she couldn't bring herself to deny this newly developing affair. She also couldn't wait to take whatever physical pleasure he would give her.

Josie thought about getting high one last time to calm her nerves, bargaining that she'd be more likable, more at ease. They'd both have a better time. But she didn't want to disappoint Tristan.

She was a nervous mess. What did Tristan expect from her? Even with her nerves, Josie suddenly found herself wanting to spend time with him outside of the protective walls of her apartment. She wanted to be seen with him and claim him for her own. She took a seat on the edge of the bathtub and put her head in her hands. Monica knelt before her and pulled Josie's hands away from her face. She held them up and smiled.

"No charcoal, no paint," Monica pointed out.

Josie nodded.

"I worked all afternoon on them."

Monica looked into Josie's eyes next.

"You're not high either."

"Nope. I do feel like I'm going to puke, though," Josie said.

"Listen to me. No matter where you go tonight, it will still be you and Tristan. Just like when you're here."

"No, we'll be out there, with people watching us. What if I embarrass him?"

A date meant restaurants and crowds. A date meant being vulnerable and honest and learning to rediscover her humanity. Until now, Josie had been free to be a societal vagabond, answering to nothing and no one. She never felt like she could operate within the realm of the law-abiding, white-bread squares of today's population. She feared that no matter what clothes she wore, they would see straight through to what she really was—trash.

"I have a feeling you could never embarrass him, Josie. You certainly don't see yourself clearly."

"What the hell am I'm doing?" Josie cried.

"Josie, calm down. Tons of girls go on dates every day. I've probably been on hundreds of dates. Look at me. It eventually led to Mr. Right. You'll be fine."

"I'm not tons of girls," Josie said, taking a deep breath. "I'm Josie Banks, fuckup extraordinaire."

Monica cautiously placed a hand on each shoulder and looked into her brown eyes. She stilled her gum chomping and gave Josie a smile.

"You are not a fuckup. You are fierce and intelligent and one of the strongest people I've ever known." She pulled Josie up and spun her toward the mirror. "You are stunningly beautiful and mysterious and every other thing that men love."

The two women's gazes met through the mirror's reflection, each wishing to understand the other more clearly. Josie longed to see the things Monica saw. She wanted to believe those praising words and attach them to herself like tags.

"Something's missing. Oh! I know!" Monica screeched, startling Josie.

Monica dug into her oversize bag and pulled out what looked like a tackle box. Josie watched with amazement as she rifled through the thing, picking through each compartment in search of a specific item.

"There," Monica said as she stepped to Josie and slid a silk flower barrette into her hair.

Monica stepped to the side and turned Josie toward the mirror. The girl's eyes landed on her reflection, and for a moment she couldn't identify the stranger staring back. This time, she could see a beautiful and happy girl. Having no patience for daydreams, she pressed her fingers to the glass to verify that it was real. There was a new light to her eyes, an unfamiliar lift to the corners of her mouth. She could almost pass for human.

A knock jolted her out of her scrutinizing. Her heart drummed against her chest and she felt pulled across the room toward the door. She could already feel his energy, his fantastical command over her body. The clicking of her heels against the hardwood floor counted off her steps toward Tristan. After sliding all the locks free, she threw open the door.

Tristan stood with his hands in his pockets, nervously jingling his keys. Her eyes started at his feet, noticing his shoes, then his jeans, then losing all patience and skipping directly to his face. He'd shaved his face clean and now the edge of his jaw looked so sharp and masculine, like it had been chiseled free from one solid piece of stone. His eyes shone like emeralds.

"Wow, you look amazing, Stems."

Her smile turned up in reaction to the nickname. Tristan's eyes took in every inch of her form, from the black top clinging to her hips down to her red high heels. Her brown eyes, lined in thick black lashes, seemed to shine. The red flower in her hair lent sweetness to her otherwise sultry appearance.

Monica came barreling past, an enormous bag slung over her shoulder, stopping between the two of them.

"Here," Monica said, handing her a small red clutch. "I put all your essentials in there, so you shouldn't need anything else. I'll get my stuff back from you sometime next week."

Monica spun to face Tristan, completely shocked by his appearance. He was not what she had expected. His presence was grand and masculine while his smile made him appear beautiful and almost childlike.

"I'm Tristan," he said.

"You certainly are," she answered, slipping her hand into his. "I'm Monica. You guys have fun tonight."

Monica trotted down the steps and out of sight, leaving the two alone in the doorway.

"Ready?" Tristan asked.

She nodded and locked the door, taking his hand as they descended the single flight of stairs. Tristan led her to his classic car parked at the curb. He opened the door and let her slide in before making his way around to the driver's seat.

Josie felt something beneath her and scooted up to retrieve another one of Tristan's books. She held it up to him as he took a seat.

"Do you read in the car?" she asked.

His lips curled up on one side, a wordless answer. Josie tossed the book onto the backseat and shook her head.

"I guess I should be happy you're addicted to books and not something like crack whores."

"Nah. I gave them up for Lent this year," Tristan joked.

"Are you Catholic?" Josie asked.

"No, but I've read the Bible."

"You mean you have that entire book memorized?"

"Ephesians 6:12. 'For we do not wrestle against flesh and blood, but against the rulers, against the authorities, against the cosmic powers over this present darkness, against the spiritual forces of evil in the heavenly places.'"

"Wow," Josie said. "How do you do that?"

Tristan laughed and turned the key.

"I don't do it. I'm just built that way."

The car rumbled to a thunderous start. He glanced at Josie's reaction, watching her denim-covered legs cross and then uncross. His baby always had that effect on ladies. At first, they'd be dazzled by her cherry red paint, clean lines, and whitewall tires. It wasn't until they were seated in the plush vinyl seat, and she kicked to life, that they fully understood her appeal.

Josie fidgeted nervously, stunned by the feel of the pulsating seat beneath her. She let her mind drift to their possible destinations and felt her anxiety go into overdrive. The idea of being in a crowded place with tons of whispered conversations surrounding them terrified her. Too many people, too many faces and eyes to see her. The thought left her reeling.

"Where are we going?" she finally asked, blowing out a breath.

"A quiet place with a fantastic view," Tristan answered, slipping his hand over hers.

She took a deep breath and exhaled again, letting her apprehension and worries slip away into the black night sky. His words and touch soothed her. It was as if he knew what she needed before she did.

9. ALBEDO
A MEASURE OF REFLECTIVE POWER.

They sat at the last table on the patio at Edgewater Grill. The restaurant wasn't crowded, but the low hum of surrounding conversations was enough to give the couple a sense of sociability. Utensils wrapped in soft linen sat just below the water glasses. A single candle marked the center of the table, its flickering warm light washing the two in swaying shadows and a honey-yellow glow. Sporadically, the salty breeze would drift in from the bay, bringing with it the cooler ocean air and a breath of repose.

Tristan ordered a Stella Artois and Josie asked for a glass of red wine.

"What kind of red would you like, miss?"

Josie glanced at Tristan and back at the expectant waiter; she didn't know the answer. Monica had advised her that self-respecting women ordered wine at dinner and did not get so drunk they had to be carried out. Just as panic began to overwhelm her, Tristan rescued her from embarrassment.

"She'll have the 2007 Talisman Vineyard Pinot Noir. Thanks."

"Of course," the waiter said before smiling tightly and turning to fetch their drinks.

Following more of Monica's instructions, Josie unfolded her napkin and laid it across her lap. She kept her elbows off the table and sat stiffly in her chair. Glancing over the menu, she felt a bit overwhelmed by the choices and the prices attached to them.

"Relax, Josie," Tristan teased, nudging her foot beneath the table.

She loosened her posture just a bit, wondering if everyone could tell she didn't belong here. Selections were made, food was ordered, but conversation was mostly absent. Tristan wondered why Josie was at ease with him within the confines of her apartment, but here she seemed unreachable.

Josie's eyes scanned the bay, the black glossy surface dotted with specks of light on each ripple. Boats sailed by, returning from their sunset cruises, cutting through the water with no resistance. Josie had never before noticed the sleek lines and curves of these vessels and suddenly longed to sketch them out on her pristine napkin. She recognized her need to return to consoling habits, but with no tools available she sipped her water instead.

There were so many sets of eyes here and she felt like all were bearing down on her. Josie resisted checking the faces at each table. She knew that *they* weren't here, the eyes of her longtime demons. This place was too refined for them, for her too, if she was being honest. Like a shadow that followed her even in darkness, Josie always feared running into her foster parents. She knew they still lived here, though she'd made sure they couldn't take in any more kids. Most of the time she could ignore that they lived in the same city.

"Are you okay?" Tristan asked.

"Yeah, I'm fine," she offered.

" 'I'm fine' is the biggest white lie ever told."

"Because it's easy. Usually, when people ask how you are, they don't really care about the answer anyway. So they take for granted that you're telling the truth," Josie said. "And what is a white lie? Why white? Are there other color lies?"

"No, it's based on the idea of opposites. White meaning good and black meaning bad. White lies are thought to be harmless and trivial, lying without ill intent."

"Harmless. That's a joke. I've told that lie hundreds of times and no one cared enough to call me out on it."

"I care," he said softly.

Josie shifted in her seat. Her eyes scanned the restaurant again, getting stuck on a familiar face.

"I know that guy."

Tristan turned toward the main dining room.

"Which one?" he asked.

"The Asian waiter with the glasses."

"How well do you know him?" Tristan asked.

Josie smirked, loving how easily he was baited.

"Well enough to know that he wears boxer briefs and likes to be spanked."

Tristan felt the possessive anger bubbling up inside and it was all he could do to not growl when the kid passed by.

"Something wrong?" she asked, feigning innocence.

"No. I'm fine," he hissed. "We all have a past. It doesn't matter who you've slept with."

"Good, because I don't remember half of them."

Tristan slid closer to the corner, allowing his leg to lean against hers. Beneath the frosted glass tabletop, she watched as his hand slid from his own thigh to hers, resting just above her knee.

"I know what you're trying to do, Josie. It won't work."

"And what is that?"

"You're trying to make me jealous. I'm not a dog pissing on my territory here. I don't need to sleep with you to prove that you're mine."

Josie scoffed at the idea. Of course he needed to sleep with her. How else would anyone believe that he was with a girl like her?

"Do you believe that people, in general, are good?" Josie asked, abandoning one heavy conversation for another.

"I guess it depends on how you define good. I don't think there's any genetic predisposition toward the idea of being good. I mean, Nazi youth were considered righteous, suicide bombers are honored by supporters of their cause. Does that make them good? I think becoming a good person has more to do with your environment, your caregivers, and society."

"Look at my environment, my caregivers. How could I possibly be good?"

Tristan was confused by her question. Of course she was good. She was everything.

"Buddha said, 'Neither fire nor wind, birth nor death can erase our good deeds.' Before you suffered at the hands of those evil people, you were raised by two loving parents. Even though you may not remember it, I believe those ideas and values are ingrained into who you are."

Josie looked down at his hand still covering her thigh, his thumb tracing a small sweeping arc across the denim. She could feel the heat coming from his palm, the slight squeeze as his fingers curled around her. It was hard to believe that she was good, but she wanted to. She wanted to be good for him.

"Tristan, there are things that you don't know about me. Things that . . ."

Just as the words stuck in her throat, the waiter appeared, sliding their dinner onto the table. The sight and smell appealed to her starved senses and she forgot what she wanted to say.

As much as Tristan wanted her to open up to him, this was not the place. He knew that Josie thought she could scare him away with her past, but she underestimated his dedication.

They ate in silence, though it wasn't the uneasy kind. It was peaceful and amicable. The wine was flavorful and Josie never remembered tasting food so good. She wondered if the company had anything to do with it.

During dinner, Tristan tried to keep himself from staring. She was always beautiful, but tonight she was otherworldly. Even with the anxious energy, she was the most stunning creature he'd ever seen. Sometimes it still floored him that she was here, alive and in his life. He often became overwhelmed when holding her or kissing her, remembering how he'd once begged for such a gift.

"Do you ever think about what would have happened if I'd never moved away?" Josie asked.

She'd thought about nothing else since she'd learned of their connection. She imagined a different life, where she could become someone her parents would have been proud of. She could have been on the honor roll and yearbook staff. She could have gone to college and studied art. She could have ruled the world with this man by her side.

"I've thought about it a lot since the day you left."

"Tell me," Josie requested, folding her napkin and laying it on the table.

She let her fingers trace over the ink on his skin, outlining the trunk and limbs just below his cuffed sleeve. Tristan smiled at the hundreds of memories surrounding the old oak.

"The night before you moved to New York, you came over for dinner. My mom made your favorite fudge peanut butter brownies for dessert. My parents tried to make us enjoy ourselves, but you were a mess and I was really angry. We spent the whole meal sulking."

Tristan took a cleansing breath and finished his beer. Just the memory of losing her made his chest ache again.

"After dinner, we went to sit in our tree. You wore my favorite blue shirt and the jeans with holes in the knees. I remember pretending to play with the hanging threads just for an excuse to touch you. We sat in silence for a while, ignoring the time counting down. When it got late, your dad called to say he was coming to pick you up. My mom yelled for us to come inside, but you wouldn't budge. You clung to me and begged me to stay up there with you. You figured if you didn't come down, you'd be able to stay in Louisiana."

"Sounds like my logic," Josie said sarcastically.

"An hour later, after threats from your dad and a million promises between us, we climbed down together. That was the last time I saw you."

Though Josie couldn't recall the scene like Tristan could, it hurt her all the same. In a way, she felt lucky that she had none of those memories. She wasn't sure if she could have survived all the old hurt and new hurt. It may have killed her long ago.

"Did I cry? I bet I was a crier."

"No. You didn't. You were so strong."

As Tristan paid for dinner, Josie wondered where that strength had gotten her, half dead and with no memories.

They walked hand in hand through Seaport Village, pausing to window-shop, though neither one paid much attention to the items. Tristan focused on the way her tiny fingers wrapped around his, the *click-clack* rhythm of her shoes against the pavement, and their distorted reflection in the shop windows.

"What does this one represent?" Josie asked, tapping her finger over a watch face tattooed on the inside of his left wrist.

"My birth, the exact minute I joined the living."

"What about this one?"

Josie reached up to the side of his neck, running her thumb along the two lines of script below his ear.

"'Everything was beautiful and nothing hurt,'" he said. "Vonnegut's protagonist in *Slaughterhouse-Five* coins the phrase regarding death. Sort of something to look forward to."

Josie's eyes searched his own, getting lost in his ability to make her understand such complicated notions.

"Come on," he said lightly, tugging on her hand.

He dragged her into a hat shop, where they tried on hats and laughed at each other until their sides hurt. Tristan stuck an enormous beach hat onto Josie's head and tugged on the floppy brim. She smiled and slid a fedora onto him. He pulled it down over one eye, and they stood in front of the large framed mirror.

"You look hot," she said, staring at his reflection.

"Sold," Tristan replied, winking at her.

Josie blushed and placed her hat back on the shelf while Tristan paid for his. She found it odd that despite all the deviant things she'd done, she'd never felt timid. Tristan could bring these alien feelings to the surface. He had a way of making her believe she was worthy of innocence.

When they stepped into Upstart Crow, a coffeehouse and bookstore, Josie could see how Tristan delighted in being surrounded by the written word. She just knew he could spend hours scouring every shelf for books. While she didn't share his passion, she loved seeing him happy and in his element.

"Don't worry, I'll limit myself," he said, placing a kiss on her cheek.

He pulled her down row after row of books. When something caught his attention, he would examine the cover as if studying a painting. Then he'd flip to the back and read whatever review or description was there. Last, he'd fan the pages a few times. Josie marveled at the ritual and smiled every time he handed her one to buy.

Thirty minutes and four books later, they shared a piece of cheesecake and an iced mocha in the coffeehouse.

Tristan persuaded Josie to ride the carousel with him, so they parked themselves on the bench surrounded by parading animals. The golden lights and mirrors reflected the couple, and Tristan couldn't help but think about what a sight they were. As the ride began to move, he pulled her in closer with his arm around her shoulders.

"Did you know carousels were first used as combat training devices by the Turkish? There's proof of their existence all the way back to 500 A.D."

Josie smiled at his fact reciting, loving all the useless information.

"Really? Tell me more," she teased.

Tristan rolled his eyes and placed a soft kiss below her ear. They watched as children bobbed up and down on their horses and tigers. The organ music lulled them into a state of ease as they spun, like two lovers rotating around their own axis.

When the ride was over, he led her to the water, where they stood beneath one of the lamps dotting the bay. One by one, the shop windows went dark. The day finished with CLOSED signs and locked doors. Tristan leaned against the rail, his back to the water, and pulled Josie in against him. He tilted his chin down and captured her lips. Josie moaned into his mouth as his hands slid down to her lower back. She could feel his racing pulse against her body, his warmth and heat surrounding her. She wanted more. She always wanted more.

Tristan spun them and held Josie against the rail, trapping her with his arms on each side. His body pressed into her back as she sighed and looked out over the water. The lights from Coronado shone from the island, bouncing off the water like rippling ribbons. The sky hosted a blanket of stars and the waxing moon shone just for them. Josie closed her eyes, wanting to memorize every bit of this moment. She just knew it would never get better than this.

(

Rob met Monica at her apartment. They'd made plans to stay in and watch a movie. She had no need for formal dates and grand gestures. They'd just skip over the usual dating rituals and get right to the heart of it, time alone and lots of it.

This feeling that engulfed them and held them to each other was powerful. Monica found it easy to be herself around Rob, though for so long she wasn't sure who that was. She was so consumed with work and the children that she didn't know what things made her whole.

He leaned against her door frame, his dirty blond hair hanging in his eyes. His casual stance was pure confidence. The way his baby blues lit up when Monica was near made her want to run away with him and disappear into the night. Rob stepped aside and let her unlock the door while he peppered kisses on her neck from behind. Her attention faltered as she fumbled with her keys. When she finally unlocked the door, he pulled the giant bag from her shoulder and set it down inside.

"Damn, babe. What do you have in there? A dead body?" Rob asked.

"No, not today. Today it's just clothes and accessories. All the essentials for a perfect date. Well, not my date, of course. Josie's date. She's a friend. Well, kind of a friend. She met this new guy, only he's not new. She knew him before. Well, before some crazy shit went down. I was just helping her get ready."

"Don't even ask me to recap that," Rob said, grinning.

Monica felt just a little reprieve from the suffocating guilt usually associated with Josie Banks. She'd done a good deed today. She'd been so excited when Josie called asking for assistance. Anything she could do to make amends with this girl, she would. If there was something Monica had practice with, it was dating. She'd been on so many in the last decade she'd lost count. While not all of them had been miserable failures, none of them had felt right. Not like Rob. He felt perfect and final, like the end of her searching.

"Can you believe I had to go shopping today because someone stole almost all of my underwear yesterday?" Monica yelled from her bedroom.

"What?"

"Yeah, I brought a load of laundry down to the basement but forgot my quarters for the machine. So I left it. Ran up here to get the money. By the time I got back down there, the entire basket was gone. Oh! I was so pissed off. I mean, who would want dirty laundry?"

"You have some weird neighbors," Rob answered, troubled by the missing laundry.

"No shit," Monica said absently, flipping through her mail.

"What movie did you get?"

"Some horror movie where everyone gets hacked up and no one gets out alive," she answered. "I'm sure all the standard rules apply. Never say 'I'll be right back.' Don't go check out that strange noise." Monica entered the living room and smirked at him. "And never, ever have sex. That's a sure way to get yourself dead."

"Those killers must be advocates for celibacy," he muttered. "The idiots."

"Well, we could just skip the movie and hump like bunnies," she offered.

"Only if you can ensure our safety from psychotic serial killers, darlin'."

"There are no guarantees," Monica teased, unbuttoning her blouse as she backed slowly toward the bedroom.

"Well, ma'am. I'll take my chances."

☾

As Tristan drove home, he found himself humming along with the radio despite not knowing any of the pop songs. If it weren't so pathetic, he'd laugh at what this girl had turned him into. Though he still had his edge and always his pistol, he felt his sharp attitude beginning to retreat. It was a glimpse of the boy he used to be, before he'd been betrayed and hurt. He felt lighter and hopeful again.

He was in luck, finding a parking spot on his block. Tristan retrieved his gun from under the seat, secured his car, and lit a cigarette for the short walk.

It had been so hard to leave Josie's apartment. He'd tried to be a gentleman, but when she pulled him by the collar and attacked his mouth, he'd lost all control. There, against her door, he'd ground his hips into hers, introducing every bit of his need. She rocked against him, and it was all he could do not to take her right there.

Josie had invited him in, begging to continue their evening. He knew what she wanted. Hell, he wanted it too, but not yet.

Not before he could make her believe that she was worth it. Thankfully, Alex had come home, cutting through their sexual tension and wishing them good night. Tristan wanted to thank him and kill him at the same time.

"Fallbrook," a familiar voice called out as he approached his building.

The sound of that voice made Tristan's stomach drop and he immediately reached for his piece. He spun to find Padre parked on a bench outside his building. He was shorter than Tristan but just as intimidating. Always wearing a stiff button-down shirt and Dockers, Padre more closely resembled a Wall Street executive than a deadly assassin. His smile was sinister and sharply interrupted by a maroon scar that carved down the left side of his face. He was Tristan's former assistant and a man who'd left the priesthood to carry out revenge for his murdered brother. He'd never returned.

"Nice hat," Padre said, grinning.

"Fuck you," Tristan replied.

They embraced in a one-armed hug and stepped back to a safe distance. In this business, people who were once your allies didn't always remain that way.

"Long time, no see, *vato*."

"I had to get out," Tristan answered simply.

"Yeah, well, I guess I should be thanking you. I was promoted when you bounced."

"Congratulations. I'm guessing this isn't a friendly visit."

"Moloney sent me to give you a message."

The air shifted, a serious rope of threat surrounded the men, tying them to each other.

"So get on with it," Tristan spat, losing his patience.

"He says no one leaves the operation alive, but he's feeling generous. He'll let you live if you find and kill this girl."

Padre handed him a folded photo with torn edges. Tristan felt nauseous as he looked into the eyes of a young McKenzi Delaune. Using every bit of strength he possessed, he kept his face indifferent.

"This girl is dead."

"Nah, man. Moloney says she's alive and well. He has it on good authority she's here in San Diego. I was just told to deliver that. Of course, there's another employee looking for her, but if you find her first, you live."

"I'm not spending my time chasing ghosts!" Tristan shouted at the man's retreating form.

"I'm just the messenger, Fallbrook. Don't make me come back here."

Just like that, he was gone. Tristan knew this was not just a scare tactic. Moloney would never waste time or money on idle threats. The message was loud and clear. If Tristan didn't deliver, they'd come back and take payment from his flesh.

It had been three miserable, sleepless hours since Padre left Tristan standing confounded on the sidewalk. He'd dropped a figurative bomb and disappeared into the aftermath's smoke. Now Tristan lay in bed, the old photo of McKenzi still clutched in his fingers. An innocent, unscathed face stared back at him from the glossy paper. This was the girl he remembered, the girl he'd grieved for. In all honesty, this girl was dead. As if featured in one of those campy daytime soap operas, the part of McKenzi Delaune was now being played by a darker, forbidding Josie Banks.

He'd been a wreck since learning of the hit out on Josie. First, anger hammered at his chest and he tore through his apartment breaking everything within reach. It wasn't a fit of calculated rage, more of an unrestrained therapy of destruction. Shattered glass dotted the floor, while his treasured books lay in a jumbled heap beneath an overturned shelf. There were holes in the dry-wall, a broken trail leading to his bedroom, where he'd finally collapsed. Maroon ribbons of dried blood twisted around his fingers and he scoffed at how symbolic they were. His hands were tied.

When his fury had dissipated, he was left only with mind-numbing fear. Not for himself but for Josie. Without a second thought, he knew that he would make any sacrifice if it meant that she'd go unharmed. He would never turn her over to that monster of a man, but that didn't mean someone else wouldn't. Padre had told him that there was another person out there look-ing for her. If they were on Moloney's payroll, they were good. It wouldn't be long before she was found.

There was no escape from the business, no calling it quits without some sort of payment, flesh or monetary. Even when he had run away, Tristan knew this. At the time, he'd rather have been dead than stay near Fiona and her unfaithful heart. How lucky he'd been to find his long-lost love perched on a fire escape.

Tristan wondered if Moloney had somehow connected him to Josie, if he'd ordered the hit only as a punishment or a test. He wondered about all that dark space in Josie's memory and what could possibly warrant her death. Mostly he wondered what he was going to do about it.

He'd be willing to bet that Moloney was responsible for her fa-ther's death and Josie's amnesia. What other reason could Moloney have for wanting her dead? They must be connected through her father.

He thought about running. He could pick up Josie, force her if necessary, and drag her away to some far-off country where they would hide out among the locals. Realistically, Tristan knew this plan would never work. They'd be checking over their shoulders for the rest of their lives, just waiting for the axe to drop. Josie deserved a better life than that. What he needed was a bargaining chip, something Moloney wanted more than Josie. He huffed and rolled over, tucking her photo beneath the cool underside of his pillow, and finally drifted off to sleep.

10. PERIGEE

POINT IN THE MOON'S ORBIT WHERE
IT IS CLOSEST TO EARTH.

The night air was cool as Alex made his way to the Darkroom. When the sign came into view, he wished that he'd done research on what kind of place it was. He suddenly felt like a roughneck among suits. Not that it mattered. He was on a mission. He knew what he was doing was going to sound cliché and dramatic, but he just couldn't help himself.

Ignoring the incredulous looks, Alex took a seat at the bar and waited for Tristan. A blond waitress placed her tray on the bar and sighed. As Tristan filled her drink orders, Alex was momentarily distracted by the way her ass moved beneath her skirt.

"What can I get you?" Tristan asked.

"I'm not here for a drink," Alex answered.

"Well, you're parked at my bar, so I say you are. How about a light and fruity cocktail?"

The two men eyed each other in an unspoken standoff.

"Nah, man. Shout-out to my homeland with a Dos Equis," Alex ordered.

Tristan opened the bottle and set it on the pristine bar.

"Actually, Dos Equis was started by a German man who immigrated to Mexico."

"Whatever, man."

Alex took a few bills from his pocket and laid them on the bar. Tristan slid the money back to Alex.

"On the house."

"Look, I came here to talk to you without Jo around. She'd be pissed if she knew."

"So I guess this is the part where you tell me to stay away from her. I'm not good enough, right?"

"Nah. Neither one of you assholes would listen. I'll make it simple, Don Perfecto. I know you care, but this girl's got issues."

"I don't need your advice on how to handle her issues."

"If you hurt her, I'll come after you," Alex threatened.

"Ah, the 'I'll kill you' speech. I judged the approach all wrong. Consider me warned."

"I'm serious. I took care of her before you showed up," Alex said, raising his eyebrows to insinuate more than he would dare say.

"I'm sure you did," Tristan bit out between clenched teeth.

"I'll be there long after you're gone, *vato*."

"I'm not going anywhere," Tristan sneered.

"I can afford to have you killed."

"Get in line." A stiff air sat between them, electrically charged with passion and intended warnings. "I would never hurt her. Thanks for stopping by."

Just like that, Alex had been dismissed. Tristan walked to the other end of the bar and, with his mask of a smile in place, began filling orders again.

Satisfied his message had been delivered, Alex threw a few bills on the bar and left his untouched beer where it sat. By the time he made it back home, Alex was exhausted. He settled in bed with SportsCenter on the television and drifted off to sleep.

Hours later, Alex woke to the sound of screaming. He sprang from the comfort of twelve-hundred-thread-count sheets, ready for confrontation. Within seconds of his feet hitting the floor, his pistol slid from the nightstand into his familiar grip. Soon he realized the sound was just Mrs. Thompson yelling at her cat again. He laughed and crawled back into bed, settling his Beretta back into its home.

Sleep escaped Alex as he lay in bed. His mind worked to piece together the coming day. There was a delivery to pick up, which would need to be inventoried and distributed. One of the downsides of being a one-man operation is that he had to play the roles of CEO, Sales, and Accounting. Job responsibilities kept him busy for much of the day. After lunch, he'd head down to Chula Vista to take care of a debt. He let no one take advantage of his generous nature. Alex would be paid. One day, these punk kids would learn that he was not to be fucked with.

Alex wasn't sure how he landed in the game he played so well. It seemed to be a path carved out for him since birth. He was a thug now, a true-to-life dealer. Most transactions were with the rich kids of Bankers Hill, the middle-aged uptowners, and the queers in Hillcrest. Though his mother wished for a better life for her children, it was hard to provide that with no male role model in the house. His father sold drugs and his oldest brother did too. They'd both paid the price. His brother was killed for the contents of his wallet and a dime bag while his father was incarcerated for most of Alex's childhood. When he was released, he tried to teach the boy about being a man. He showed him how to fire a gun, how to outsmart the streets, and how to keep women in their place. The lessons had not been lost on an impressionable boy.

For as long as he could remember, Alex had had the same basic priorities in life: wealth, power, and pussy. Not necessarily in that order. He'd accumulated a hefty savings, a sizable collection of drug and blood money washed clean of its sins and folded neatly in an uptown bank. Power had always come easy to him, his hulking size and self-appointed authority ensured that. Pussy was a whole different story.

Alex rolled over and huffed. He was pissed that the old lady had disturbed him from his sleep and, consequently, a hot dream involving twins. It had been two weeks since he'd gotten laid, but what worried him the most was that he didn't even care. Sex was usually just a means to an end. Call up one of his regulars, drill her until she was speechless, and leave before her head hit the pillow. His skills soon pushed cringe-worthy words and phrases from the lips of satiated women. *Date, dinner, boyfriend.* When the girls became too attached, he would attack their vulnerable side and, when needing the big guns, insult their sexual prowess.

Relationships were unheard of in his business. Trusting someone enough to hold your secrets and know your innermost thoughts was not practical. Alex was happy where he was, alone with his fifty-inch flat-screen television, free weights, and imported beer. At least that's what he told himself.

It took seeing Tristan and Josie together to force him to face the truth of his loneliness. Alex had never seen such substantial love between two people. Every time Tristan looked at the girl, Alex burned with such jealousy that he couldn't be in their presence for long. It wasn't that he had developed feelings for his neighbor; he was simply resentful of their connection. Jealous of what he hadn't even known he wanted. For the first time in his life, what Alex coveted couldn't be bought or sold, no matter the amount of wealth, power, or pussy he possessed.

(

Josie woke feeling better than she could ever remember. There was a crackling electricity in the air, a heat radiating from within her own body. Her lips still tingled with the memory of Tristan's teeth scraping against them. Her body still burned where his hands had gripped so tightly. The midday sun greeted her through the window, doing a shadowless rainbow dance across her legs. She felt unfamiliar, like a stranger was living inside her. Something was different, not bad, but different. Her hands slid up her body, over her stomach and eventually up to her face, where she found the distinction immediately. She'd woken up with a smile.

While still a creature of habit, Josie recently found herself deviating from her norm more and more. She'd been sketching less, the faces no longer calling out to be recorded. She hadn't been out tagging in a while. While she loved the cloak of night, the whooshing sound of paint, and the vibrant images she left behind, she didn't need it like she used to.

She now made eye contact with strangers and waved at her deranged old neighbor, Mrs. Thompson, when passing at the mailboxes. She still visited Gavin, though less frequently. She felt herself disconnecting from her old life and clinging to something new. Alex still came by, bringing food and staying until she ate. She found comfort in his protectiveness and longed to thank him, but she could not imagine anything appropriate.

It had been three days since Tristan and Josie's date, but already she grew nervous at the separation. The air was harder to process in his absence. The lights seemed dimmer and the emptiness made her queasy. If Tristan wasn't within the paper-thin walls of her apartment, she didn't want to be there either. She questioned if it was healthy to feel this attached to someone so quickly. She decided she didn't care.

For hours at a time, she would sit on the bare mattress of her bedroom and stare at the pencil-drawn faces before her. There were so many versions of Tristan, each so detailed and true to life. Josie wondered how she'd ever forgotten him.

Her mother had the kindest smile, just like Josie imagined every mother should. Warm eyes stared back, the roughly drawn charcoal lines doing nothing to diminish her softness. Tristan had described Josie's mother as a fun, free spirit who cared deeply for her family. She had died in a car accident a year before they moved away.

Her father was handsome, but his eyes seemed to reflect worry and sadness in every drawing. Perhaps her only memory of Earl had been after her mother's passing. She wanted, so badly, to remember what his hugs felt like or the timbre of his voice.

Tristan's parents were represented on her wall of memories as well. His mother, Bitsy, and his father, Daniel, were such beautiful people. It was easy to see how Tristan had turned out so stunning. There was anger and sadness in his voice when he spoke of them, but Josie knew he missed them. From what he'd told her, they were good people who had only wanted the best for their son. As outsiders, they were able to see the poisonous future that lay ahead with Fiona and had tried to warn him against it.

The sun was setting on another day, and as the fiery glow flooded her apartment, she thought of endings and beginnings. Josie recognized the need she had for Tristan, the need to end her aimless wandering through life and begin again with him. Fear ate away at her, making her feel undeserving of such notions.

Josie wanted to call Tristan and ask him to come over, but she didn't want to scare him off by being too clingy. She suddenly hated being alone. Before he had come along, when Josie got this feeling, she would go out and find someone to bed. It was always easy on her end, a tiny flirt, a lingering gaze, and they'd be putty in her hands. All she wanted was a warm bed and protective arms around her. Orgasms and various drugs had just been a bonus.

This wasn't an option anymore. She didn't want just any arms around her, she wanted his strong inked arms. She wanted to devour and consume him. She wanted to exist for Tristan and only Tristan.

Resigning herself to a night of tagging, she threw on Tristan's hoodie, grabbed her bag, and tied a bandanna around her neck. It wasn't a fashion statement, it worked for covering her face while writing. She was searching the apartment for her shoes when a knock sounded at the door.

Running across her apartment, her socked feet having trouble gaining traction against the hardwood, she skidded to a stop and threw the door open. The relief at seeing Tristan standing there was more than she could handle. Josie leaned against the door frame to keep herself upright.

"Don't ever just open your door like that, Josie. At least fucking ask who it is first," he grumbled at her.

Her face fell as his harsh words struck her with the force of fists. Tristan barreled into the apartment, slamming the door behind him and locking it up. He threw himself down on her sofa, crushing random sketches beneath his feet with no regard.

"Thirty-eight percent of assaults and sixty fucking percent of rapes happen in the home. Do you want to be another statistic? I can't stand the thought of you being measured using some goddamned algorithm compared to a set of data on the San Diego crime rate scale."

Unsure what to do with herself, Josie approached him care-fully. She'd dealt with irate people too many times to count and considered herself schooled in the ways of diversion. Not so long ago, in a house that she'd been forced to call home, it had been a way of life. She'd become an expert at dissolving hostile situa-tions with minimal damage.

For some reason, she was clueless about what to do with Tristan. He had never spoken to her so harshly before. Tristan scrubbed at his face, taking a deep breath and blowing it out slowly. Josie thought he looked like he needed a cigarette. She cursed the fact that she didn't have any. So she gave him all that she did have.

Crawling into Tristan's lap, Josie straddled his legs. She took his worried face between her hands and looked deep into his eyes. She placed herself at his mercy, wanting so badly to deci-pher his thoughts, to ease his mind.

"What's wrong? What did I do?" she whispered.

Tristan shook his head, disgusted with himself. His careless ac-tions had made her feel like she'd committed some sort of crime. Her words only fueled his anger, creating a desire to punish him-self for his ill manners. Tristan needed to make her understand just how much she meant to him. He needed to make her see that the girl from his past and the girl before him now owned his heart. She always had. His temper had gotten the best of him and he'd misdirected it at the one person who would never deserve it.

"Nothing, Josie. You did nothing. I'm just an ass. I'm having a bad day," he answered, placing a kiss on her forehead.

Tristan leaned back against the cushions and closed his eyes, trying to calm his overactive mind. His heart raced at her near-ness, the warmth of her body on top of his. His mind was staggered with thoughts of approaching danger and impossible choices. A treacherous situation had been presented, and for now, he could see no way out.

"Let me make it better."

Her nimble fingers worked quickly, skillfully unlatching his belt buckle. When it was pulled free, she popped open each button of his fly. Slowly, with purpose, she traced the length of him.

"Josie, you . . . you don't have to," he stuttered before being distracted by her touch.

"I want to."

For too long he had denied physical satisfaction with Josie, and he would punish himself no more. He felt as though she might need this just as much as he did. For a few minutes, he could forget about the threats on McKenzi and focus on the talents of Josie.

Tristan cleared his throat, causing Josie's eyes to meet his own. The apartment was eerily silent as they absorbed each other's breaths and desire. His eyes were dark and hungry and begging for more. *More,* Josie chanted in her head, *more.* She wanted to give him more. She wanted to be more.

Tristan fisted the sofa cushion, a breathy grunt escaping his lips as he watched Josie descend onto him. While this was far from his first blow job, it was certainly his most intense. He'd come over in a foul mood, unable to stay away from her any longer. He was confused and frightened for Josie's safety. He was tired of just existing in a swirling mess and not living. With Josie's soft lips wrapped around him, he lived.

Josie had never wanted to please someone so badly. She'd never wanted to give so freely. She knew this meant more than just the physical act itself, but she couldn't admit what it was. Soon, Tristan's hips rocked, rising up to meet her. His fingers wrapped tighter in her hair.

She felt the ache in her jaw, the burn and shake of her arms holding her over his lap, but she ignored the discomfort. Tristan climaxed almost violently, calling her name on labored breaths.

She had given more and taken more. She had a feeling, with Tristan, it could never be enough.

"That was not why I came over here," Tristan said as he tucked himself back into his pants. "Though I must admit your powers of distraction are amazingly effective."

Josie remained quiet, refusing to excuse the most exquisite orgasm she'd ever been witness to. Instead, she pulled in closer, squeezing tight around his ribs. Tristan exhaled heavily as ran his fingers through her hair.

"I'm sorry I yelled at you. I just really needed to see you," he admitted.

Josie sat up so that she could look into his face. She ran the tips of her fingers over his brow, smoothing out the worried lines there. His expression displayed guilt and she wanted nothing more than to erase it.

"You do see me. You always see me. That's what's so scary."

He kissed her lips, at a loss as to how to make her understand that she didn't need to be scared, not of him, anyway. Tristan had debated whether to tell her about the threat from Moloney. He didn't want to make decisions without involving her, but he didn't want to be responsible for pushing her too hard. His biggest fear was that she would disappear again. He knew, without a doubt, that he'd never survive it a second time.

Mort had spent three days combing through Balboa Park looking for the girl. He'd even dressed in torn and dirty clothes to try to assimilate himself into the band of vagrants. During the day, most of them hid away in the shadows of the canyon or panhandled downtown. By night, they roamed the park freely in search of food or anything else worth having.

He made small talk and asked around, but never did he find Josie Banks. Sometimes he would swear that he'd seen her face, but it always turned out to be some other girl with dark eyes and a tortured past. Poverty and hard luck had no predilection for a certain type of person. Teenagers, kids, even whole families of every race and color found themselves in its hopeless grip. It was easy enough to imagine himself in their position had he never found the employment of Dean Moloney.

It was by chance that Mort seated himself on the very bench that Josie often visited. He was bent over, his elbows on his knees, head in his hands, when he felt someone sit beside him.

"You're new here."

Mort nodded, not looking up.

"I'm Gavin, your concierge for the evening. Whatcha looking for?"

"A girl."

"Well, today's your lucky day, handsome."

Mort sighed and sat back before sliding his eyes over to his new friend. She looked tired and weathered, but something in her eyes was content.

"A specific girl."

"Oh, well, I get it. I'm not your type. No worries, you're not mine either."

"A girl named Josie," Mort said through gritted teeth.

"Josie? Why didn't you just say that? Haven't seen her in a couple weeks, but you're definitely in the right place."

Gavin pointed to the elaborate JayBee signature on the bench between them. Mort's spine straightened severely and he tried to keep the look of triumph from his face.

"Cool. That's cool."

"What you want with her?" Gavin asked, suddenly wary.

"I owe her some money. You know where I can find her?"

"Uh, I might. But I don't know you, dude. What if she don't want to be found?"

Instantly, Mort's expression morphed from innocent to sinister. He pulled his switchblade and held it against Gavin's throat.

"You'll tell me or you'll fucking die."

Gavin's mind ran wild as she felt death grab hold. This man would end her, she knew that. If she didn't tell him what he wanted to know, her life would end here on this bench. She eyed one of Josie's drawings, a simple self-portrait. There was no decision to make.

"Then I guess I'm meeting my maker tonight," she answered in a firm voice.

There was no scream as the blade penetrated her flesh. She didn't beg for her life. There was no change of heart. Gavin closed her eyes and slipped away silently beneath the lush green canopy.

An hour later, Mort returned to his apartment, where he washed the blood and disappointment from his hands. When he was clean again, he lay in bed and pondered what his next move would be. Just as he began to doze off, his phone buzzed.

"Mort," he answered.

"Any word on the girl?" the sinister voice asked.

Mort glanced at the phone, as if the man could come through and grab him by the throat if his answer was not satisfactory.

"All I've got is a lead on her case worker."

"Be aggressive. Those fuckers in New York really dropped the ball on this," Moloney sneered.

"I've got this."

"I have a former employee looking for her as well. If he finds her first, you are out of luck, my friend."

The line disconnected, and Mort slumped against his pillow. The word "friend" resonated through the air, dripping with disdain and anything but camaraderie. He'd dedicated so much time to this job, and just like that, Moloney would send someone else to finish it. Mort recognized this for what it was, a motivational threat. He needed this money, his whole future depended on it.

Throwing his phone onto the table, he vowed to step up his game. Mort hacked into the internal archives of the Child Services office. Within minutes he was logged in as a registered user and began his search for Josie Banks.

He pulled up her file and noted the assigned case worker was Monica Templeton and smiled satisfactorily. He followed Josie's path through the failing child protective system, noting the methodical check-ins every twelve weeks.

First she was placed in a girls' home in north San Diego County. After six months, she was put into a foster home with Mr. and Mrs. Spangler. The couple lived in a decent uptown neighborhood and seemed an ideal family on paper.

Mort scrolled through the folder, finding it pathetic that almost four years of this girl's childhood could be so easily accounted for and condensed into this small file. As he read the notes detailing the horrific abuse she suffered, it hit him like a suffocating blow.

"Mr. and Mrs. Spangler were charged with criminal negligence and physical abuse while serving as Josie Banks's guardians. They were both convicted and served time separately. Denise, released early in March 2010, and her husband, Stephen, released in November 2010, remain residents of San Diego County. See notes below for parole information," Mort read, sickened by the words.

The details of the case stated that none of the abuse had been discovered until Josie had turned eighteen and was no longer a ward of the state.

He felt a wave of nausea shoot through his body. In the business he was in, Mort had seen many things. He'd experienced enough blood and carnage to last him several lifetimes. This was something entirely different. He too had suffered abuse at the hands of adults he'd trusted, an unforgivable act in his book. These people were monsters.

While he felt sorry for Josie and all that she'd endured, he had a job to do and it would be best if he just viewed her as a paycheck. He knew he needed to act quickly, otherwise he might be thwarted by Moloney's other man. He quickly logged out of the program and shut down his computer.

11. UMBRA

A SHADOW THAT BLOCKS OUT ILLUMINATION.

It was raining in Southern California and no one knew how to behave. Pedestrians scurried down the streets, taking cover under the eaves of various restaurants and secondhand bookstores. The strangers huddled so tightly together that personal space and physical boundaries were breached. The falling rain assembled into puddles along street curbs and on the dry fronds of palm trees.

Monica huffed at the inconvenience as she hurried down the sidewalk. The coffee shop sign lured her in, the neon glow immediately reminding her body of its requirement of caffeine. She weaved in and out of the crowds, sometimes darting through the downpour to reach her destination. The man before her, the one dressed in appropriate rain gear and designer shoes, swung the door too hard, knocking her over. Monica yelped and grabbed his sleeve to keep from falling, only to send them both careening to the ground.

"Shit!" Monica exclaimed, feeling the water seep through the seat of her pencil skirt.

"I'm so sorry," he said, jumping up quickly, offering his hand and an apologetic smile.

She took it and let him pull her in beneath the shelter of his jacket. Once inside, Monica tried to assess the damage. She knew her ass was wet and maybe bruised, her hair was a mess, and she'd broken a nail. That shit always happens just when you get them all to the same length, she thought.

"Are you okay?" the man asked, concern lacing his voice.

His face was a bit round and childlike while still remaining handsome. His curly brown hair was cropped short, while his devious smile hinted that there was more beneath the surface. His oxford shirt hugged his chest, indicating a muscled body beneath such common clothes. Soon, for no reason at all, Monica found herself smiling back.

"I'm fine, really."

"Well, if you're sure. Hey, let me buy you a coffee. Pick your poison," he said, gesturing to the menu.

Monica blushed and stepped to the counter, placing her usual order. He followed and ordered the same. There was a recognized silence between them as they waited for the drinks—a lingering glance, the faintest smile, all telltale signs of flirting. Even though all she could do was compare this man to Rob, Monica was flattered.

"Can you believe how people freak out when it rains?" he finally said.

"I know, right? It's like I want to scream at them, 'It's just water!'"

He laughed wholeheartedly, his dimples deepening, further softening his face. Their order was called and they retrieved their cups from the counter.

"So you must not be from here." she said.

"Nah, I'm from Tacoma. What gave it away?"

"You're wearing a raincoat, an item that none of us locals even own." She twisted the cup nervously in her hands. "So you should be an expert, right? I hear the sun never shines up there. People have vitamin D deficiencies and it, like, rains every day?"

He shook his head and grinned at her. "It's not quite that bad."

"Well, thanks for the coffee. . . ." Monica paused, waiting for his name.

"Evan."

"Evan," she repeated. "I'm Monica. Thanks again, and good luck out there. Try to stay upright for the rest of the day."

"You too," he countered, raising his cup and grinning triumphantly at her retreating form.

Josie let Tristan's statement sink in. Her crazed eyes could almost see the words breeze across the room and enter her head. He'd said them so matter-of-factly, so interestingly, as if reciting more of his random facts.

"You're telling me that Dean Moloney, crime lord, wants me dead? Not only that, but he's asked you to do it?" Josie screeched.

"Yes," Tristan answered calmly.

"Why me? Who is this other person looking for me? Do you know him? Does Moloney know that you know me? He couldn't possibly."

"I'm not sure if he's connected us to each other yet. We were just kids back then. But I bet this has something to do with your amnesia. We can assume that he may be responsible for your father's death and your disappearance. Would you be willing to try hypnotherapy to recover your memory?"

"Been there, done that. Nothing has worked." Tristan watched Josie's grip tighten on the edge of the kitchen counter. Her elbows were locked, her shoulders high and tense while her head hung down between them. "What am I going to do?" she whispered.

The words poured from her mouth and circled the drain before slipping away.

"We," Tristan corrected.

"What?"

"What are *we* going to do? I think I should go back to New Orleans and see what I can find out, but I don't want to leave you here alone."

"Take me with you," she offered, turning to face him.

"Absolutely not! The chances of anyone recognizing you are low, but if they did, word would spread fast. Then you'll be on his turf. You've got to stay here. Not to mention I'm not exactly on his good side. If Moloney finds out I'm there . . ." He trailed off.

"I want to help. I can't sit around while you run off risking your life, Tristan!"

"Just don't leave the four walls of this apartment. I'll talk to Alex and have him keep a closer eye on you while I'm gone. Whoever is looking for you hasn't found you yet, so it's best to just stay put. It's eighteen hundred seventy-two miles from here to New Orleans. If I leave in the morning, avoid big-city traffic, and maintain the average highway speed limit, I can make it there by Tuesday evening."

"Shit," Josie muttered, slumping down into one of her wobbly kitchen chairs.

Tristan watched as she absorbed the bad news. He knew it would be rough on both of them, but he was almost relieved not to have to deal with it on his own anymore. Josie curled into herself, the tips of her fingers rubbing at her temples.

He'd never been around someone who made him feel so whole and inadequate at the same time. She brought out the best and worst in him. She made him question everything he'd ever known and still he wanted to crawl at her feet to serve her every need.

When he'd said good-bye to her as a child, he never imagined he'd get a second chance. Now was the time to make things right, to build her up and tie her to himself. They would never get back the years they missed, but they could start over if she'd only surrender.

Pulling her to the sofa, Tristan wrapped his arms around her. She climbed into his lap and tucked her head beneath his chin. Her fingers dug into his skin relentlessly, feeling like if she let go, he would vanish.

Tristan's eyes roamed over the meager apartment and he couldn't help but cringe at all the drawings carved into the walls and door frames, the paint-and-ink signatures on every surface.

"The drawings in your bedroom are one thing, Josie. You've got to stop marking up your apartment. You'll never get your security deposit back."

"Who says I paid a security deposit? I may have negotiated my way out of that."

Tristan looked down into her eyes.

"I am very persuasive when I need to be. I have my methods." He flinched at her implication. "Besides, I like it. Maybe I'll never leave. When I die, I'll be so famous that people will come to visit this place. It's like a big memorial."

"You will not die in this shitty apartment. I promise," Tristan said.

"You don't know that, Tristan. You can't make that promise."

"Promises are my best intentions."

"Then promise to say nice things and tell stories when I die," she said.

Tristan pushed that thought from his mind. It would be a cruel and terrible punishment to lose her after just finding her again.

"I remember the day of your memorial at school. It was so humid that it felt hard to breathe. It was the second week of school and everyone had already fallen right back into their cliques."

Tristan took a deep breath, closed his eyes, and let that day play out against his eyelids. So clearly he could envision the sympathetic teachers, the looks from his peers.

"They asked me to say a few words and, at first, I refused. I was angry and knew that these people didn't know you like I did. Then I figured I wanted them to know you better, so that I wasn't so alone. I stood in front of the assembly and told them who you were and what you meant to me."

Josie reached for his hand and laced her fingers through his. The vibrant ink that ended and wrapped around his wrist was such a stark contrast to her pale, clean canvas skin. They were contradictory and stunning together.

"'McKenzi Delaune was my best friend. We met when we were seven years old. She was smart and witty and the prettiest girl I've ever seen. You all knew her as the shy girl who studied during lunch and never joined clubs, but she was so much more than that.

"'McKenzi climbed trees. She wrote secrets in a purple diary kept between her mattresses. She loved old black-and-white movies. She always danced around her living room with her mom, blasting music so loud that it shook the windows. Most of all, McKenzi loved to draw. Sketches of family and celebrities covered her walls. Sometimes she made up entire stories to go with her pictures, stories about dragons and aliens and superheroes.

Every story had a common theme, happy endings. McKenzi believed in fairies and heaven and love. I hope that wherever she is now, she's been reunited with her family and has found her own happy ending.'"

Tristan's throat became tight and restricted with the words that he'd spoken as a teenager. Josie remained still on his chest, her breathing slow and steady. For a moment, he wondered if she'd fallen asleep.

"I can't believe you remember that speech," she said softly, sitting up so that she could see his face.

He smiled at her and couldn't believe that she thought he'd ever forget it.

"I know things are shit right now. Our whole lives have been crazy, but I need you to know that I'm here to stay."

Josie wondered how such passionate declarations could be made by a man who had suffered so much heartache. She looked at him, really looked at him, and could see now that he had made himself vulnerable. He was so unlike every other person she'd ever met. He wore his battered heart on his sleeve. Even after all the hurt he'd endured, he still had faith in love, whereas her faith had never existed.

She slid off of his lap and to the other end of the couch now, needing separation. Josie pulled her knees up and wrapped her arms tight around them, a defensive move she'd perfected years ago. A battle raged in her mind, a fight between what she wanted and what she needed.

"Tristan, I'm not that girl you remember. I'm not McKenzi. You're infatuated with the memory of who I used to be, not who I am. You don't know me."

"I want to, Josie. If you'd just let me. I want to know everything," he pleaded.

She shook her head and balled her hands into fists. He'd never want to know who she was now. She'd never compare to his perfect childhood memories.

"No you don't, Tristan. No one wants to know those things."

Tristan stood and began pacing the room, trying to keep his temper under control. He hated that she doubted his word. He hated that she didn't trust him to keep her safe. But what he hated most was that he honestly didn't know if he could.

"Yes, I do," he said looking into her eyes, challenging her. "I need to."

Josie shot off the couch, losing the last bit of restraint she had.

"Fine, Tristan. You want to know? I'll fucking tell you. You want to know about when they found me, I was so dehydrated and malnourished I barely survived the night? I spent days in a hospital, and when I finally woke up everyone was a stranger! You want to know how I was shipped across the country to a state home, where I didn't know anyone? You want to know how, at night, when the adults were asleep, the older girls would force themselves on me, and in me, while the others stood as lookouts? Is that what you want to fucking know?"

Josie yelled at him, she raged at him, she wanted to stop, but she couldn't. Tristan just shook his head, helpless to soothe the trembling girl before him. Every statement stabbed at him like a serrated knife, destroying his heart.

"How about when I was so lucky to be placed in a foster home? You want to know how for the three years I lived there, I was kept in a nine-square-foot closet, even though there was a perfect little room upstairs staged with boy band posters and frilly pillows? Oh, I bet you want to know how that asshole beat me every time I spoke without permission."

"No," he whispered. "I can't believe . . ."

"Yes! This isn't one of your books, Tristan. This is my life. It's real."

Tristan wanted to go to her, he wanted to take away all the suffering she'd endured. He took a step toward her, but she held up her hand to stop him. Josie's chest was heaving now, her breaths shallow and unfulfilling. The room began to spin as her heart crashed against her chest and pulsing blood deafened her ears.

"I slept in the park and stole to survive until Monica found me. Do you want to know that I've fucked so many people that I've lost count? Men, women, anyone who would give me what I needed. I did it for food, for a soft bed, and for a few pills."

Tristan shook his head, unable to imagine the things she described, unwilling to accept that she'd endured those horrible atrocities.

"Don't shake your fucking head, Tristan. You wanted to know, now you do."

Her voice was only a whisper now, a tortured plea for solitude.

"None of that was your fault, Josie. None of it. You can trust me. I want to help."

"You can't help me, Tristan. No one can. This is who I am, now. I'm fucked-up and I can't be fixed. Not by you or Monica or anyone else. Just go."

"Josie."

"Go!" she yelled, pointing at the door.

When he didn't move, she yelled again, her face stamped with pink splotches and pent-up emotions. Tristan found himself on the edge of a precipice. He wanted to make her happy, but leaving would appease her only for the moment. He knew, more than she did, that she needed him to stay. Tristan squared his shoulders and prepared for battle.

12. TIDES

THE RISING AND FALLING
LEVELS OF THE OCEAN.

With heavy footsteps and infallible conviction, Tristan charged toward Josie. Her eyes widened in surprise as he approached. She'd told him to leave. She wasn't prepared for resistance.

"No!" she shouted, pushing at his chest in a futile effort to keep him away. "Get out before I throw you out!"

He remained silent as he fought off her flailing arms and empty threats. Tristan's large hands enveloped her wrists, stopping her assault midair. He pinned her hands to her sides and wrapped his arms around her, trapping her in his viselike grip. She struggled against his hold, her strength fading with every effort.

"Let me go! Leave me alone! Just go! Why won't you just go?" her weakening voice yelled.

Tristan squeezed her tighter and lowered his lips to her ear.

"Because I love you."

Josie's body sagged against his in defeat, and she rested her forehead against his chest.

"You can't," she whispered. "You can't love me."

"I do," he insisted.

She blinked a few times, trying to focus her blurry vision, straining to understand his words. They made no sense to her. She'd never heard them directed at her before. It felt terrifying.

"Show me."

Tristan crushed his lips to Josie's. He didn't have to think or plan, he only had to feel. He felt the wetness on her cheeks as his skin moved against hers. He felt the hot, soft flesh of her tongue push and pull against his. Releasing his hold on her, he slid his hands up to her shoulders and brought her flush against his chest. She felt so good, fit so perfectly. Tristan couldn't imagine a physical pleasure more fulfilling than her touch.

Josie felt crazed and overwhelmed with emotion. She scratched and clawed at his body as if trying to climb inside him. Over the lines of his ink, she raked pink trails with her fingernails. Tristan hummed at the fulfillment of her pain becoming his.

Josie felt his hands trace down the curve of her body. Tristan grabbed the backs of her thighs and she hopped up, wrapping her legs around him. She celebrated the electrifying buzz of every part of her body being touched by every part of his.

A low, satisfied hum vibrated through his chest as he walked them to her never-used bedroom. The only light came from the moon filtering in through the dirty window. Tristan dropped to his knees, Josie still clinging to his body. In a tangle of limbs, Josie fought her way out of her shirt and jeans while Tristan helped.

They ventured into unfamiliar territory for Josie. It was strange and intimidating and completely welcomed. Josie usually held all the control in these situations, taking what she wanted and then abandoning her conquest. With Tristan, she was happy to surrender.

Josie lay before Tristan, her skin glowing silvery blue in the moonlight. With her eyes hooded and her chest rising and falling so quickly, she looked like a beautiful waiting sacrifice. She was heavenly and entirely his. Here, in the quiet of this room, beneath the light that shone only for them, she was not damaged, she was faultless and brilliant.

Lowering himself, he let the weight of his body press her into the mattress. He placed soft kisses on her chest and neck, dragging his tongue across her pulse point. The rapid thumping of her heart kept him grounded, otherwise he felt as though he might float away.

"Tristan, please," she begged, pulling up on his shoulders so she could see his face again.

Josie rocked her hips against him, loving the feel of rough denim against her bare flesh. Desperate for the heat of his body, she tugged at his shirt until he sat up and removed it. The planes of his chest were artfully defined by the colorful images that curved and clung to his muscles.

She let her fingers trace over each pattern before dropping down to the fly of his jeans. Expertly, Josie slid each button through its hole, while her lips pressed kisses against his neck. He tasted like salt and adoration.

The muscles and tendons of his shoulders were rigid. Her tongue ran over the stubble of his jaw and she hummed at the delightful scrape of it against her lips. With his jeans undone, Tristan slipped out of them easily. Josie smiled at the revelation that he wore nothing beneath them.

Again, he lowered himself onto her, but this time the feeling was quite different. Hot flesh against hot flesh and worshipping hands made them each feel as if time had stopped. Josie vowed to keep her eyes open, not wanting to miss a second of his loving, lustful face.

Tristan placed his lips on her body, sucking and biting until she was a hopeless mess. He slid his hand into hers to hold his weight. Josie treasured the feeling of being pinned beneath him, being held down by not only his body but also by his affection. She'd never wanted to belong to anyone until this moment.

Josie watched in fascination as his brow furrowed and his eyes fluttered when he finally slid inside her. She felt her body stretch to welcome him and wanted to commit the feeling to memory. Once fully joined, he stilled and placed a sugary, chaste kiss against her lips.

"Perfect," Tristan whispered.

He began a steady rhythm, a greedy pace set by his body and not his will. Sex had always been good for him, easy and pleasurable. But it had never been this. This was unexplainable and foreign. It was the rejoining of two lost souls to make each other whole again, immeasurable love.

"Tell me again," she whispered.

Knowing exactly what she wanted, Tristan whispered the three words that gave her the only strength she had.

"I love you."

His declaration sent her hurling over the edge. A fiery orgasm ripped through Josie, every muscle unyielding and taut as she chanted his name. She felt drunk and dazed and completely addicted.

Tristan groaned at the sight before him, her eyes squeezed tight, her lips parted in a silent scream. He'd never seen anything more stunning.

Josie hated that those three tiny words could invoke so much joy and so much fear inside her heart. As much as she felt that it might be true, she could not find the strength to reaffirm their more-than-physical connection. Instead, she kept with what was familiar to her.

"Oh God! So good, Tristan."

Josie knew her words were harsh and unromantic, but they were easy. She couldn't offer him the same profession that he'd given her, so she stayed true to the wild desire between the two of them. Tiny whimpers escaped Tristan's lips with his climax, his own erotic melody.

Tristan rolled them over and wrapped his arms around her. Slowly, their breaths became slower, their pulses calmed. Bathed in the glow of lunar beams, they fell into a deep slumber surrounded by the pencil-sketched faces of their past.

The next morning, in the Clairemont neighborhood, swimming in their own postcoital glow, Monica and Rob exchanged their own confessions.

"It seems soon, but I just know that you're it for me," Monica said, tracing the light trail of hair leading from his belly to the waistband of his boxers.

"It's the same for me. I love you like biscuits and gravy."

"Ha. You better really love biscuits and gravy," she teased.

"Of course, ma'am."

"Seems like some people wait for love their whole lives. Some people never expect to find it. How did two people like us happen across each other? Destiny or a higher power maybe," Monica said, her voice trailing off.

Rob nodded, silenced by her ideas of destiny and otherworldly forces responsible for their union. He believed in no such thing. Still, he pulled Monica in close and kissed the top of her head. He wouldn't question her ideals. All he knew was that he wanted her to be happy and he would do anything in his power to make that happen.

Later that afternoon, when they had rehydrated and fed themselves, the couple ventured out to Balboa Park. Rob lay in the grass with his jacket folded beneath his head. In the warm light of the late-day sun, he hummed as Monica ran her fingers through his hair. They watched children play and dogs chase after them. Couples walked hand in hand, enjoying each other and the impossibly beautiful weather. When massive jets swept over, they raised their faces to the sky to enjoy the roar of the engines and the momentary eclipse created by their shadows.

They talked about love and life and changes to come, planning their future as if it were guaranteed. Rob admitted to never being in love before. While Monica couldn't admit the same, she was sure that it had never felt quite like this. Rob complained about the unrealistic expectations of his job and his fears of failure. So much responsibility sat on his shoulders and the weight of it felt crushing at times. Monica admitted that, though demanding, she loved her job.

"It's so fulfilling," she confessed. "I mean, these kids, who have been abandoned in some form or another, have no one to look out for them. That's where I come in. It's my job to make sure that they're safe. I want them to have a fair chance to reach their potential."

"Yeah, but don't you get tired of taking responsibility for other people's children? Don't you just wish parents would be parents?"

"I do wish people would be accountable for their children, but I feel a responsibility to help," Monica answered.

For her, it was simple. She was capable of helping, so she did.

"When I was younger, I thought I could save them all. I was stupid. I made mistakes that were covered up by my superiors, swept under the rug with a slight slap on the wrist. It makes me sick now to think of me getting off so easy when this innocent girl paid the price."

Monica felt tears prick at her eyes. She blinked quickly, willing them away.

"What happened? Is she . . . ?" Rob inquired but couldn't finish the thought.

Monica shook her head. "She'd had a really rough life already. She lost both of her parents, then she was shipped cross-country. She was only my third assignment. I placed her in a foster home with this couple who seemed perfect. They had a safe home and full-time jobs and an older son who was about to leave for college. They wanted to offer their home to a teenage girl. I put her there. I did that to her."

The tears rolled down her cheeks now, and she didn't care to stop them.

"It's okay," Rob whispered, clutching her hand in his and running his thumb back and forth in a sweeping motion.

"It's not okay. They did horrible things to her, Rob, things that you can't even imagine. It was my fault for not seeing through their lies. It was my fault."

This had been the subject of nightmares, the cause of therapy, a never-ending black cloud looming over her. No matter what, Monica could not let go of the guilt and shame associated with Josie Banks.

"Can you imagine being responsible for something so horrible?"

"It's not your fault those people were terrible."

"It's my fault she had to live with them, my fault that she was too scared to tell me the truth about them. She's twenty-two years old now. She uses drugs and sex and God knows what else to avoid having any real relationships. She's so damn talented, an artist. I check in on her, always trying to guide her toward a better life, to save her from herself. Josie doesn't want to be saved, though. I guess I'm just being selfish. Because if she turned out okay, that would mean I didn't fail."

She broke down again, this time losing all control. She sobbed against his shoulder, painting his shirt in misshapen circles of salt water. Monica clutched his arm, needing to feel and consume his strength. She sighed when she felt his hand rub comforting circles on her back. The feel of Rob's love made it easier to manage.

"Darlin', you did what you could. I'm sure she knows you didn't intend for any of that to happen."

Monica swiped at her eyes and took a deep, cleansing breath. She forced a smile down at Rob's worried face, regretting burdening him with such tragedy.

"I know. I do. I just want her to be happy. I almost feel guiltier now that I've found you."

"Monica?" a deep voice called from a few feet away.

She looked up to find her coffee beau, Evan, standing there. She forced a smile and glanced around, trying to figure out where he had come from. Feeling vulnerable, she wondered if he'd overheard any of their conversation. Rob sat up quickly but remained relaxed as Evan approached.

"Hi, Evan. Fancy seeing you here," she said, shielding her eyes from the sun so that she could look up at him.

"Yeah, I was heading to the museum with some friends when I spotted you. You're looking much better than the last time I saw you."

Both Monica and Rob looked around for his friends but found no one waiting.

"Yeah, a day off will do that," she said. "Oh, Evan, this is Rob. Rob, this is Evan."

Evan stepped closer, enjoying how he towered over the seated man. He offered his hand in a gesture of forced politeness. It would gain him points with Monica if he remained casually friendly to the boyfriend. Rob gripped his hand and Evan almost grunted from the force of his hold. The corded muscles and tendons of Rob's forearm were evident as he kept his expression indifferent and his hand crushing Evan's.

Rob nodded and released his grip from the would-be suitor, hoping that his warning was clear. *She's mine.*

"Evan knocked me on my ass the other day in the rain. He bought me coffee to make up for it," Monica offered, completely unaware of what had just transpired between the two men.

"Did he?" Rob asked.

"It was the least I could do," Evan acknowledged. He looked around, wringing his hands together before turning back to address the couple. "Well, I'd better get going. It was good to see you again, Monica. Rob, nice meeting you."

"Likewise," Rob spat at his retreating form.

When he was out of sight, Monica turned to Rob only to find his gaze still trained to the empty space where Evan had been. His blue eyes were slits and his face was contorted into a menacing scowl.

"Rob? He's gone, you can stop crushing my hand now."

Rob snapped out of his jealous daze and released her hand. She smiled at him and shook out her fingers, exaggerating the pain just a bit.

"That guy's a douche bag."

"Aww, sweetie, you're jealous," she teased. "That's so cute."

"No, I'm not," he denied.

Monica straddled his lap and kissed him on his forehead, then his nose, then his lips.

"Yes, you are, but it's adorable. The green-eyed monster suits you."

"You could have introduced me as your boyfriend, you know."

"Is that what you are?"

Rob shrugged, suddenly aware of their unidentified relationship.

"Boyfriend seems so juvenile. You can be my partner, my lover, my special guy," she sang in a dramatic declaration.

Rob chuckled, letting his anger slip away.

"Regardless, I don't like Khaki Pants Church Clothes Evan. I want you to stay away from him."

Monica laughed and placed more distracting kisses on his face along his hairline. She combed her fingers through his hair and gave him an obedient smile.

"He's nobody. I'll never lay eyes on him again," she promised, though she couldn't know how far from the truth that statement would prove to be.

Tristan lay awake for nearly an hour, holding Josie close and memorizing her sleeping face. When she began to stir, he placed a kiss on top of her hair and inhaled. He found her intoxicating.

"Good morning," he whispered, his lips still pressed into her hair.

Josie hummed in response and squeezed him closer. Perfect, she thought, everything is perfect. She marveled at how soundly she'd slept and how utterly content she felt.

"REM sleep usually only accounts for twenty-five percent of our sleep, but with you it seems much higher. Do you remember your dreams?"

"I used to just see all those faces, yours, my parents', but now I don't remember anything. I bet they're mostly about you."

"I hope so," he answered, running his hand down the curve of her spine. "Josie?"

"Yeah?"

"Didn't you ever want to know about your life before amnesia?"

"I would sometimes think that I wanted to know, but I was too scared to face it. I thought, what if it's worse than what I *do* remember? I was happy to leave it alone. That way I could imagine it was a good life."

"It was a good life," he confirmed.

"Thanks to you, I know that now," she answered, smiling.

"When we were thirteen, you forced me to go see the movie *A Knight's Tale*. You were obsessed with Heath Ledger. I begged you to go see *Joe Dirt*. I couldn't stand the thought of sitting in that theater for two hours while you sighed and drooled over that guy."

Josie laughed.

"Well, he was beautiful. I was crushed when he died."

"Anyway, I gave in and went to see your movie. You went on and on about how hot he was. I was so jealous," Tristan said, laughing at the memory. "It worked out in my favor, though."

Josie lifted her head and rested her chin on his chest.

"How's that?"

"After the movie, you were so worked up that you dragged me into the bookstore and attacked me in the self-help section."

"I attacked you?"

"Yes, attacked. It may be the only time in my life that I was oblivious to books. The best parts of that night were the smell of paperback books and your perfume combined, the shelves cutting across my body and my hands in the back pockets of your jeans. We made out until one of the employees busted us. You gave me my first hickey and let me feel your boob. By thirteen-year-old-boy standards, it was epic."

Josie laughed and lay her head back down, wishing she could remember the moment. She wanted to see his adolescent face surprised by her aggressive behavior. More than anything, she longed for that connection to a boy who had shared so many of her firsts.

"It also happens to be the same night my mom caught me masturbating," Tristan added.

"Ha! No way!"

"Yes, it was traumatic. I don't think I looked her in the eye for a month."

She let her fingers trace his ribs, tapping out a soft rhythm like pressing piano keys.

"Stay with me for another week," Josie whispered.

"I can't. The sooner I find out what's going on, the sooner you'll be safe."

"Five days?" Josie begged, placing a kiss over the red-and-blue anatomically correct heart tattooed on his chest. "Imagine how many times we can do this in five days," she teased, shifting her naked body against his.

"One day," he bartered, trying to remain unaffected by her charms.

"Three," Josie countered, nibbling gently on the edge of his jaw.

Her fingers drifted down his body, beneath the sheet, tracing invisible patterns below his navel. She lowered her hand and continued with a feather-light touch to where he wanted her most.

"Deal," Tristan barely got out.

Josie grinned triumphantly and kissed his lips. He smiled and pressed his lips back to hers, wanting nothing more than to devour her again. Now that he'd tasted the sweetest flesh, he would never settle for anything less.

Josie shifted her hips. She usually felt empowered by the way she could coax physical reactions from the men she subjugated. Josie would become drunk on the power of seduction. With

Tristan, it was different. His body moving beneath hers and his salty inked skin alone made her euphoric. She'd gladly relinquish all authority just to be with him.

Tristan sat up in bed holding Josie. Her legs straddled his lap and she wrapped her arms around his shoulders. Skin to skin, they cradled each other in a warm embrace, each breathing in the other and wishing to never leave the moment.

"Can we stay like this for the next three days?" Tristan asked, reaching behind her to pull back the curtain.

Bright morning light flooded the room, highlighting their combined form like a spotlight. Josie's messy hair glowed a fiery red in the white-hot light, the wavy tendrils like flames. She stared into his eyes, which were usually dark emerald but in the sunlight had become the color of springtime grass. The hair on his face gave a beautiful shadow that look stippled in by pencil.

"Yes," she answered. "Forever."

Mort slid stealthily through the apartment. The sound of the shower running let him know that he had approximately ten minutes to complete this search. His shoes made no sound against the tiled floor as he glided from room to room. Ghosting his fingers along the kitchen counter, he paused briefly to flip through a few pieces of mail, finding junk and several bills. Next, he entered the small office nestled next to the den and opened her idle laptop. It was password protected, so he closed it and moved on.

Slipping into her bedroom, he could now smell the floral scent of her soap and shampoo, mixed with the steam escaping from the cracked bathroom door. He didn't bother checking her dresser or nightstand; he knew that those searches never revealed much more than perverted sexual secrets. Instead, he was drawn to her logo-emblazoned designer bag, sitting on the corner of her bed. Still comforted by the running water, he dug through the cavernous purse and fished out her smartphone. All he needed was a contact, some kind of physical connection to Josie, and he would be set.

He knew for sure that she was still here in the city, and that Monica still had contact with the girl. He couldn't believe his good fortune when he'd discovered that little gem, courtesy of a Monica Templeton breakdown. The poor woman hadn't even known she was confessing the much-needed information and it took Mort only a few seconds to connect the dots. Scrolling through her contacts, he came across Josie's name. He entered the number into his own phone before returning Monica's to her purse. With today's technology and a small fee, this number could be used to track down Josie's exact location.

The water cut off, and through the door he could hear Monica's soft voice singing Lady Gaga's "Poker Face." He smirked, imagining her petite, curvy body covered in water droplets and steam coming off her skin. He adjusted himself, took one last look around, and slipped out of her room.

Monica emerged from the warm confines of her bathroom to find absolutely nothing out of the ordinary.

13. PHASES
DIFFERENT ILLUMINATIONS THAT THE MOON
UNDERGOES DURING ITS ORBIT.

Josie left Trader Joe's loaded down with bags. Tristan was working his last shift at the Darkroom, so she didn't have the convenience of a car to carry them in.

She liked Gavin and she liked making sure the kids down at the plaza had enough to eat. When she was comfortable in her apartment with running water and a roof over her head, she felt guilty for having things they didn't. Her time on the streets had been short compared to most of them. Many had been homeless for years.

It had been during those nights of wandering empty streets

that she'd noticed graffiti. At first she saw the big pieces, entire walls or top to bottom on a train. They were always such a stark contrast to the whitewashed bricks or gray metal. The way each one had a identifiable style amazed her. Later, Josie started to notice the smaller pieces. Someone's name thrown up on a bus shelter or one-word mantras on freeway signs. She realized that it was everywhere.

Soon she stole her first set of permanent markers and was tagging JayBee on every pristine surface she could reach. Then she moved on to paint markers. She adored the bigger selection of colors and the way the glossy paint looked when it was dry.

While sneaking through the streets of San Diego, she'd run into a couple of other taggers. There was never any animosity, only an understanding that this was their art. A mutual appreciation for self-expression and attack against society was their binding force. There were rules to this art, though, and through trial and error, she learned them. Gangs claimed parts of the city and Josie avoided them at all costs. She was just a girl putting herself out there; she didn't want to fight their fight.

As she turned onto Sixth Street, Josie noticed a small piece thrown up on the side of a Dumpster. It was a three-color job. The outline was messy and ran down in tiny dripping rivers. She smiled and shook her head. This was someone just starting, just learning how to control the flow. Eventually, he or she would learn to cut the caps or tighten the wrist movement.

Josie had bought a few extra things, and the weight of the bag handles were cutting into her palms. She flexed her fingers and shifted the bags a bit to relieve the ache. Taking the familiar path through the park, she was surprised to find no one there. Usually Gavin would be sitting on the left side, her large frame and dirty clothes covering the green slats. Every drawing and inked word was visible on the empty bench. It chilled Josie to the core.

She set the bags on the bench and looked around.

"Gavin?" she called out.

She didn't want to be too loud. In these late hours, hidden away from the main path, sometimes people you didn't want to find, found you.

Josie sat on the bench and waited for her friend. After an hour, she was annoyed. She felt like maybe Gavin didn't appreciate what she brought. Maybe Gavin was upset that Josie came around less these days. Nigel came by offering his usual products, but Josie declined.

"Have you seen Gavin around?" Josie asked.

"Nah. Not last week neither."

"Shit."

"No worries. I'm sure she just found a sugar momma to take care of her. It's a shame too. You two were my regulars. Now I don't got shit."

He left disappointed and unconcerned with Gavin's whereabouts.

After two hours, Josie was scared. It was a feeling that sank deep into her gut. It made her nauseous and shaky. Those kids down at the plaza were important to Gavin, she wouldn't just abandon them. Something had to be wrong.

Josie didn't want to bother Tristan at work, but she had a really bad feeling. She stared at one of the streetlamps off in the distance. Even from here she could see the moths fluttering around it and throwing themselves toward the light. It reminded her of Gavin's approach to life. She was never afraid of the streets. She'd try anything. She'd throw herself into a fire if it meant she'd feel something.

After three hours of waiting, Josie decided to head home. She left the food bags tucked under the bench, not having the heart to take them with her. Maybe Gavin would come later, or one of the kids. When she got to the sidewalk, she turned and checked one last time, but the bench remained empty.

$$\smile$$

"Hello," Rob said, smiling at his phone.

Monica huffed, her end of the line unusually silent.

"Monica?"

"I miss you," she answered.

"I miss you too, Button."

Monica squished her face up at the nickname, unable to decide if she liked it or not. In all her years, Monica Marie Templeton had never had a nickname, or anyone to give her one. Her parents had been stiff, formal people who never called her anything but her given name. It never occurred to her to mind.

"I hate when you work late," she said, walking to the fridge and grabbing a beer. "Can't you just be at my disposal? I mean, any Southern gentleman would pride himself on doing that."

"Well, ma'am, I do have to make a living. I'm finishing up now."

"I had the worst day. First there was no Internet for like four hours. They shut us down because of a security breach or something. Then I got locked out of my building because I lost my work ID tag."

"I'm sorry, darlin'. Tomorrow will be better," he promised.

"Well, I guess I could say any day I make it home without a pending lawsuit or a threat on my life is a good day."

"I'll make it all better when I see you," Rob answered, his voice trailing off.

"You sound distracted. I'll let you go. Please get here with a quickness. I need you."

"Yes, dear."

Monica hung up and took a long sip of her beer. Time flew by quickly as she prepared dinner. An hour later, a tap at the door interrupted her stirring. She threw open the door and pulled Rob down for a searing kiss.

"Damn, that was quite a greeting," Rob said, panting against her lips.

Monica dragged him inside and pressed him against the wall, her tiny body acting as a wedge to keep him in place.

"I told you I missed you."

"Well, I'd say that was obvious," Rob answered, chuckling.

"I'm home alone and you're not around. I have to sit here and entertain myself with reality television and tabloid magazines. It's torture."

She fetched a cold beer and handed it to him. Rob took the bottle and downed half of it in one swallow. She watched as a drop of the amber liquid seeped from the corner of his mouth, carving a path down his chin and neck and soaking into the collar of his T-shirt.

"Subjected to bad TV and trashy gossip. What's a girl to do?" he asked.

"Well, I suppose I could always *entertain* myself, but I like it better when you do it."

He smirked and picked her up by the waist, placing her on the counter. Rob loved the feel of her tiny body enfolding him. He loved how her large personality was wrapped into this tight little package of dynamite. He loved her curly dark hair and cheerful eyes. She was devious and spunky and always kept him on his toes.

"Now that's something I'd like to see."

They kissed deep and hard until Monica had to come up for air. She recovered quickly, hopped down from the counter, and returned her attention to dinner while Rob parked himself in front of the television.

While her rice dish simmered, she went to check on Rob,

finding him asleep on the sofa. Monica hated that his job was so demanding. Some days she could sense the stress in his body, feel it in his tense embraces. But not now. He was fully relaxed and it made her heart happy to see him so untroubled. His forearm was thrown over his eyes as he slept. She sighed at the sight of his handsome pout.

A shrill noise cut through the air and she recognized the ringing of her cell phone. Running to her purse, she answered out of breath.

Monica fell into the closest kitchen chair, stunned by Josie's voice on the other end. There was no chitchat, only Josie requesting a double date tomorrow evening. She felt as though the room swirled around her feet. This was Tristan's doing, she knew that, but she would take redemption any way she could get it. After ending the strange yet thrilling call, she sat in a daze of hope and absolution.

"Button? You okay?" Rob asked, suddenly appearing in the doorway.

Her blank expression shifted to an enormous smile as she nodded and leapt into his arms.

"Are you working late tomorrow night?"

"Nope."

"Good. We have plans."

"Oh my God, that conversation was painful. Why the hell did I let you talk me into that?" Josie whined, clicking her seat belt into place. "Seriously, I feel like I need a Xanax after that phone call."

"She can't be that bad," Tristan said, laughing. "Besides, I want to get to know your friends."

"I told you, I don't have any friends."

"Tennessee Williams said, 'Life is partly what we make it, and

partly what it is made by the friends we choose.' Friendships are
the cultivation of relationships with people who are like you, believe in you, and share your burdens. You have Monica and Alex.
That's more than I've got."

Tristan started the car and watched as Josie crossed her legs
tightly, appreciating the rumble of the engine. She closed her
eyes and laid her head back against the seat.

"I fucking love this car," Josie whispered, not sure if she meant
to say it out loud or not.

She slid her hands down the tops of her thighs and back up
again, concentrating on the rough feel of the denim vibrating
beneath her fingertips. Tristan eyed her actions, almost losing his
breath at the sight.

"She's got a 396-cubic-inch, 325-horsepower turbojet V-8 engine with a Muncie 4-speed."

"I have no idea what any of that means."

"It's a sixty-seven Impala. A classic."

"It's fucking hot."

Tristan delighted in the purr of both his girls. He tried to con-
centrate on the road in front of him instead of on the vixen by his
side, who suddenly looked like she wanted to devour him.

"So I'm finally going to see your place? I bet you have everything covered in plastic so that cleanup is easy when you kill
your victims," Josie teased, looking to Tristan. His expression
remained unchanged. "Maybe there are whips and chains with
leather-padded tables and shock collars?"

"That doesn't sound so bad," Tristan answered.

"Not bad at all," Josie replied, playing along. "I've seen worse."

Tristan gave her a devious smile.

"Oh! I know! You're a geek, right? You have six thousand *Star
Wars* figurines worth a small fortune displayed on custom shelves
around your house?"

He shook his head, "Wrong again. I'm afraid you'll be disappointed."

Josie smiled and couldn't imagine ever being disappointed in Tristan. She watched the city pass by, morphing from the dark alleys of her life to the amber- and neon-lit streets of his. The sidewalks got cleaner, the buildings looked nicer, and the kids hustling on each corner vanished with each passing block. She didn't mind living in the seedier part of the city, she was comfortable there. Josie wondered if she'd always been that way.

"Dean Moloney lives right outside New Orleans?"

"Yeah, in Gretna. That's where we lived."

"So he had to have known me back when we lived there. I was a kid. What the hell could I have done to him?"

"I don't know," he said. "I've been asking myself that for days now. It has to be related to your dad. I'll take a look at any court cases Earl was involved with and see if I can make a connection."

"I wish I could remember," she whispered, the desperate longing in her voice painful to Tristan's ears.

Tristan watched Josie stare out the window again. He would give anything to be inside that head of hers, to jar those trapped memories loose so that she could remember her parents and how much they loved her. He reached for her hand and held it beneath his on the gearshift, knowing it would bring her some comfort.

They came to a stop and Josie looked around, amazed at how much their surroundings had changed in such a short drive. He hopped out and grabbed Josie's bag while she took in the building before her. It looked like a typical San Diego apartment, surrounded by palm trees and wrapped around a courtyard. It's stucco façade looked aged under the streetlights.

"I've never been tagging in this neighborhood. Looks like it could use some flair."

Tristan frowned and led her across the street. They climbed a

set of stairs, where he fumbled with his keys before finally entering apartment 2D.

"I'll just put your bag in my room. There's beer in the fridge if
you want."

To say Josie was surprised by his home was an understatement.
Sure, the walls were white and the carpet was tan, but that is where
the generic appearance ended. There was a built-in bookcase lining
one wall, with a space cut out for a television. The entire thing was
filled with books. New books, old books, hardbacks, paperbacks,
every kind of book she could imagine created a patchwork mosaic
look to the otherwise plain space.

There was an open laptop on a small wooden table with two
mismatched chairs parked beneath it. A well-worn sofa graced
the living room. Besides that, there was no other furniture. She
stepped to the bookcase, trailing her finger over the spines of the
books. None of the titles was familiar to her, and suddenly she felt
small and far out of her league.

"My collection."

Josie jumped at his proximity. She turned to face Tristan,
leaning against the shelf.

"I can see that," she answered.

He eyed her as though she were a fixture, a lovely piece of art
hanging on his wall. His eyes stayed glued to hers as he stalked
forward. His gaze pinned her there. Tristan stopped mere inches
from her body. His large arms grabbed the shelf behind her, caging
Josie in like the willing prisoner she was.

"I love having you here, in my space," he said, ducking his head
and whispering against her neck.

"Your space?"

"Yeah, you know, the boundless, three-dimensional extent in
which objects and events occur and have relative position and—"

"Tristan," Josie interrupted. He raised his eyebrows. "Shut up."

She closed her eyes and reached for him. Sliding her index fingers into the belt loops of his jeans, she pulled him closer. As always, a blaze consumed her, and she wondered if this feeling of longing would ever be satisfied. After what seemed like a lifetime, Tristan met her lips with his own, placing sweet, simple kisses there. Every so often, his tongue would trace across her lip and she'd forget to breathe.

"There's something I want to show you," he said.

Breaking away, Tristan reached above her head and pulled down a book. He led Josie to the sofa and drew her down next to him.

"It's our freshman yearbook," he said, answering her questioning eyes.

Josie looked on with anticipation, eager to see a tiny glimpse into her past, a past that apparently had been happy and normal. While she was thrilled to learn about her early childhood, normalcy was something she couldn't even fathom.

As they went through each page, Tristan excitedly pointed out their friends and favorite teachers. Sometimes he had stories to accompany the candid photos and stories to accompany those stories. Josie listened intently, soaking in every word he said and staring at the frozen gray faces on the page. When they got to the student section, she noticed some sort of bookmark sticking out.

"What's that?" she asked.

Tristan flipped the page to reveal a small metal barrette snapped onto the page.

"It was yours," he said. "I found it in my room about a week after you moved."

He ran his finger down the page until he stopped at her face. Josie looked on, intrigued by the younger, fuller face and familiar eyes.

They continued flipping through the book, Tristan pointing

out some candid shots of her. These were much happier. She looked carefree and shy. Josie grinned back at the photos, wondering if, back then, her smiles were genuine and unrehearsed.

Next, Tristan turned to his photo, not even caring that Josie laughed until her side hurt. The sound of her genuine laughter made him want to capture it and hold on forever.

"You were so skinny! Your hair was out of control!"

"I was prepubescent. You loved my hair," he countered. "And you loved me."

She looked down at her lap, stunned by his words. A heavy silence fell between them until Josie worked up the nerve to ask what she wanted to know.

"Did you love Fiona?"

"Yes, I did. I would've never stayed with her if I hadn't. It was different, though. Different from this," he said, motioning between them.

"I kind of hate her," Josie said softly, focused on a hole in her jeans.

"Yeah," Tristan said, dropping his arm around her shoulders. "But why?"

"Because she hurt you. Because she had you for all that time and didn't appreciate it."

Tristan placed a kiss right below her ear and whispered, "It should have been you."

This time the silence felt different. It was warm and comforting, a blanketed feeling of desire and love.

"Do you have a picture of her? I want to see."

Tristan reluctantly nodded and went back to the shelves, pulling out an envelope from between two books. He took his seat next to Josie again and opened the envelope, pulling the photo from inside.

Josie stared at the picture. The girl was beautiful, with blond hair and sparkling blue eyes. She was everything that Josie wasn't. She tried to associate this girl with the hurt and pain that had been inflicted on Tristan but failed to make the connection. There was an innocent happiness imprinted on the glossy paper. Fiona was smiling and hugging a boy who wasn't Tristan.

"Who's he?" she asked.

"That's her twin brother. I never knew him. He died when they were sixteen. I stole this photo when I left her. It was stupid. I just did it to hurt her."

Josie nodded, understanding completely.

The next morning, Josie woke to find herself in a real bed with clean sheets and fluffy pillows. Her head lay on Tristan's bare chest while one arm and leg were thrown across his body. She stifled a yawn and rolled onto her back, stretching the muscles in her arms and legs. The room was flooded with sunlight and she couldn't believe that she'd slept so late despite it.

She turned toward Tristan, her eyes memorizing every nuance of the man before her. He lay on top of the covers, his bare feet crossed at the ankles. His black pajama pants sat low on his hips, immediately coaxing her eyes upward. Each peak and valley of his muscled chest and abdomen were highlighted by the sun's rays, causing golden shadows across his skin. The vibrant shapes and twisting lines of ink clung to his arms as if they never could belong anywhere else. Long fingers wrapped around a weathered paperback book that was folded over on itself. His hair was growing out now and had become a bit of a zigzag-patterned mess. The stubble on his jaw caused a slightly darker shadow to his face, and she hummed at the memory of what it felt like beneath her fingertips. Tristan's mouth was open just slightly, his pink tongue sliding back and forth across his bottom lip keeping time with his eyes on the page. Perched halfway down his nose sat a pair of black-rimmed glasses.

"You're staring," he said without looking up from his book.

"Since when do you wear glasses?"

"Oh," he said, instantly reaching to pull them off. "Sometimes when I read."

Josie grabbed his hand, halting his movements and smiled up at him.

"I love them."

"Really?" he asked.

"Yep. You've got that hot nerd thing happening."

"Hot nerd? Isn't that an oxymoron?"

"What did you just call me?" Josie teased.

She placed a kiss on his lips and hopped over, heading to the bathroom. Tristan shook his head in disbelief, loving how she always had a way of surprising him. Marking his page, he placed the book on the nightstand and closed his eyes, trying to clear his mind.

He'd been up since dawn, his thoughts reeling. Josie was in danger, and he needed to know why. He couldn't believe that he let her talk him into staying three extra days. This time could be better spent assuring her safety.

She emerged from the bathroom and instantly he understood exactly how she'd persuaded him. Her mere presence sang to him, called to his weaknesses. Josie was beautiful with her tousled hair and endless legs standing at the foot of his bed. It had been awhile since he'd wanted to share his life with anyone, but here she was and Tristan cherished the sight of her.

Mort stepped into the shower and let the water run over his face. He leaned his forehead against the cool tile and grinned, still excited about yesterday's find. He had sat outside Josie Banks's North Park apartment the previous day waiting to catch a glimpse of her. He couldn't wait to lay eyes on her, if for nothing other than to confirm that she did exist. He stared at the building with loathing, begging it to reveal her.

Finally she'd come trotting down the steps with a large bag slung over her shoulder. She was a dark and brooding beauty compared to the teen girl in the photo he'd memorized.

She was small, an easy target for someone like himself. But she hadn't been alone. The guy by her side was young, probably her age. His arms were covered in tattoos. His smile for the girl was easily recognizable as one of affection.

Mort had snapped a few photos of the couple and watched as they disappeared down the block. He grinned sinisterly at the idea of being rid of her. Hell, killing her would probably be doing her a favor. After all the shit she'd been through, she might even welcome him like an angel of mercy. He'd never spent this much time and effort on a job and felt a bit put off that he'd become so attached to the girl. Not that he wouldn't carry out his mission, but it would definitely feel different from every other kill.

Stepping out of the shower, he dried off and swiped at the mirror. His speckled, foggy reflection stared back. But he wasn't sure what he saw there. He seemed changed in a way.

After getting dressed, he forwarded the photos of Josie to Moloney, confirming that he'd found her. Adrenaline pumped furiously through his veins as he beat his fist against the wall in triumph.

All he had left to do was case the place for a couple of days to determine if she had any kind of schedule. He would set his internal clock in sync with hers, trying to connect them in any way possible.

It was always best to make the kill out in public, away from the home. It seemed less personal that way. Though he knew that murder, in any location, was personal. There was always a bigger chance for witnesses out in the open, but Mort never worried. In all his years in the business, he'd perfected the art of being invisible when needed.

Just as Mort walked out the door, his phone buzzed. He checked the ID and smiled.

"You saw the photos?" he asked calmly.

"There's been a change in plans," Moloney's voice sneered. "Don't kill her. Bring the girl to me alive." Mort froze, his heart beating against his chest. The silence grew longer between the men. He hated being taken by surprise. It rarely happened. "Is there a problem?" Moloney asked.

"No problem."

"Good. Ticktock."

14. REVOLUTION

THE MOVEMENT OF ONE CELESTIAL BODY
AS IT ORBITS ANOTHER.

Tristan and Josie sat in the beer garden at New Orleans Creole
Cafe. It was a charming place nestled in historic Old Town.
Tristan sipped an Abita Turbodog while Josie fought the urge to
pull the marker from her bag and tag the seat of her chair. It had
been awhile since she'd thrown up a significant piece, and the
urge to do so scratched at her.

"What are you thinking so hard about?" Tristan asked.

"Going out writing. It's been awhile."

Tristan frowned and set his bottle down on the table.

"I hate that you do that," he said, staring past her.

"I know. It's not dangerous like you think. I've never gotten caught."

"'In a closed society where everybody's guilty, the only crime is getting caught.'"

"Hmm. Who said that?" she asked.

"Hunter S. Thompson. A man so avant-garde that his suicide note was published in *Rolling Stone*."

"Wow."

"I read this book called *Engaging Art*. It was commissioned as a study, but it's an interesting read. It talks about how art participation, of any kind, in today's society will encourage future generations to do so."

"See? I'm encouraging future generations," Josie said.

"Encouraging what, though? Vandalism? It also discusses people's motivations behind their own artistic expression. So what's your motivation?"

"I don't know, Tristan. I like the idea that there are permanent parts of me out there. It's like being able to communicate without having to say anything. You know?"

Tristan nodded and finished off his beer.

"You're talented. You always have been. You could express that talent in other ways, legal ways. If they catch you, they can link every piece you've ever done."

"Don't worry so much. It'll be hard to connect all my work since I changed my writing name a few months ago. I used to sign everything JayBee."

"And now?" he asked.

Josie looked away, a smile stretching across her lips.

"Bundy."

Tristan laughed and slid his arm around her shoulders.

"Josie!" Monica called out when she spotted the couple.

She ignored Josie's groan as they stood to greet her. Monica could barely contain her excitement. She wanted to wrap Josie in a hug and thank her for giving their relationship a chance, but she knew that personal boundaries should not be crossed. Instead, she offered a nervous wave.

"Sorry I'm late. I got held up at the office. I swear, I have to file paperwork every time I take a bathroom break. We like to kill trees apparently. Anyway, you two look great."

"Thanks," Tristan answered, though it sounded more like a question.

He took a few seconds to process Monica. Their last meeting had been brief, but he could tell she was what his mother called high-spirited.

"Where's your boyfriend?" Josie asked, scanning the sidewalk.

"Ugh," Monica grunted. "He can't make it. Work again. Some big real-estate buyout mumbo jumbo. I don't know. I guess it's better to be busy, right? Job security and all."

As much as she hadn't been looking forward to a date with Monica, Josie had a decent time. It sucked that Rob had to work late. Josie was curious about any man who could tame the unstoppable force of nature known as Monica Templeton. Expectedly, Tristan was a pro at making Monica feel included and comfortable. She rambled on and on about nothing in particular. With Tristan there, Josie found it easier to keep her eye rolling and huffing to a minimum.

Dinner was casual, and after two glasses of wine, Josie found herself less annoyed and more entertained by Monica's effervescent personality. Tristan didn't seem to be fazed by her dramatic flair in the least. He was kind and engaging and as charming as ever.

"Well, thanks for a lovely evening," Monica said.

Josie snorted at her formal statement. Tristan nudged her with his elbow.

"It was a pleasure," Tristan answered with his special crooked smile.

"Oh good Lord, you're adorable. You better hold on to this one," Monica said to Josie before winking and trotting off down the sidewalk.

(

Monica hadn't been ready to head home when dinner was over. She knew Tristan and Josie were eager to be alone, so she said her good night and walked down to a nearby bar for a drink. She sat at the bar and ordered a margarita, the specialty. Monica couldn't help but smile as she took in the decor around her. The festive colors and music seemed to further encourage her mood. She sent a text to Rob, letting him know where she was. He promised to meet her there soon.

She had been disappointed that he missed dinner, stuck at the office yet again. As happy as Monica was with Rob, she hated that he wasn't always available to her. She knew he was an executive at a corporate real estate company, but she never asked about his work. It seemed to be the only topic that caused him stress. All she could do was become his distraction. Monica had never been so important to another human being before and she absolutely adored the feeling of being needed.

After assessing the thin crowd, she sipped her drink and watched the bartender mix some fruity concoction and flirt with the tourists.

"Monica?" a familiar voice said from behind her.

She turned to find Evan standing there, eyeing her like prey. He was dressed in dark-wash jeans and a black button-up shirt, looking handsome and a little dangerous. His warm brown eyes sparkled from beneath a baseball cap. Even through his charm, she could sense that his thoughts were anything but pure.

"Evan," she said, giving him a cautious smile.

He took a seat next to her and ordered a whiskey. Immediately,

Monica was racked with guilt just for being in his presence. She wavered between wishing that Rob would show up and wishing that he'd stay away.

"I was in the neighborhood. What are you doing here all alone?"

"My boyfriend had to work late, but he'll be here any minute," she said confidently, hoping Evan could not sense her half-truth.

"Good, good. You seem to be in excellent spirits. Did you have a good day?"

"Yep. I just had dinner with a friend and her boyfriend. Well, she doesn't really consider me a friend, but I think we are closer now. Hopefully, I'll see her again soon since her boyfriend is going out of town tomorrow. Maybe I'll stop by and surprise her or something. Oh my God, I'm rambling."

Monica promptly shut her mouth and motioned for the bartender to bring her another drink. She had no idea why she became a blabbering fool around this man. She hadn't suffered from word vomit like this since she was in high school.

Evan laughed and took a long pull from his drink, enjoying the slow burn of the whiskey down his throat. He leaned in close to her, barely catching the scent of her floral perfume.

"Do I make you nervous, Ms. Templeton?"

"Uh, no, I just—wait, how do you know my last name? I don't remember mentioning it."

Monica eyed him suspiciously, suddenly uneasy under his hungry gaze. Evan shifted in his seat and emptied his glass. His eyes darted back and forth, as if searching for an acceptable answer.

"Well, I'm embarrassed to admit that I read it off of your work badge when we met at the coffee shop. I may have found you on Facebook as well. So I know where you work and where you play," he said, gesturing to the bar, "but where do you live?"

"I think I'll hold on to that tidbit of information for now," she joked, feeling more nervous than before.

"Aww, I'm not a bad guy," he said. "Just for good measure, I'll tell you where I live. Ocean Beach."

"I love O.B. Spent a lot of time there when I was a teenager. We used to get there early and spend all day on the beach. We'd eat lunch at Hodad's and get ice cream before walking over to the tide pools in the afternoon. Good stuff."

Evan smiled and motioned to the bartender for a new drink.

"Well, hey, you should come over sometime. We could grill and you could help me decorate my new place. I know you're good at it."

"How would you know that?" she asked.

"Well, uh, you always look impeccable. I bet that spills over to your home too."

Monica felt slightly flattered but leery of his words. She took a swig of her drink and smiled at him, playing with the placement of her lips, not wanting him to read too much into her polite smile. Believing that she was overthinking things, she decided to just be pleased by his admiration. It wasn't often that Monica had male attention.

"So, about this friend who is not a friend but may have become a friend." He paused, hoping she'd catch on to his teasing. "It's very considerate of you to spend time with her while the boyfriend's away."

"I owe her so much more than that."

"Hmm, that seems loaded for someone who is barely a friend."

"It's complicated," she answered quickly, finishing her drink.

"Well, I'm all ears if you're aching to talk."

"She's not achin' for anything from you," Rob's harsh voice cut in.

The two spun around to find him scowling down on them.

Evan straightened his shoulders, sitting taller on the stool now, while Monica looked meek and a little bit guilty. Darkness clouded Rob's face, his gaze murderous.

"Rob, you remember Evan, right?" she asked, gesturing to her drinking partner, feigning innocence. He nodded but kept his hands at his sides and his lips pressed together in a harsh line.

"He was just leaving, right?" Rob sneered.

Evan leaned back against the bar, making himself at home.

"Actually, I just got here."

Fury blurred Rob's vision as he rushed at the man and pulled him from his seat. His fist twisted Evan's collar as he held him upright.

"I said, you were just leaving," Rob's voice said in an eerily calm tone.

"Rob!" Monica shouted, surprised by his sudden hostility.

He ignored Monica, waiting for Evan's compliance. With a tight nod, Evan relented. He threw a few bills on the bar and said good night before leaving. Monica didn't watch him go, more concerned with the seething man seated next to her now.

"Everything okay?" the bartender asked.

"Jameson, neat," Rob said before turning his attention to Monica. "What was he doing here?"

"I swear I just ran into him. I don't think it was a coincidence, though. He creeps me out."

Rob nodded stiffly and threw back his drink, motioning for another one instantly. Monica had never seen him this angry before. While it was a bit frightening, it was also incredibly sexy. She almost felt guilty at the lust swirling inside of her.

"Monica, I told you that I don't trust him. I know it's just a gut feeling, but I expect you to respect that. I don't share."

She was his, in every way, but hearing it come from his lips was somehow empowering. She decided to provoke him even further. The fact that he thought she would stray so easily was starting to piss her off.

"Oh, well, that's too bad. I was just about to hop on his lap in the middle of this bar before you got here," Monica taunted. "It was just conversation."

They left shortly after, Rob driving erratically through the city. He hadn't spoken a word to her in nearly thirty minutes, and to say it was driving her insane would be an understatement. Once inside her apartment, he flew at her. At first Monica cringed away, unsure of what to expect from his attack, but she knew in her heart that she had no reason to be afraid.

Like a caveman staking his claim, he tore at her clothes while kissing her. What started out as rough and obsessive slowly morphed into slow and sensual, where he placed soft heated kisses against her lips and whispered his apologies against her skin. Their intertwined bodies became a declaration of infatuation and mutual understanding.

Monica fell asleep to the feel of his strong arms and the sound of his loving whispers around her.

☾

Back at Josie's apartment, Tristan undressed for bed while Josie washed her face. Tristan had insisted on bringing some things from his place back to hers. So he wrapped her mattress in new clean sheets and stacked pillows at the head. He settled in and started on his book while he waited for her.

"So, you're leaving in the morning?" Josie asked from the bathroom.

Tristan looked up from his book and eyed her reflection in the mirror. She looked nervous. He wanted to smooth the lines in her forehead and tell her that everything would be okay, but he hated to make unrealistic promises. The last three days had been heavenly. They had existed in their little domestic bubble, behaving as if there weren't evil plots and assassins out to get them.

"Yeah, I plan on driving eight to ten hours a day, so I should get there by Saturday night."

Josie stood in the doorway to her bedroom, watching him watch her. She smiled at the sight of Tristan on her mattress with his paperback book and his glasses firmly in place. He fit here with her; she couldn't imagine anyone else ever doing so.

"Just let me finish this chapter and I'll get the light," he mumbled, not looking up from his page.

She crawled in next to him and lay back against the borrowed pillow. Josie loved the new sheets and fluffy pillows. It was a luxury she hadn't even known she'd missed.

Tristan closed his book and folded his glasses, placing them both on the floor. He turned to Josie and pulled her closer, wanting nothing more than to memorize the feel of her arms wrapped around him. They'd spent so much time together lately, he wasn't sure how he'd survive time apart.

"I'm going to miss you," he said into the quiet room, squeezing her tighter. "It's going to be a long, lonely drive back to Louisiana."

Josie avoided eye contact and any real emotional declarations.

"Do you think you'll be able to find out anything? It could be dangerous. I don't think you should go."

"I'll be fine. I have connections there, people who can help."

Josie nodded, knowing he felt like he had to do this. She wanted to scream and cry and beg him to stay, but she knew her effort would be futile. So instead she sat up and placed kisses on his chest. She brought his forearm across his body and traced the lines of their tree on his skin.

"Is that my old hoodie?" Tristan asked, spying the black article tucked into the corner of the room.

"Yeah. I used to sleep in it, but it doesn't smell like you any-more." Josie took a deep breath, exhaling slowly to kill her build-ing panic. "Please come back to me," she whispered.

"I promise," he answered, lifting her chin so that she was forced to meet his eyes.

"Promises are only your best intentions," she reminded him.

For the rest of the night, they alternated between making love and sleeping. Each time he touched her, they would ravage and cling to each other, whispering words of devotion. In the early hours of morning, just before sunrise, Josie woke him one last time. This time, with tears of desperation, she begged him. She didn't want soft and sweet, she wanted hard, possessive fucking. She longed for her body to remind her of this night with bouts of soreness and aching thighs.

Tristan gave her what she wanted. When she was passed out, he wrapped her in the cool sheets and placed a kiss on her temple. He was exhausted but forced himself to shower.

As the early light tried to push its way through the thick cur-tain, Tristan stood at the foot of the mattress, watching Josie sleep. Even in her slumber, she called to him. He eyed his packed bag waiting by the door. Tristan summoned his strength and whispered his good-bye. Remembering his old hoodie, he grabbed it and threw it on, knowing that it would be as close as he could get to being wrapped up in Josie.

15. OCCULTATION
THE ACT OF ONE CELESTIAL BODY
OBSCURING ANOTHER.

Tristan had done some hard things in his life. He'd faced his own demons and those of others. He'd been shot at, threatened, and survived heartbreak, but nothing had been harder than leaving the girl he loved.

In her slumber, her face was no longer stamped with hardness and doubt as it was when she was awake. Her lashes cast tiny shadows on her freckled cheeks. Despite the way they turned down into a natural frown, her pouty lips had begged to be kissed. Like some kind of foreshadowed tragedy, Tristan had got this feeling in his gut that he'd never see her again. It's what made it so hard to leave.

In the dark and dingy hall of her building, he'd pounded on Alex's door until rousing the man from his sleep. The door swung open and a Glock was pointed directly at his head. Tristan didn't even flinch as he waited for Alex to recognize him. He knew what being on the business end of a piece of steel felt like, and through the years he'd grown indifferent to it. Alex smiled and dropped the gun to his side.

"Damn, man. What the hell couldn't wait until the sun comes up?" Alex asked, gesturing for Tristan to come in.

Tristan declined.

"I need you to keep an eye on her, more than usual. There's a hit out on her. A professional. I'm heading back home to see what I can find out."

"I'll kill anyone who comes near her," Alex growled. "Why not bring her?"

"I can't take her with me. It's too dangerous. I thought about taking her to my place, but they know where I live. She'll be safer here."

Alex leaned against the door frame and crossed his arms, exhaling loudly.

"You know I got her. You fuck with me, you fuckin' with the best!"

"Nice, Tony Montana."

The two bumped fists in solidarity, a silent vow between them to trust each other unreservedly.

As Tristan traveled east on the I-10, he found himself frustrated with the amount of time he had to spend alone. He wasn't sure how closely he was being watched by Moloney's men, so he stuck with driving back to Louisiana instead of flying. It was easier to stay off their radar this way.

For the past thirty-eight hours, every waking thought had been of Josie. Trapped with no one to converse with but the open road, he became a prisoner of his memories. There were no distractions here, just the rhythmic passing of mile marker signs and his fellow travelers tucked away in their vehicles. He wondered where they were headed and what they expected to find when they got there. He wondered the same for himself. Sometimes he'd drive for hours without even recognizing where he was or where he'd been.

As he navigated away from the West Coast, he felt the shift in the air as it became warmer and denser. The South presented the familiar scene of more trees than buildings. Pine and oak and cypress flew by in a streaked green blur past his window. It felt like home.

Home was where his parents lived, in their ostentatious Victorian-style house on the West Bank. It was where he'd lived his entire childhood, surrounded by the same common faces and same group of peers. Home was where all the memories of McKenzi began and ended. It was where Fiona entered his life, where he made hasty decisions and had thrown away his future. It was where he sat on the leather couch in their living room and broke his parents' hearts.

Tristan had debated whether to call his mother and father to let them know he was coming. Eventually, his cowardice won out and he decided to just surprise them. A sly grin crept across his lips as he thought of the heart attack his father would have at the sight of him. The prestigious Dr. Daniel Fallbrook would surely not embrace his only child looking like a common criminal. Tristan knew, though, that his mother wouldn't care one bit. She would cling to him and bathe him with her tears, just happy to have him back. Suddenly, he didn't dread heading back home and he pushed the accelerator down.

Just before eleven o'clock in the evening, Tristan turned down the long driveway lined by hundred-year-old oak trees draped with Spanish moss. His nerves got the better of him and he wiped his sweating palms on the thighs of his jeans. His pulse quickened, and he struggled to understand why anxiety was plaguing him. Then it occurred to him—he was afraid of rejection.

He parked behind his father's car and killed the headlights. For a full two minutes he sat there debating whether to back out and find a hotel in the city. It was then that the old, familiar tree came into focus. Sitting at the edge of their property, it was barely visible with no moonlight filtering through the cloudy night sky. It sent a warm feeling through his chest, and he remembered that he'd come here for Josie above all else.

"Stop being such a pussy. Rejection is to discard as defective or useless. They wouldn't do that," he told himself.

Tristan shook his head, threw his bag over his shoulder, and decided to leave his pistol beneath the driver's seat. He climbed the steps to the front door and took a deep breath before ringing the bell. It felt odd, considering he'd never rung the bell at his own house before.

Time passed slowly, each second exponentially increasing his unease. He rang the bell again and exhaled, needing to get this part over with so he could focus on Josie. A few seconds later, he heard shuffling feet and whispered conversation on the other side of the door. The red door creaked open and both of his parents stood there gawking. Tristan squared his shoulders and shoved his hands deep into his pockets, waiting for the moment of recognition.

They looked tired and weary. His mother was as beautiful as ever. Even huddled behind her husband in her nightclothes, not a hair was out of place. Tristan's father looked a bit older, the graying hair at his temples giving him away. Their eyes started at his feet and did a synchronized dance up his frame, lingering on the art on his skin and finally reaching his face. His mother gasped aloud, her trembling hand flying to her open mouth.

"Tristan?" Daniel's crackling voice barely got out the words.

"Hi," Tristan answered, shuffling his feet while one hand rubbed at the back of his neck.

Bitsy pushed her husband aside, no longer frozen from shock. With tears in her eyes, she threw herself at Tristan, burying her face in his chest. Tristan wrapped his mother in a firm embrace.

"You're here? You're really here?" she whispered between sniffles.

"Yeah, Ma. I'm here."

Tristan placed a kiss on top of her head just as she released him and took a step back. Daniel watched the reunion with conflicting emotions. Elation, concern, and relief billowed around his head, making a conscious decision impossible. Instinctively, he held out his hand and hoped it would convey his forgiveness.

"Son," Daniel said.

"Dad," Tristan answered, taking his father's hand and shaking it.

Without letting go, Daniel pulled him in for a hug. Despite their disagreements in the past, this was his child, his flesh and blood, and he loved him unconditionally.

Bitsy ushered them inside, immediately assuming her motherly responsibilities again. She felt so first-rate in that role, so fulfilled. Tears filled her eyes as she watched Tristan sit at the bar practically inhaling the sandwich she'd made. Her boy had become a man. He looked different, so grown-up. He looked like a stranger sitting in her kitchen.

Daniel joined his wife and watched their son in fascination. Of all the paths he'd imagined for Tristan, he wondered which one the boy had ventured down. He wondered which one had led him to become this man, the one with cropped hair and tattoos.

"Tristan, it's really good to see you." Daniel spoke softly, not knowing how to broach the subject of Tristan's motives. "What brought you back to us?"

Tristan stopped midchew and stared at his father. Of course they deserved an explanation of his sudden arrival, but he couldn't bring himself to share the entire story just yet. He threw the last bite of sandwich in his mouth and swallowed quickly.

"Can we talk tomorrow? I just drove for three days. I really need to crash."

"Of course," his mother answered, a sad smile pulling at her lips.

"We *will* talk in the morning," his father said, daring Tristan to refuse.

Without another word, Bitsy led Tristan up to his old room, where he discovered that they hadn't changed a thing. His eyes scanned the room and he smiled at all the memories he found there. Each shelf was still filled with his book and music collections, not a speck of dust covering them. Too tired to explore, he fell onto his bed, facefirst.

"Do you need anything, baby?" his mother asked.

"No, I'm good. Just tired. So tired," he mumbled into the mattress.

"Okay, well, you know where we are if you need anything. Throw a rock."

Bitsy smiled at the sight of his large frame sprawled out across the bed. His feet hung over the edge and his spread arms touched each edge. She wanted to go to him, tuck herself in beside him, and hold him, but she knew he'd have none of that. She resisted the urge to kiss him good night and quietly closed the door behind her.

That night, as they all slept the deepest of slumbers, the Fallbrook house, made of brick and mortar, magically transformed back into a home.

☾

Feeling like a hostage, Josie paced the perimeter of her apartment for the twentieth time. She'd never had a problem with confinement before. She'd spent so much time in small spaces, so much time alone that she should be used to this. She knew it had everything to do with the fact that both Tristan and Alex had forbidden her to leave the apartment. Solitude was okay only when it was on her terms.

This was the third morning she'd endured since Tristan had left. While she tried to remember what her life was like before she'd found him, she couldn't. All she knew was that she wanted him here. She wanted him safe and happy. She just wanted him.

A bang at the door jarred her from her inner ramblings. She flew across the living room to open it. She had two of the locks undone before she remembered to ask who it was.

"Alex, *mami*," he shouted.

Josie let him in the apartment, along with the delicious-smelling breakfast calling to her from a Styrofoam container.

"Ohhh, what's that?" she asked, holding out her hands.

He gave her the food, took a seat on her couch, and propped his large boots up on her coffee table.

"A breakfast burrito from Sombrero. *De nada*."

"Thanks," she mumbled around a mouth full of food.

Alex nodded and flipped on her television, grumbling about her lack of channels.

"Maybe you should come stay at my place. At least I have cable."

"No way. The fact that I'm stuck inside till further notice is enough of a punishment."

"Fine, whatever. You heard from ya boy?"

"He sent me a text last night, telling me that he made it to his parents' house, but that's it," she answered, trying to keep the disappointment out of her voice.

"No worries, Jo. He'll be fine."

"I know."

But she didn't really know, she only hoped. Josie had never been one to pray, but the last two nights she'd found herself pleading for his safe return. She tried to reason with herself, knowing that he was intelligent and had been hardened by the streets, but it offered little solace.

"With me here, you're safe. No one's gonna mess with this cobra."

Alex flexed his large arm and curled his fist around, imitating a snake's movement. Josie rolled her eyes.

"Know the difference between this and a real cobra?"

"No, but I'm sure you'll tell me."

"If a real cobra gets ya, you might survive."

He laughed at his own joke and lay back against the couch cushions. Josie shook her head and decided to make no comment. She didn't want to encourage him.

"Ya think he'll find somethin' down there, Jo?" Alex asked.

"I don't even care anymore. I just want him back here with me. We could take off. Try to outrun them. Or, if it's inevitable that they're going to find me and kill me, I'd rather spend the time I have left with Tristan."

"That's heavy. You miss him, huh?" Alex asked, his eyes studying her closely.

She looked down at her lap and her suddenly unappealing breakfast before answering.

"I love him."

☾

After swearing them to secrecy, Tristan sat his parents down around their dining room table and told them everything he knew. He relived his introduction to a life of crime, his breakup with Fiona, and his life-changing discovery of McKenzi Delaune. They remained silent the entire time, processing the details of the story he told. When he was finished, Tristan sat back in his chair and exhaled, relieved by no longer shouldering this burden alone. Daniel and Bitsy remained quiet, letting the facts and implications sink in.

"I need to find out how Moloney is connected to Josie, why he wants her dead. I don't want to involve either of you. I don't want to put you in danger. Just know that I have to do this. I won't lose her again."

"I can't believe she's alive," Bitsy whispered, reaching across the table to rest her hand on Tristan's.

"Most days, I can't believe it either," he said solemnly.

"Organized crime, Tristan? You can't be serious," Daniel said. "You could have done anything!"

"Honey," Bitsy said, placing her hand on Daniel's shoulder.

"I just don't understand how we lost you," he said defeatedly.

Bitsy wiped tears from her eyes before they could slide down and ruin her makeup. She looked at her husband and then at her son, not knowing how to mediate this battle.

"That's not important right now, Dad. Can we focus on why I'm here?"

Daniel took a deep breath and let it out slowly.

"What's your plan, Tristan?" Daniel asked.

"I'm going to go talk to anyone at the station who was working when Earl was there. I also know a few people who work for Moloney in the city. I don't want to alert him to my presence, so I'll try them last."

"This is dangerous. I don't like the idea of you getting involved," Daniel warned.

"I'm already involved."

"I knew Moloney was dicey, but I never dreamed it reached this far."

"How did you know about Moloney?" Tristan asked, his curiosity piqued by his father's statement.

Daniel sighed and folded his arms across his chest. He hadn't planned on ever having to tell this story. He slid his eyes toward Bitsy, knowing she'd be displeased that he'd kept it from her.

"The spring before your sixteenth birthday, Dean Moloney's son, Dean Jr., was diagnosed with a heart deformity. It was somehow undetected for years. After a consultation with his parents, we all agreed that surgery was the only way to give him a fighting chance. I performed the procedure, assisted by Dr. Marcus. He flat-lined twice on my table, and the second time, we couldn't get him back."

"Atrioventricular septal defect?" Tristan asked. Daniel nodded, proud and nostalgic at the memory of his raven-haired boy sprawled across the floor of his office, reading through medical journals like comic books.

"Fiona never told me what happened to him," Tristan murmured.

"When I explained to the family that we'd lost him, Moloney went ballistic. He told me, 'You will pay for this. An eye for an eye, my friend.' His tone was maniacal. I still remember the look in his eyes. I just assumed that it was an empty threat fueled by grief."

"Jesus, Dad, you think this would have been useful information when Fiona and I started seeing each other?"

"Would it have made a difference?"

"No," Tristan admitted, shaking his head.

They sat in silence, each absorbing the heavy weighted words laid out before them. Bitsy immediately performed the sign of the cross and squeezed her eyes shut. The Lord's Prayer whispered across the room and echoed off the walls. Then Bitsy opened her eyes as if remembering a secret of her own.

"There's something else," Bitsy whispered, breaking the

rhythm of her prayer and abandoning its purpose. The men's eyes shot up to her remorseful face. "I'll be right back."

Tristan and his father sat in silence, surrounded by Audubon prints and Bitsy's finest china displayed in an antique cabinet. Tristan's eyes stayed trained on his drumming fingers along the tabletop while Daniel openly observed every detail of his son's appearance.

Bitsy reappeared carrying a large manila envelope. She took her seat and sighed, letting the guilt and regret absorb into her words.

"I should have given you this a long time ago," she said, sliding the package across the table to Tristan. "It came about six weeks after they moved."

Tristan retrieved the envelope and turned it over. A purple bound book dropped heavily onto the polished wood table, the sound of it echoing through the room like a slap to his face.

"I'm sorry for keeping it from you. I don't even know why I still have it. I just figured that it was better to make a clean break. I never thought that . . ."

Bitsy's voice became empty jumbled sounds as Tristan's pulse raced through his ears.

"This is McKenzi's diary," he finally said, running his fingers over the cover. "How could you?"

"I'm sorry," was her only answer as she cringed away from his angry words.

He turned the envelope over to find his address scrawled in McKenzi's fourteen-year-old handwriting. Tristan jumped up from the table, clutching the diary, and raced to the comfort of his room. He locked the door behind him and sank to the floor. There he sat for hours, reading the words of his childhood best friend, each entry sending him further into her world before the hurt.

Moloney sat on the antique chaise in his mother-in-law's family room feeling emasculated by the very fabric. Its pink floral pattern looked humorous as a backdrop to his large frame and scowling face. He sipped his Jameson and tapped his fingers impatiently on the padded arm of the chair. He'd wanted to leave hours ago. Moloney wasn't used to not getting what he wanted. The thing holding him here, his only weakness, was his beautiful wife, Jane.

She was a vision, growing more beautiful with age. Her long strawberry blond hair curled around her shoulders, a perfect frame for an angelic face. Moloney grinned as she told a story so animatedly that her hands flung about in a precarious manner. He loved her spunk, her fire. He loved that she loved him unconditionally. Jane made no rules when it came to their life together. She'd promised her devotion and would gladly endure whatever life Moloney provided.

Not that she suffered. Through racketeering, weapons, drug trafficking, and gambling rings Moloney had provided a cozy life. They had prize-winning horses, a private estate, and a beautiful home. All that was missing was a family.

Moloney poured the last of his whiskey into his mouth and swallowed. The burn of the alcohol slid down his throat and past his frozen heart before settling in his stomach. With all his wealth and power, he still didn't have what he'd wanted most—a successor. His boy was gone and his daughter was across the country living a new life.

He frowned down into his empty glass and shifted on the uncomfortable piece of furniture. He found it hard to stay in the present conversation when there were so many more daunting things to worry about. Barry had phoned earlier with more news of Gino Gallo strong-arming Moloney's clients into doing business. As if the Italians weren't enough, Tristan and Josie were longtime thorns in his side.

The girl knew secrets that could surely bring down his whole operation. Her father, Earl, had been stupid enough to go to the feds, and now she would pay for his mistake. When Moloney's men had kidnapped and held the chief and his daughter, she'd been a witness to their rather archaic torture methods. For days, they had poked, prodded, burned, and bled that man, asking questions about what he'd told the feds. Josie had screamed and begged them to stop, but they were machines, immune to a child's pleas. Eventually, they got all the information they needed. Moloney shot and killed Earl Delaune himself, in front of his daughter. With a quick warning that she was next and instructions to his men to finish her off, he'd left the Brooklyn warehouse and boarded a plane for home.

It wasn't until eight years later that Moloney found out his men had failed in New York. One of those bastards had drunkenly confessed to Barry that the girl had escaped. Even though there was an official report from the NYPD that the girl's body was recovered three days later in a subway terminal, he knew better. His gut told him so. He suspected that the FBI connected her to him and hid her away. He'd never been so angry to be right.

Once he was rid of Tristan and the girl, there would be nothing stopping him from crushing the Italians and solidifying his reign in New Orleans. He would not be run out of town by these greasy Wops, he thought.

"And then Myrtle confessed to sabotaging Sally's flowerbeds!" his mother-in-law exclaimed.

Moloney smirked, knowing it was time for such insincere actions.

"We really should be going," he announced.

There were hugs all around as he nodded for Frank to fetch the car. Moloney held Jane's coat as she slid her arms inside. She kissed her mother's cheek with a smile and promised to return soon.

As the couple stepped outside into the cold air, Frank pressed the automatic start on the car. The heater would warm the interior before they'd even entered. It was the small luxuries that Moloney appreciated, things his poor and meager parents never knew.

When the electronic signal left Frank's hand and reached the car, a spark shot through a device attached to the undercarriage. A loud explosion rang in their ears as fire and smoke engulfed the car.

Moloney hovered over his wife, protecting her from debris, as she screamed into his shoulder.

"I'll call the police," his mother-in-law shouted.

"No," Moloney answered.

The harshness of his retort left her frozen on the front stoop. Though she was not used to taking orders, she knew not to disregard this man. He was dangerous. If it were not for his undeniable love for her daughter, she would have turned him in long ago.

"What happened?" Jane asked, panic making her voice falter.

The red-orange flames reflected in his eyes and he could utter only two words.

"Gino Gallo."

16. FAR SIDE
THE SIDE OF THE MOON THAT IS NOT VISIBLE.

Mort sat on his front stoop, staring up at the few stars visible above the nighttime city lights. His leg bounced nervously as he flipped his cell phone over in his hands, staring at it for the answers to silent questions. He remembered when he was a kid, he'd had a Magic 8 Ball. All you had to do was ask a question, shake it up, and wait for your answer to appear in the small liquid-filled window. If only life were still that simple.

Taking a deep breath and exhaling slowly, he decided to suck it up and make the call. Mort knew that when it came to Dean Moloney, if your information was important enough the time didn't matter.

"Moloney."

"I'll have the girl within the week."

"Excellent," Moloney answered firmly.

"When this job's done, I'm out. Retired."

"Are you telling me or asking me?"

Mort gritted his teeth and squeezed his eyes closed.

"I'd like this to be my last job."

"Are you joining Gallo's crew?" Moloney asked.

"No. I wouldn't betray you like that. I just want out."

"I'm not sure that's in our best interest," Moloney answered.

"I just want to disappear," Mort begged.

"Be careful what you wish for."

The line went dead before Mort could continue. You don't just declare yourself out of the business. You either die or you run. Mort wanted to avoid both. He couldn't imagine living the rest of his existence in fear or servitude. He knew to remain cautious.

Some guys were meant for this life. They were born into it and trained to succeed. Mort had just been good at it. He was young when one of Moloney's men had recruited him straight out of high school. Frustrated by living under the same roof as his abusive parents, he'd hauled ass and never looked back. Living on the street wasn't easy, but it was better than living with their tyrannical rules and severe punishments. Barry had taken him in and shown him how life could be sweeter if he just pledged his allegiance to Moloney. Mort hadn't thought twice about it. He was in.

All the promises of fat living and easy money were fulfilled, but he hadn't been prepared for living for the job. He soon realized that his life was not his own. He was owned by Moloney and was reminded of that on a daily basis. Eventually, Earl Delaune had wangled up charges against six of Moloney's men, Mort included, landing him in prison for a short time. He served his time quietly, fueled by anger and plans for retribution.

Years went by in the blink of an eye, and he found himself with the reputation of a heartless killer. Mort didn't mind, though; it secured the respect of his associates and kept his enemies in check. When this job was thrown at him, he was only too happy to oblige. Not only would it supply enough money to retire with, it would allow him to carry out his vengeance on a dead man. After almost a year of digging and chasing and loathing the idea of this girl, he'd finally found her. Despite all records, McKenzi Delaune lived and breathed. Not for much longer.

17. EARTHSHINE

SUNLIGHT THAT IS REFLECTED BACK FROM EARTH ONTO THE MOON.

Tristan lay in his childhood bed, his phone trapped between his cheek and pillow. Josie's purple diary sat propped open before him.

"'August 3, 2002. New York is like so chaotic I sometimes feel like I can't breathe.'"

Tristan read aloud. He could hear Josie's anxious breath over the phone.

"'I've never met our neighbors, but I do know that they have a loud dog that lives there. Dad and I have made the trip to my new school a few times so that I could get comfortable with the bus and the walk. It's a big brick building that looks nothing like Gretna High School.

"'I probably won't be able to make friends here. But who cares. Just three years and then I'll head back home. I miss all the green and the trees. Central Park is the closest thing I have to home and I find myself wanting to go there all the time. I miss Tristan so much. Talking on the phone just depresses me because I can't see him or kiss him. God, I miss kissing him. Plus, we've got a ten-minute time limit, so I barely have time to tell him anything! Daddy says I'll get over it, but he's wrong.

"'August 8, 2002. Dad and I got into a huge fight yesterday. I cried and screamed at him and blamed him for making me miserable. I hate this city. He held me while I cried and tried to explain his reasons. He said that we'd had to move because we were in danger from a powerful man because of a case he worked on. He said that he was trying to make it all better. Later, I heard him on the phone telling someone he thinks this man was responsible for my mother's death. I don't understand how that's possible when she died in a car accident. I miss her so much.

"'I want to call Tristan and have him tell me that everything is going to be okay. I want to hear that he misses me half as much as I miss him. I want to climb into our tree and kiss him until he makes that humming sound in the back of his throat. Meanwhile, I'm stuck in this fifth-floor walk-up, listening to Vanessa Carlton's "A Thousand Miles" song over and over. I can just hear Tristan complaining to turn it off because he's sick of hearing it. I bet Tracy Veltin is thinking of ways to sink her shiny, glittered nails into my boyfriend. Stupid frosted-hair-C-cup Tracy Veltin.'"

"That song is awful. Who is Tracy?" Josie asked.

"Just some girl."

"Huh. Some girl who wanted to hump you?"

"Maybe," Tristan said.

"Was she pretty?"

"I don't remember, Josie."

"Liar. You remember everything."

Tristan laughed and quickly moved on.

"This is the last entry. 'August 13, 2002. Dad called this morning and told me not to leave the apartment today. He sounded bad. It kind of freaked me out, but he told me not to worry. He's been working longer and longer every day, and I feel like we never even see each other.

"'Some men in suits came by last night, and he sent me to my room so that they could talk. I hate how he treats me like a damn child all the time. I'm practically an adult.

"'This is the last page of my journal. Who knew that I'd ever fill up this entire thing with my nonsense? I'll admit, some pages just have drawings on them, but mostly it's filled with the last two years of my life. Good times, bad times. There's only one person I'd ever share it with.

"'Tristan, please keep this journal. From this far away, it is the only thing I can give you. Save it, and when we are together again, you can return it. Love, McKenzi.'"

"Wow. I was such a whiny twat," Josie said, laughing uncomfortably.

"You were a kid, Josie. I think you were probably a typical fourteen-year-old girl."

"Yeah, I guess. So, your mom had this the whole time?"

"She thought a clean break would be best for me. What a fucking joke. Now she's created parental trust issues."

"Translate."

"I no longer believe my mother knows what's best for me."

"What kid does?"

"I mean, she hid away the only connection I had to you."

"She was only trying to help."

"I know." He sighed and closed the diary, setting it on the nightstand.

"You think that my dad was involved with Moloney back in New Orleans and we moved to escape him?"

"Yeah, I think that much is clear. The fact that your dad was suspicious of Moloney being responsible for your mother's death would be enough to scare him across the country, especially if he thought you were in danger."

"Moloney caught up with us in New York?"

"It's a theory."

Josie sighed and mumbled something about theories. Tristan could hear the weariness in her voice. He longed to hold her and kiss away all her fears, but again, distance was their enemy.

"I miss you," Tristan said into the phone, staring out his window blackened by the night sky.

"God, I miss you too. I hate being stuck in this damn apartment with my only human contact being Alex. His idea of fun is counting pills and doing pull-ups on my door frames."

"You could call Monica. You guys could do a girls' night or something."

"Do I come across as someone who enjoys having a girls' night? No, what I want is to go back to Seaport Village with you. We could ride the carousel again and I'd let you buy me a hat this time."

Her frustration was palpable. On instinct alone, Tristan wanted to grant her wish. He never wanted to deny her anything, but safety deemed that she stay put.

"I'm sorry. When I get back, we'll do that."

"You bet your fine ass we will."

Tristan chuckled and felt relieved at her teasing tone.

"You think my ass is fine?" he asked.

"I think all of you is fine," Josie said dryly.

"By what ratio do you like my ass compared to the rest of my body, considering it only represents approximately 9 percent of my 575 inches of overall body surface area," he teased. "Is my ass your favorite part?"

"No. Your dick is my favorite part. It's so perfect I want to construct a twenty-foot statue in its honor so that I may kneel before it and worship every day."

Tristan was stunned by her words, and a deep sensation stirred in his groin. He finally released the breath he'd been holding and fumbled with the phone.

"Fuck, Josie," he breathed out.

"Good night, Tristan."

"Wait! What? You're hanging up?"

"Yeah, I've got to go wash my hair or something. Smooches," she teased, barely holding in her laughter.

"Uh, bye."

The line disconnected before he'd even uttered his pathetic parting words.

☾

The breeze was warm and damp, but it felt like a reprieve on Tristan's heated flesh. He sucked on his cigarette, needing its toxins more than air. He'd brought one of the old books from his room to read, but he couldn't bear turning on the harsh porch light. He loved the dark of this land. No city lights glowed here. Crickets serenaded one other and he found a sense of calm in their song.

Bitsy stepped lightly across the porch and took a seat beside him. As much as it pained him to do so, Tristan didn't acknowledge his mother's presence.

"I know that you're upset with me, Tristan. I know what I did was wrong. I can see that now," Bitsy said softly. "Back then, honey, I was only trying to protect you. You were already in such a fragile state and I just couldn't add to that hurt. I wanted to take away your sadness and I just didn't see how prolonging your connection with McKenzi would do that."

Tristan exhaled, watching the smoke float between their faces, creating an effective curtain that, in reality, had always been there. His mother had never really seen him. Like everyone else, she'd never looked past the charming façade and the brainy performances. For most of his life, Tristan had felt like Bitsy was more like an adoring fan than a mother. She'd always said how smart he was, how handsome and polite, but she'd never really gotten to know him. She sure as hell didn't know him now.

"I didn't understand what she meant to you, Tristan. I wish I could go back and do things right. You know what they say. If wishes were horses we could all ride away."

Bitsy looked out over the dark yard, the treetops creating sharp silhouettes against a gray clouded sky. She sniffled and dabbed at her eyes before the tears could fall.

"I'm sorry, baby. I'm so sorry."

"I know you are, Ma."

Bitsy sat back, smoothing her hair and swiping at the black makeup smeared beneath her eyes. She always said a Southern woman must look her best, even at her worst.

"It doesn't change anything. I'm not ready to forgive you."

Bitsy looked back toward the house, as if searching for Daniel.

"Do me a favor and don't tell anyone I'm in town."

Tristan stood and made his way to the back door.

"To err is human; to forgive, divine," Bitsy said to his back.

Tristan kept his eyes on the door.

"'We are each our own devil, and we make this world our hell,'" he responded.

Tristan left his mother on the porch, alone with her tears and the words of Oscar Wilde.

☾

The street was quiet as Mort made his way around the house. He checked each door and window, finally finding one that was unlocked. Once inside, he let his eyes adjust to the dim lighting and began his investigation.

The house was typical of a single man. Not much decor, not much food in the fridge, and not much security. He made his way through each room, finding nothing out of the ordinary. When he pushed the door open to the small office, Mort had to press his lips together to keep the foul words from escaping. On one wall sat a small desk and a laptop computer. The adjacent wall held hundreds of photos of Monica Templeton taped and stapled to the wall, forming a collage. Photos of her leaving work, leaving her apartment, in her car, eating lunch, and having drinks. Among the photos were random items attached to the wall as well. Gum wrappers, a pair of lace panties, and her missing work badge.

In slow, calculated movements, Mort removed every photo, every item from the wall and placed it in a small bag to take with him. He had come here for information, but now his plans had changed. He would have to dispatch this nuisance.

Satisfied when the wall was bare, he pulled his piece from his waistband and made his way toward the bedroom.

"Wake up, bitch," Mort spoke loudly into the quiet room.

The man stirred in his sleep but failed to realize that he was not alone.

"I said, wake up!"

Evan shot up in bed, panicked by the booming voice. When

his eyes adjusted to the dark room, he found himself at the end of a very large gun.

"What the . . . ?" he shouted, scrambling back, trying to press himself into the headboard. Evan's panicked voice cracked like a pubescent boy's.

"Go ahead and try to run, it will only make this more enjoyable."

The voice was cold and sickly evil. It sent a terror-filled chill down his spine when his eyes finally landed on its owner. He could barely see the man standing over him in the shadows, but his identity was unmistakable.

"Rob? How did you get in here?"

Dread settled in his stomach, making him nauseous. Fear prickled across his skin, and he knew his time was limited.

"I found your little shrine to Monica," Rob said, waving his gun toward the hall. "I took it all down. Don't want a piece of shit like you to be connected to my girl in any way. You're quite the fucking stalker."

"No. It's not what you think! I swear!"

"What is it, then? You working for Moloney?"

"Who?" Evan asked.

"That's what I thought. How long?"

"How long what?" Evan's eyes scanned the room, searching for an escape.

"How long have you been stalking her?"

"I haven't been stal—"

Mort placed his gun to Evan's forehead.

"I dare you to finish that sentence."

"Ni-nine months," Evan stuttered.

"Ah, so in all fairness you did find her first. Too bad. I just needed her for a job. She was my link to someone else. But she got me. I couldn't help but want her."

"So you understand," Evan hedged, "her appeal. How amazing she is."

"I understand her in a way you never will."

"I'll stop. I swear. I'll leave her alone. Just let me live," Evan begged through heaving breaths.

"Such a fucking coward. That's not dedication. You're willing to give her up to save yourself. She's worth way more than that. It's too late for you."

"What can I do? What do you want?" Evan asked, thinking he'd trade anything to save his own life.

"I wanted you to stay away from my girl, but you just couldn't help yourself."

Rob placed the end of the silencer to Evan's forehead and before the man could even beg for his life, he pulled the trigger. He didn't wait around to watch the light fade from Evan's eyes, he didn't need to. The kill itself had been more satisfying than anything he'd ever felt. This man was a thief, out to steal his most prized possession.

The next evening's news would report that Evan Randal, thirty-eight, was found dead in his home by his housekeeping service. There were no signs of forced entry and no witnesses. The police had no suspects.

18. TERMINATOR

THE BOUNDARY BETWEEN NIGHT AND DAY
ON A CELESTIAL BODY.

Barry stood near the corner of Chartres Street and Ursulines, awaiting the arrival of his former colleague. He leaned against the building, cupping his hand so that his cigarette would light in the night breeze. Though he'd never left the South, he hadn't grown jaded or indifferent to its charms. He enjoyed the damp city air and the jarring horns of the passing river barges.

When not working for Dean Moloney, he loved to pass the time fishing. There was a peace to being in the space between water and sky. He felt small and insignificant there. It was a calm feeling, void of responsibility. His daughter always worried when he went out alone. She would tell him to wear his life jacket and to not drink too much beer and always bring his cell phone. He would laugh at their role reversal and ask her how a cell phone could prevent him from drowning.

Sometimes Barry imagined sinking into the warm brackish water and letting it fill his lungs. He thought it wouldn't be such a bad way to go. On the other hand, it was also easy to imagine himself living out his last days drowned in women and whiskey from the Quarter.

He was an old man now. His graying hair and leathered face left nothing up for debate. His waist size and his bank account had expanded over the years, but not much else. What his physical age hadn't taken from him, his time in the business had.

Moloney shared secrets with Barry. He confided in him and trusted him. While Barry respected and had pledged his life to this man, he knew the sentiment was not returned. Most days, he felt like an overdressed errand boy. This business was messy and dangerous. Anytime Moloney didn't want to get his hands dirty, it became Barry's job. He'd been taking orders for thirty years and was resigned to do so for the rest of his life.

Barry was uneasy about this meeting. His insides were churning as he thought about anyone catching him here. He was taking a huge risk meeting with Tristan, but he owed it to him. The boy had twice saved his ass during deals gone sour. It was the least he could do.

In all his years, he'd never met anyone like Tristan. The kid was smart—not just street smart but genuinely gifted. He had a cool head and a sharp eye. It hadn't surprised Barry in the least when he'd quickly climbed through the ranks. Of course, it didn't hurt that he was banging Moloney's daughter. The news of Tristan's departure from the organization had shocked Barry; he had figured him for a lifer.

As if on cue, Tristan rounded the corner, his appearance taking Barry by surprise. He was much larger now, a man in every way, and his tattoos had multiplied over the years. His trademark mess of inky black hair had been shaved down. Barry didn't understand why kids these days wanted to look like damned hooligans. He was more of a tailored suit and silk tie kind of man.

"Barry, good to see you," Tristan said, offering him a one-armed hug.

"You too," he replied, stomping out his cigarette. "Shall we?"

Tristan nodded and followed him inside. The hostess, recognizing the regular, sat them in the back corner and immediately returned with two cold beers.

"Wow. Great service," Tristan pointed out.

"You have no idea," Barry answered.

They both laughed and fell into an easy conversation summarizing the last couple years. When this was done, Barry found himself at the bottom of his beer and the end of his patience.

"Down to business, then."

"Well, the short version is that Moloney wants my girl dead and I need to know why."

"I know he has a hit out on some cop's kid, but nothing else. You remember Chief Delaune from Gretna, right? Ah, you would have been a youngster then. Back in the day, he couldn't get anything on Moloney himself, so he ended up arresting a group of us for stacked misdemeanors. Delaune shut down business for nearly six months."

Tristan nodded silently, wanting to extract as much information as possible.

"After the conviction, Moloney had Conners take out the chief's wife. Made it look like an accident. Ol' Earl Delaune must have gotten the message loud and clear because he took his kid and hauled ass across the country."

Tristan almost growled at the dismissive way Barry spoke about Josie's family. The rage built so rapidly, he felt a burning flush consume his body. He took a deep breath and calmed himself before speaking.

"Why is he after her? How could she possibly be a threat?"

"Ah, you know. Moloney has his reasons. Once he makes a decision, that's it. Earl was talking to the feds, so we took him out. Was supposed to off the kid too, but she escaped. Pretty clever too. She broke a window and then hid up in an air duct. Moloney's men thought she had squeezed through the bars on the window. When they left to search for her, she really escaped. Bested by a little girl."

"She doesn't remember anything."

Barry's eyes shot up to meet Tristan's, a look of genuine shock on his face.

"How would you know?"

"His daughter, that's my girl."

"No shit? What a small world!" Barry exclaimed. "Damn, man, that's too bad. He's had Mort on her for a while. How'd she stay under the radar for so long?"

Tristan eyed his former associate. He knew that the man was fishing for more information. He ignored the question.

"How close is Mort to finding her?"

"He's in San Diego."

"Shit," Tristan whispered, scrubbing at his face with his rough palms. "That fucker would slit his own mother's throat for the right price. He's the typical model for dissociative detachment. I bet he's even got psychotic symptoms."

"I'm not sure what all that means, but he's ice-cold, that one. Look, all I can tell you is that there's been pressure on us lately to tie up loose ends. The Italians are not happy with Moloney's growing business. Gino Gallo moved into town and he's been trying to recruit us. Offering more money and a pardon for allegiance. He's determined to eliminate the competition."

Tristan nodded again because he knew exactly what Barry meant. Gallo was legit Italian Mafia. Moloney had flown under their radar for a while, but apparently his operation had gotten too big and they considered him a threat now.

"What are Mort's orders?"

"I don't know," Barry answered.

"That's bullshit, Barry. You know everything that goes down. Give me something!"

"Watch yourself, boy. I'm telling you the truth. This is personal for Moloney. He's handling everything himself."

Tristan cursed again and stood to leave.

"Thanks for the information."

"Forget it, Fallbrook, consider us even. Get back to your girl and you two disappear. I don't know, head down to Mexico or something."

"I was never here," Tristan said, knocking his knuckles on the table.

"Of course not."

Barry watched the kid leave and groaned. He had given just enough information. And when the time came, Tristan would fall right into place.

(

Monica sat folded in half on Josie's couch, painting her toenails a deep purple color called Pump Up the Jam. Josie watched Monica with curious fascination. She'd never seen a woman more in her element than Monica was now.

"I'm glad you asked me over," Monica said, smiling to herself. "Rob and I had plans, but I told him we'd have to hold off. I need to hang with my girl."

Josie smudged her penciled line on the paper, shading Monica's face just so. She'd never been anyone's girl before. She wasn't sure how she felt about it. What did being someone's girl entail? Was she expected to gossip about boys while they braided each other's hair? Would she need to have Monica's back in a bar fight? These were things that, being a twenty-two-year-old woman, Josie thought she should know.

"You didn't have to blow off your boyfriend to come over."

"It's okay. I see him every day. I hardly ever see you."

Josie wanted to roll her eyes at Monica but couldn't risk offending her. She was so glad to have another human's company that she'd do almost anything to keep her here. Somehow, Monica made Josie feel more normal than anyone else. She sighed and wondered when she'd become so obsessed with normalcy.

Monica leaned over and grabbed a book from the floor.

"You're reading J. D. Salinger?" she asked.

"That's for Tristan. They're all over the apartment."

"Oh."

"Hey, do you have any cigarettes?" Josie asked.

"No, Josie. You know I don't smoke."

"Anything better than cigarettes?" Josie hedged, knowing she'd get a reaction.

"Are you seriously asking me for drugs?"

"Relax. I was kidding. I haven't done anything besides smoke an occasional joint since meeting Tristan."

"Is he one of those 'Just Say No' guys?" Monica asked, intrigued and thrilled by Josie's confession.

"No. He would never be so judgmental. I think when he's around, he fills all those holes that I usually try to block with risky behavior."

Josie grinned and shook her head, amazed at how she now echoed the words of every therapist she'd ever seen. She wondered why on earth she would share this information with her almost-friend, Monica. A pressing weight sat on her shoulders and she hated that the conversation had just taken a serious turn.

"So he fills your holes, huh?" Monica asked, eyebrow raised in amusement.

After a few seconds of stunned silence, both of them burst into a fit of giggles. The air around them grew light again. When she finally was able to catch her breath, Josie genuinely smiled. Maybe this was what being somebody's girl was all about, knowing and providing what you need when you need it. Josie feared that she'd never be able to carry out such an important responsibility.

Alex, hearing a ruckus through the paper-thin walls, came barreling in to find Josie wiping tears from her eyes. Shocked by the man barging into the apartment, Monica gasped, pointing her nail file toward him.

"What's wrong?" he asked, alarmed.

"Nothing! Calm down. You can't come barging in here like a Power Ranger. We were just laughing."

"Oh. Well, that's why. Never heard that shit coming from this apartment before," he answered. "Power Ranger, Jo? Those guys *son jotos*! Coulda made me something cool, like He-Man."

"Oh, yeah. He was so straight in his loin cloth and classic bob haircut," Josie answered, rolling her eyes. "Anyway, I don't presume to know what you do in your personal life."

"*Mamacita*, you of all people know that I like the ladies," Alex responded, a victorious lilt to his voice.

Josie blushed.

"Oh, this is my . . . friend. Um, Monica. Monica, this is my neighbor-slash-warden, Alex."

"Hi," Monica said, waving her nail file at him.

"Nice to meet you, Um Monica."

Josie flipped him off and refocused on her drawing.

"What were you gonna do? File me to death?"

Monica smiled and returned her attention to her nails.

"Heard from Tristan?" he asked, glancing back and forth between the two women, not knowing how much Monica knew.

Another involuntary smile graced Josie's lips at the mention of Tristan.

"Yeah, I talked to him for a while last night. There have been some interesting developments."

Alex assessed from Josie's strained code language that Monica didn't know anything.

"Okay, well, I'll give him a call when I get back."

"Where are you going?" Josie whined.

"Heading downtown. I'll be back soon. Stay inside and out of trouble. For the last time, lock this fucking door!" he warned, pointing his enormous finger at her.

Josie huffed and waved him off. The door closed behind him and she scurried over, locking all three locks with an overdramatic flair before turning and crossing her arms in defiance. It wasn't that she didn't care about her safety, she just hated being told what to do. At some point, one of her shrinks had diagnosed her with oppositional defiant disorder. Of course, she'd argued that he was a quack with no logical explanation for this imaginary disorder. She'd told him to fuck off when he pointed out that she'd proved his point.

"Did he say to stay inside? What? Are you grounded or something?" Monica joked, wiggling her painted toes in admiration.

"Uh, kind of. Not really. Maybe a little bit," Josie responded uncomfortably, tucking herself onto the sofa.

Monica looked up, suddenly aware of Josie's conversational avoidance maneuvers. She'd come up against them more times than she could count.

"What's going on?"

"I'm kind of in some trouble," Josie answered, not meeting Monica's worried gaze.

"Trouble? Like I stole a pack of gum trouble? Or I killed a hooker trouble?"

"Like we think we know who was responsible for my parents' death and now he's after me trouble," Josie spit out.

Monica's strangled gasp cut through the air and her trembling hands reached to embrace Josie. After the initial shock had worn off, Josie told Monica everything she knew. She hadn't realized how much of a load she'd been carrying around by keeping the secret. When she was finished, she sat in silence, trying to calculate Monica's reaction.

"Josie, we've got to go to the police," Monica said.

"No! Monica, this is so far beyond the police. It would only make things worse. Tristan will figure something out. I know he will. I'll understand if you want to leave. I mean, it could be dangerous to be here."

Monica shook her head, knowing that she'd never bail on this girl.

"I could call Rob to come over?" she offered.

"No! You can't tell anyone about this!"

"Okay, okay. I won't say a word," Monica promised, though it pained her to do so.

The rest of the evening was spent in nervous silence. They each kept to their menial tasks, Josie sketching Monica's worried face and Monica filing her already perfect nails. When it was far past Monica's bedtime, she bid Josie good night, promising to come over the next day. She kept her brave face firmly in place until she reached the bottom of the stairwell. Within seconds Monica was on the phone with Rob, begging him to meet her at her apartment.

That night, Rob held Monica while she cried for the unpredictable fate of her friend. As she dug further into his embrace she was racked with crippling guilt, because she knew across town, Josie slept alone.

C

Josie woke the next morning, still bothered by the late-night phone call from Tristan. He had forced casual conversation on her, but she could feel something was off. His voice had been tense. Not wanting to add any stress, she kept things light. Josie told him about her night spent with Monica and how she hadn't hated the experience. After a few minutes, Tristan said he needed to go but would call to check on her soon.

She stretched across her empty mattress and ran her hands over where Tristan should be. The material was cool to the touch and saddening. Josie crawled out of bed and dragged herself to the kitchen, hoping that Alex would be by soon with some breakfast or coffee. In nothing but a tank and boy shorts, she felt a chill in her apartment. It was uneasy, like when a stranger's eyes linger on you for too long.

With only one foot in the room, Josie froze. The sight of a man seated at her kitchen table had her feet bolted to the floor.

"Hello, McKenzi," the man said, not moving from his casual place at her table. "Or should I call you Josie?"

Panic seized her, making every muscle in her body rigid. Her head felt fuzzy and she couldn't quite focus on the man before her.

"How the hell did you get in here?"

Her eyes darted to the door, all three locks firmly bolted. Quickly, she tried to calculate the probability of making it to the door, getting the locks undone, and out into the hall before he could catch her. She was no genius, but it was obvious that the odds were not in her favor.

"You can't make it," he said, answering her thoughts. "Please, have a seat."

Rob pointed to the chair opposite him, but Josie still hadn't moved. He placed his hand around his gun and lifted it from the table.

"I said to have a seat."

Josie let out a squeak and hurried over, falling into the seat.

"That's better."

"Who are you?" Josie asked.

"Who I am is not important. What is important is why I'm here. Do you know why I'm here?"

Josie nodded her head, her eyes flashing to the gun still in his hand and back to his face.

"Good, then we don't have to worry with introductions. Go put some clothes on."

"You won't do it," Josie said.

Rob cocked his head and smiled.

"Do what exactly?" he asked.

"Kill me. You don't look like a killer. I don't think you'll do it."

"Neither did your little friend in the park. Now, go get dressed."

"Gavin? You bastard!" she shouted. "What did—"

"I'm not answering your questions. See this gun?" he asked, waving it between them. "This gun means I'm in charge. Now go!"

Josie stood and crossed her arms. She glared at him. If she was going to die, she was going to do it on her terms.

"Fuck you," Josie spat. "I'm not going to do shit."

Rob shot up from his chair, making her flinch. He grabbed her roughly by the arm and dragged her to the bedroom, throwing her down on the mattress.

"I don't like repeating myself," he said.

That's when the nauseating panic and fear took over Josie. Flashbacks of unwanted touches and rough hands sent flashes of terror through her.

"Please don't touch me. Just kill me," she begged while tears soaked her shirt.

Rob looked away, his jaw clenched in anger and uncertainty. He admonished himself and raised the gun so she'd take him seriously.

"Shut up," he growled. "I'm not here to kill you. My orders are to take you back to Moloney."

"Anything, just don't touch me, please."

Josie's broken words sent a jolt of guilt through him. The unfamiliar feeling left him with more fear than he'd ever experienced, fear of failure and perverse compassion.

"Get up! We're leaving."

She crawled from the mattress and wiped the tears from her face. As she crossed the room to her closet, she could feel his gaze searing her flesh. It felt invasive and so wrong. She managed to throw on some jeans and a T-shirt before heading toward the bathroom.

"Where are you going?" Rob asked.

"I've got to use the bathroom."

He took a step toward her, as if he would follow her into the small space.

"Are you going to help me change my tampon?" she said quickly.

Rob frowned and walked down the hall toward the kitchen.

"I'll wait in here," he said. "You have three minutes."

Josie slammed the door closed and leaned against it. She ran her hands through her hair, scraping her nails against her scalp. *I need a weapon, something*, she thought. Dropping to her knees, she searched the cabinet beneath the sink, coming up with only one towel and a can of magenta spray paint.

"Shit," she whispered, leaning her forehead on the counter.

Knowing her time was limited, Josie stood and threw her hair into a ponytail. She opened the medicine cabinet for a hair band and spotted the pencils and paint markers inside.

Bang. Bang. Bang. Josie jumped as the man beat on the door.

"Sixty seconds and I'm coming in," he said.

"I'm almost done," she said.

Her voice sounded weak and unfamiliar. She didn't like it. She cleared her throat and tried again.

"Just a second," she said.

Josie scribbled across the mirror, for once paying no attention to letter styling or form. She flushed the toilet and emerged from the bathroom.

"Get your shoes on," the man demanded.

Josie sucked in a breath and turned to find him waiting in the hall. Her heart drummed against her chest as she swallowed and answered him.

"They're by the front door."

Josie walked away quickly, praying that he would follow. He did.

When they reached the kitchen, Rob slid his gun into his waistband and roughly gripped her shoulder.

"We're going to walk out of here and down to my car. If you try to run, you die. If you alert anyone, you both die."

Josie wordlessly nodded. After slipping on her shoes, she crossed her arms so he couldn't see her trembling hands.

"Let's move."

As they approached the door, a loud knock sounded through the apartment. Both sets of eyes stared at the door and the swinging chain.

"Who is that?" Rob asked.

"My neighbor."

"Get rid of him. Fast."

The loud knocking sounded again.

"Jo!" Alex's voice yelled from the hall.

Josie felt at war. Should she try to get help or should she just comply with her kidnapper? Her mind seesawed, every emotion heightened.

"I'll kill him," Rob warned quietly.

Josie nodded and leaned her forehead against the wood door.

"I'm sick," she said.

"What's wrong? Open up so I can check on you," Alex answered.

"No. It's gross in here. I'm pukey and . . . and I've got a fever. You don't want to come in here. I should be quarantined."

She hoped her voice sounded sick and not scared.

"Ugh, that's gross. All right, I'll check on ya later."

"Okay," she answered.

Josie turned her head and pressed her ear to the door. She listened to Alex's heavy footsteps fade down the stairs and released the breath she'd been holding.

19. APOGEE
THE FARTHEST POINT FROM EARTH
IN THE MOON'S ORBIT.

This had to be the longest day in the history of her career. At one point Monica would have sworn that time had either stopped or was moving backward only to keep her at her desk. The one silver lining was that she would see Josie again today. Two days in a row set a record for them, and she felt empowered by the bond that was beginning to grow. Since waking up this morning, Monica had felt sick with worry for the girl. The danger that hung over Josie was consuming. So she vowed to become a great distraction.

Armed with chick flicks, microwave popcorn, and ice cream, Monica found herself losing all patience outside Josie's door. She

"What's up, short stuff? She giving you a hard time?"

"I-I don't know. I can hear her phone in there, but she's not picking up and she's not answering the door. I'm worried that—" Monica stopped herself, not wanting to speak those thoughts out loud. "I'm worried. Did you check on her this morning?"

"Yeah, she told me she was sick."

"Well, did she look okay?"

"She never opened the door."

"Alex . . ." Monica whispered, worse-case scenarios flooding her mind.

"Shit!"

Alex attacked Josie's door. He rammed it with his huge form, over and over, hearing the old wood begin to splinter under his assault. Monica watched in fascination as he pounded against the door. The thunderous sound echoed through the stairwell of the quiet building. Finally, it gave and Alex hurled through, almost falling inside. Monica followed him in and they both began calling Josie's name and searching the small space.

"Alex! Come here!"

Alex ran down the hall and crowded into the bathroom with Monica. They both stared, openmouthed, at their reflections in the mirror. Thick lines of pink paint crossed over their horrified faces, lines that formed the words *New Orleans*.

"I'll call Tristan," Alex said, his voice defeated.

Monica nodded and watched as Alex placed the hardest call he'd ever had to make.

Two days of complete silence. That's what Josie had endured on this road trip from hell. She was trapped in a tin can with a very attractive assassin who, for some reason, had yet to assassinate her. Instead, he was driving her east to her former home. She pressed her forehead to the cool window and counted the street-lights that went by, just for something to do.

Josie didn't really know what to make of this bad guy. One minute, he would be unreadable, and the next, his eyes would become tiny slits staring out at the road. She could only assume that he was fighting some kind of internal battle. For the one who had the gun, he sure seemed troubled.

His phone had been ringing nonstop since yesterday. Every time it happened, he'd look at the number and silence it but would never turn it off. His foul moods seemed to coincide with the phone calls. Josie almost laughed at how observant she had become when there was nothing else to occupy her attention.

They had stopped for breaks only four times in two days. They'd eaten only once. Josie was starving and thirsty and irritated by the whole hostage situation. She was sure that she was causing irreversible damage to her bladder while her captor feigned ignorance about how women's bodies work.

Josie crossed her arms and sulked at all the waiting. She'd rather he just get it over with. She was positive that her mind was imagining a much worse fate than what would transpire. The not-knowing part was the worst. She thought about New York and how maybe it would have been better if she had just died back then. There would have been no amnesia, no horrible foster parents, and no feeling like she didn't deserve to live. Then again, there would have been no reuniting with Tristan.

"How much longer?" Josie asked.

No answer.

"What are you going to do with me?"

His eyes stayed forward, his face expressionless.

"Well, since you don't want to answer my questions, I'll just keep talking. So, I know you're the bad guy, but when did bad guys get so hot? I mean, in that older guy, daddy complex sort of way. I'm fucking hungry. Are you starving me to death? Is that what's happening here?"

He sighed and twisted his grip around the steering wheel. Josie almost smiled and wondered if she could annoy him into releasing her.

"You could let me go, you know. Just drop me off at the Mexican border and never look back. You could let me out here. Tell Moloney you killed me. I'll disappear and everybody wins."

He shook his head slightly.

"What are the odds of me surviving a jump from the car while going"—she leaned over, looking at the speedometer—"eighty miles an hour? Probably not good."

Josie took a deep breath and slammed her head back against the headrest.

"You are the worst fucking bad guy ever. You're supposed to be crazy smart and witty. Also, you're supposed spill the master plan, giving me some satisfaction before I die. Have you never seen a horror movie?"

She rolled her head toward the window and watched the trees slide by in a blur. For a second, she glimpsed her reflection in the glass and thought about the message she'd left in her bathroom. She hoped someone found it.

"It's Mort," his deep voice made Josie's head whip around, thinking that he was finally talking to her. Instead, she saw his phone pressed to his ear. "I'm three hours out with the girl. Yes. Yes. Got it."

He ended the call and cast a glance in her direction. Josie's eyes darted away quickly, not wanting to upset him. Three hours. She had three hours to live. What should she be doing with her time? More than she wanted to escape, she wanted to hear Tristan's voice just one more time.

Josie closed her eyes and prayed. She was a hypocrite just like those people who become religious only on airplanes. She didn't pray for a savior or an escape, only for Tristan to know undoubtedly that for the second time in her life, she loved him. It wasn't until all her time thinking in the confines of the car that she realized she had never said it to him. How could she have never said it to him?

Rob didn't speak to the girl unless necessary and kept his eyes on the road. At this point, he was functioning on pure adrenaline and no sleep. If he didn't have to look into her questioning eyes, he could find the strength to keep driving. For a while, he thought he might kill her just to shut her up. She asked questions, many questions. Rightfully so, she wanted to know where they were going, what he was going to do with her. Rob knew she didn't really want to know the answer, so he fought to remain silent.

He glanced over, finding her eyes closed and her hands clasped tightly together. He sighed and refocused his attention on the highway, brooding over the enormous mess. He was still angry that he'd had to take the girl instead of just killing her. It would have been an easy kill. She hadn't fought back or tried to escape, it was textbook. It had been her terrified, begging voice that had done him in. That and the vision of Monica's sad face.

Rob was in too deep, far too connected to Josie Banks and her past. The woman he loved, the woman he craved above anything else, would be crushed by Josie's death. As he drove through the night, he found himself hoping that Moloney wouldn't make him be the triggerman on this job. Now that he didn't have to kill her, he'd be able to sleep next to Monica with a clearer conscience. He'd be able to hold her and soothe her aching guilt. He'd be able to live the rest of his days, however numbered they might be, without remorse.

(

Dean Moloney sat behind his large oak desk, peering out the perfectly clean plate-glass window. On this cloudless day he could see clear across his property. The blue sky filled the top of the window canvas and spilled down until it was interrupted by green trees. His eyes skimmed over the pond, the water rippling with soft patterns. His stables rose against the backdrop of the security fence marking the perimeter of his land. He loved sitting here, celebrating all that was his.

His parents had been poor people. They had been happy with a small house and secondhand furniture. Dean always wanted more. He envied his uncle's lavish lifestyle. Uncle John Moloney, his father's brother, had been a part of the organization for as long as Dean could remember. Even at a young age, Dean knew that he wanted to follow in the man's footsteps. His parents fought him on it. They prided themselves on working hard and walking the straight and narrow. When he was a teenager, he started working for his uncle. Before Dean took the job, John warned of the importance of discretion. Dean fell into the lifestyle easily, becoming a sort of apprentice to his uncle. Only nine years later, John was killed by a random mugger. Dean clawed his way over more experienced and seasoned members directly to the top. He learned how to cover his tracks with legit businesses and how to recruit the best men and keep them.

Eventually, he'd met his wife and started a family, an ideal step along his path. Nothing was more important to him than continuing his proud Irish bloodline. He'd never been happier than when his twins arrived. He remembered running through the halls, shouting to anyone who would listen, of his healthy baby boy and girl. From that instant, he had their destinies mapped out. His daughter would be a princess, never wanting for anything, and his son would be groomed to ultimately take his place.

Dean looked at the framed photograph sitting on the corner of his desk, an unsuspecting and blissful family stared back. He wanted to grab it and yell at them, warn them of the impending danger. It was too late. With the death of his son, Dean Jr., came a darkness that he had never experienced before. Hate and fury filled his heart, turning him into the dark and sinister monster he was now. All he could think about was vengeance, wanting to punish anyone who dared to live a life free from hurt, especially Dr. Daniel Fallbrook.

This man and his faltering surgical skills had taken Dean Jr. from him, and retribution would be paid. Dean had worked out a plan, a devious, life-altering scheme. It took patience and manipulation, but it had worked out so well.

Fallbrook had taken his son, so Dean would take Tristan.

It was a joyful day when he had learned of Tristan Fallbrook's interest in his daughter, Fiona. It took convincing, but in time she agreed to see the boy. Dean didn't want him dead; that would be too easy. Instead, he wanted to take him from his charmed life. He wanted to rip him from his family and destroy every piece of his future. At the time, Dean had no idea that it would work so well.

Before he knew it, Tristan had fallen in love with Fiona. After that, it was easy to lure him into Dean's world. It was the best result he could have hoped for. Everything had worked out perfectly—except for Fiona.

She resented her father for making her stay with Tristan. When she was younger, she didn't really mind. Dean kept her well paid, a sort of bribe for her part in the scheme. When they relocated to California, she fell in love with another man. She begged her father, pleaded with him to let her break it off. But he would not agree.

Dean got what he wanted. He'd destroyed Tristan, but at the cost of losing his daughter. Fiona rarely spoke to her parents these days. She'd married a man her father never met and they live in Northern California somewhere. His need for revenge had destroyed them. Sure, there were e-mails and photos, but it was not the family he dreamed of.

Now that Fallbrook had left the organization, he would have to be dealt with. Dean kept him around for a while, waiting to see if he would be of use. His patience had worn thin and now the boy represented one more loose end that needed to be tied up.

When he received the photos of the girl from Mort, he almost didn't believe his eyes. Tristan was with her. His unmistakable tattoos had given him away.

Dean drummed his fingers on the top of his desk and wondered how he'd never connected the two before now. When he'd been after Earl Delaune, they would have been children. Dr. Fallbrook hadn't shown up on his radar until two years after the chief and his daughter fled. Another six months went by before Fiona came home talking of a boy named Tristan Fallbrook.

He'd never known that Fallbrook knew the Delaune girl, but once he learned that they were hiding out together, he dug into their past and was delighted with what he found. Now that he knew they were connected, he could use the girl to hurt Tristan. It was almost too easy. He grinned and bowed his head in amusement. The thought was so satisfying he almost screamed with joy. Of course he didn't. He was a man of restraint.

A knock at the door broke the silence of the room.

"Enter," Dean said.

"We just received word that Mort will be arriving in three hours with the girl. I've instructed him to take her to the South warehouse for holding."

Dean nodded.

"Thank you, Barry."

He waved his hand, dismissing the man, and sat back in his chair.

20. MAGNITUDE

THE BRIGHTNESS OF A CELESTIAL BODY.

After making the call to Tristan, Alex told Monica that he was heading to New Orleans. They had no idea if Josie left on her own or if she'd been taken. Either way, he had a gut feeling that Josie was still alive. Monica couldn't stand by and do nothing. She decided to accompany him.

They flew out the next morning. They spent an entire day with Tristan working out plans from downright stupid to borderline suicidal. Alex watched Tristan, who bounced haphazardly between grieving for Josie and insisting on her survival. He resembled a tiny boat being thrown about in the middle of a raging sea. They did their best to comfort him. Bitsy and Daniel gave their son and the two strangers space in their home, offering anything they could to help.

It wasn't until Tristan received a call from one of Moloney's men that he was able to regain control of himself. Barry had called to let him know that Josie was still alive and being held at Moloney's Tchoupitoulas warehouse. The trio was in the car and on their way before the phone call ended.

"How far is it?" Monica asked.

She sat on the edge of the backseat, her fingers gripping the seat in front of her. Tristan took a sharp turn quickly and she flew against the door.

"Twenty minutes," he answered. "Put your seat belt on."

Monica nodded and buckled up. She squeezed her eyes shut and held her breath when they flew through a red light. After they cleared the intersection, she exhaled and said a prayer.

"What's the plan?" Alex asked. "I don't have my piece, man. Couldn't get through airport security, you know?"

Tristan's fingers curled around the steering wheel as he eyed the upcoming intersection. He pressed harder on the gas and ignored the horns and screeching tires left behind.

"There's a pistol under your seat."

"¡Simón!"

Alex reached under the seat and pulled out the gun. He checked the clip and slid it back in.

"What about me?" Monica asked as they reached the Crescent City Connection.

The wide Mississippi River stretched beneath them as Tristan and Alex gave each other knowing glances.

"You're staying in the car, *mami*. We can't be worried about you *and* Jo," Alex answered.

"What? That's crap! I could help. I'm great at distractions."

"No," the two men answered in unison.

Monica crossed her arms and looked out the window as they entered New Orleans. It was a beautiful city and she wished that she'd come here under better circumstances.

"I've been to this warehouse before," Tristan said. "There are two doors. One at each end of the building and a large loading dock on the street side. Our best bet will be to enter through the farthest door since that one is blocked from street view."

"Okay. Then what? How many men you think they got?" Alex asked.

"I don't know. At least three. They'll all be armed. I hope they're still there."

"What if they're not?" Monica asked.

Tristan blew through another intersection, barely avoiding a moving van.

"Then we'll be too late."

The silence enveloped them and the interior of the car felt like it was shrinking. The outside world flew by in a blur of cars and buildings. Tristan's muscles ached from the intensity. He needed to be there now.

They parked a block away on a residential street. Tristan placed his own gun in the waistband of his jeans and turned to Monica.

"Thank you," he said. "For everything you did for her."

Monica shook her head, freeing the tears she'd been holding back.

"And thank you," Tristan said, turning to Alex. "You took care of her. No matter what happens, know that Josie cares about you both."

"Stop that," Monica cried. "This isn't good-bye."

"'Don't be dismayed at good-byes. A farewell is necessary before you can meet again,'" Tristan quoted. "Richard Bach."

"'Unless someone like you cares a whole awful lot, nothing is going to get better. It's not,'" Monica said, giving him a half smile. "Dr. Seuss."

Tristan crawled out of the car. Alex followed. Before shutting the door, Tristan stuck his head back in.

"Stay here. If we're not back in an hour, take my car and find the police."

Tristan dangled his keys in front of her and she took them without meeting his eyes.

"Be careful," she said.

Both doors slammed closed and Monica jumped at the sound. She felt entombed as she watched the two men jog off down the street. She followed their progress through the dark, each becoming more like a transparent shadow, until they turned the corner and were out of sight.

☾

The smell was grease and metal and stale air. She could hear the tugboats as they passed, so she knew they were close to the river. In a dark warehouse, Josie sat tightly bound to a metal chair. Her arms and shoulders cramped from the pull of the ropes even though she had given up her struggle long ago. Just in case she survived, she took in everything about her surroundings. She counted the number of skylights high above her head. She tried to make out the printed words on the hundreds of boxes and cartons stacked around her. Her mind raced with so many questions and not enough answers.

The stacked pallets obscured her view, but she could hear murmured conversation and approaching footsteps. Josie fought to keep her breathing under control while her racing heart created a countdown tempo against her chest. She couldn't help but feel robbed by this. After finding Tristan and the first inkling of happiness, she was going to lose it all.

Jarred from her reflection, she felt a hand grip her shoulder. Four men stood before her, including her kidnapper. She looked them over carefully, trying to assess which one of them would do the job. Her mind was shutting down and laughter almost bubbled out of her as she took in the sight before her. It was a scene straight out of a mobster movie, complete with damsel in distress.

"McKenzi Delaune, it's so good to see you again. Welcome home," the man dressed all in black taunted as he began to circle her. "Please excuse our lack of fanfare."

Josie followed him with her eyes for as long as possible, memorizing the scowl on his face and the venomous words that dripped from his thin lips. He was short, with a wide chest and a shirt that didn't fit his muscled arms. His skin was pale, sickly almost, and stood out beneath his black hair and beard. Icy blue eyes glared at her. His voice carried so much hate and contempt she felt as though his words alone could cause damage.

He had that dominant, soul-crushing air about him. This had to be Dean Moloney. When he was standing directly in front of her again, he grabbed her chin and roughly turned her face toward the overhead light.

"So beautiful," Moloney sneered. "You do look just like Earl, though."

Josie bit down on her lip to keep from screaming. She wanted to tell him to keep her father's name out of his evil mouth.

"Why am I still alive?" she asked.

"Because you're the grand finale," Moloney answered.

"What did I ever do to you?"

"Your father shut down my operation for six months."

Josie's gaze flickered over to the other men. They all seemed bored and unaffected by his dramatics.

"He's dead. How much more punishment could you need?"

"His punishment was the loss of your mother. Though it did look like an accident. Right, Barry?" Moloney asked.

"Very unfortunate, sir," Barry answered.

Moloney's face held a devious smirk that, had her hands been free, Josie would have slapped clear off. The anger and hurt expanded in her until she felt like she would burst from it.

"You killed my mother," she whispered, dropping her head to hide her tears.

"Of course," Moloney answered. "Your father thought he could outrun me. I found out he was talking to the feds. That is why Earl is dead. He couldn't keep his mouth shut."

Tears blurred Josie's vision but did not diminish the hateful glare she had on him. This man was the reason for everything tragic and wounding that had ever happened to her. She felt sick just being in his presence.

"Why me? Why now?"

"You know too much," he answered. "You watched as we tortured truths from your father. You begged us to stop. You cried when we killed him. And then you escaped, making a fool of me and my men."

"I have amnesia! I don't remember anything before being sent to a home in California. I don't know anything! You killed my fucking family and now you want me? Well, do it, you coward! Do it!"

Moloney laughed, his wicked cackle rising up through the building and echoing off the metal walls. Her tale of amnesia was humorous yet inventive, a smart attempt at self-preservation.

"As you wish," Moloney said, smiling. "Barry."

The oldest man nodded and pulled his pistol from its holster, raising it toward Josie. Her eyes searched his face for any sort of hesitation and found none. This was it for her. Resigned to her destiny, Josie took a deep breath and closed her eyes, waiting for the end to come.

"I love you, Tristan," she whispered, her lips barely moving as she spoke her final words.

"Drop the fucking gun!" Tristan shouted.

He appeared behind Rob and Barry, his piece pointed at Moloney. He stepped forward, making his intentions clear. If Josie dies, so does Moloney.

"Right on time, Tristan," Moloney said.

Frank reached for his gun, only to feel the press of metal to his temple.

"Don't think so, *cabrón*," Alex growled.

Josie, shocked by Alex and Tristan's presence, sat speechless as she watched the triangle of guns before her—Tristan at Moloney, Alex at Frank, and Barry still focused on her. Her eyes darted from one to another, finally staying on Tristan. The sight of him, no matter the circumstance, was comforting. Her eyes raked over his intense face and she willed him to look at her.

"I said to drop the gun or Moloney eats this fucking bullet," Tristan shouted at Barry, but the man did not flinch.

Fearless, Moloney spun to face Tristan, a Cheshire cat grin plastered on his face. He assessed the boy and the passion in his eyes. His plan had worked perfectly.

"Tristan, what an entrance. Still trying to play hero? Of course, I knew you would come. You'll never make it out alive," Moloney said.

"I don't care, as long as she does."

Tristan finally glanced at Josie and his heart broke. He'd avoided eye contact so that he could remain focused, but now he was a mess. The love of his life sat at the end of a cold, impassive piece of steel.

"Barry, drop your goddamned gun," Tristan repeated.

Moloney shook his head and the standoff continued.

Rob stood motionless, watching the situation play out before him. He knew he could draw his gun and take one of them out before anyone knew what happened. The problem was, he wasn't sure where his allegiances lay now. The tiny bit of compassion that remained inside him was fixed on Tristan. Rob imagined Monica on the end of that gun and he almost crumpled from the vision. Still, if he betrayed Moloney, he wouldn't get any of the money. He wasn't willing to risk that just yet.

"What do we do now? You want to trade your life for hers?" Moloney asked.

"No!" Josie shouted, somehow finding her voice.

"Be quiet, Josie," Tristan told her, avoiding her pleading eyes.

She fought hard against the metal chair, thrashing about to keep their attention on her. She would not tolerate them taking Tristan from this world.

"No, you can't do that! Kill me, you fucking pussy! Me! Do it, please," she screamed, tears soaking her face.

"Josie, shut up!" Tristan shouted back at her, shifting his weight from foot to foot.

"You're not in a position to offer deals, Moloney. I've got the upper hand."

"You've got nothing."

Moloney grinned and whistled through his teeth. The sound shot across the building, but nothing happened. Everyone looked around and listened for approaching danger, but silence and empty space surrounded them. Confused, Moloney whistled again, his eyes searching the darkness.

"Expecting someone?" Alex asked.

Moloney turned to Barry expectantly.

"They were in place when I came in," Barry answered.

"Like I said, upper hand," Tristan said. "Now drop it."

"Not anymore, Fallbrook," Rob said softly, raising his gun to the back of Tristan's head. "I need this money too bad for you to screw this up."

Although Rob did not possess the ability to end Josie's life,

Tristan's would not be an issue. He had no feelings for the boy and frankly believed he'd be saving Fallbrook from a torturous death at the hands of Moloney.

"Rob?" Monica's voice shouted as she emerged from between two stacks of boxes. "Why? I don't . . . What are you doing here?"

"Rob?" Tristan and Josie said in unison, turning their attention to the blond man now holding all the cards.

Monica had obeyed Tristan's command to stay in the car for almost a full five minutes. She'd worked her way down the block, checking each building before finding the right one. From her hiding place, Monica had been listening to the men's conversation, waiting for an opportunity to make her move. Sure, she was unarmed, but she had the element of surprise.

Unable to see everything, the sound of Rob's voice had shaken her and she didn't even think before emerging to investigate. Her mind reeled with the scene before her, and she fought to understand her lover's place among these men.

"Monica? What are you doing here?" Rob screeched.

"Do we have a problem, Mort?" Moloney asked.

"You're Mort? The Mort who's been hunting Josie?" Tristan asked.

"No! It's not true!" Monica screamed. Her hands flew to her head, pulling at her hair as her eyes scanned his impassive face. "Rob, tell them it's not true!"

"Get out of here, this has nothing to do with you," Rob said firmly, his trembling gun still pointed at Tristan. "Fallbrook, drop the gun. You too, big man," he demanded, nodding toward Alex.

"Damn!" Alex sneered.

Monica watched in disbelief as Alex relented first. He surrendered, not wanting to be responsible for the death of Tristan, especially in front of Josie. He knew she would never survive that kind of heartbreak even if she did escape this mess. Tristan dropped his gun, the clanking sound of it hitting the concrete floor marking the extinction of hope.

"Now that that is all squared away," Moloney said, rubbing his hands together in victory, "you three, join the girl."

Alex and Monica took their places next to Josie. Tristan rushed to her, running his hands over her hair and whispering apologies.

"I'm sorry, baby. I'm so sorry. I love you."

"I love you too," Josie said.

"Enough!" Moloney shouted. "I'll do it myself."

He pulled his 9mm from his waistband and pointed it directly at Josie. A shot rang out, a deafening break in the otherwise silent building. Barry dove for cover, disappearing from view. Josie squeezed her eyes tight and prepared for the hurt, but it never came.

Josie opened her eyes to find Monica on the floor before her. She had taken the bullet meant for Josie. She was small, but she was fast. Her tiny body lay still at Josie's feet, crimson spreading out around her like ink saturating paper.

Tristan jumped Moloney, wrestling his gun away. Frank raised his gun and fired once before Alex took him out with a bullet to the temple.

"Monica!" Josie screamed, her voice a haunting and agonizing cry.

"No! No, no, no, no! Monica!" Rob shouted, running to her side and dropping to his knees. "Why did you do that? You stupid woman!"

"I had to. I saved her," she barely got out before her throat flooded with blood.

The blood soaked into the knees of his jeans as he pulled her into his lap. Rob wailed as her breaths became shallow and her eyes fixed onto his, his howling pleas for a miracle falling on helpless ears. Monica's body arched as a cough forced crimson rivers from the corners of her mouth.

"Button. I love you," he whispered, pushing her hair back from her face.

She managed a smile, exhaled a stuttered breath, and faded away from this world.

Everyone who had been watching the scene now looked on helplessly as Rob jumped up and hurled himself toward Moloney. What began as excruciating sadness morphed into something malevolent and irate. Tristan let go of the man and stepped aside as Rob raised his gun and emptied the entire magazine. But each blast from his gun offered no redemption, no satisfaction. Even when Moloney lay dead at his feet, Rob wanted to crush him, to pound him into the earth with his own fists. He wanted to bathe in his blood, but he knew that wouldn't resurrect his love.

Rob dropped his smoking gun to the floor and disappeared into the shadows. A few seconds later, the sound of the door slamming closed jarred everyone from their daze.

"Tristan!" Josie shouted.

Alex turned to find Tristan leaning against one of the crates, blood soaking his shirt. Alex knelt beside him and looked at the wound.

"Who got you?" Alex asked.

"Frank."

"Are you okay?" Josie shouted.

"'Tis but a scratch. A flesh wound,'" Tristan said, giving Josie a reassuring smile.

Alex took his shirt off and wrapped it tightly around Tristan's biceps.

"That'll help," Alex offered.

"Any excuse to take your shirt off, huh, muscles?" Tristan said.

Alex untied Josie from the chair, his large fingers fumbling with the knots. She fell onto the floor, sobbing over Monica's body. She fought for each breath, the air feeling like razor blades to her lungs. She felt undeserving and wondered how she'd ever take a guilt-free lungful of air again.

Alex helped Tristan stand and together they retrieved Josie. She clung to Tristan, crying into his chest.

"I hate to break up the reunion, but we gotta get outta here," Alex said.

A loud smacking sound came from behind them in the dark. The three eyed each other as Alex pulled his gun and pointed it toward the sound. Another smack. Josie whimpered. Then came another and another, until the sound of a single person clapping became recognizable. From the back of the warehouse emerged a man wearing an expensive suit and matching hat. Shadow covered most of his face, making only his menacing smile visible.

"That was truly an entertaining show," he said, his voice amused and heavily accented.

The three onlookers stood motionless, curious as to the identity of this stranger and worried about what it meant for their survival.

"My name is Gino Gallo. You have done me a great favor here today."

He snapped his fingers, and Barry appeared behind him. "You saved this man from having to eliminate his former associates. You should be grateful, Barry. Are you grateful?"

Barry nodded, his eyes on Tristan the whole time.

"Yes, sir."

"Of course, we did offer a bit of help, eliminating Moloney's backup for you," Gallo said.

"What now?" Alex asked, unfazed by the man's presence.

"Let me tell you what now," Gallo said, glaring at the boy who dared to question him. "You all will leave this place. My men will

take care of the bodies and clean up the mess. Do not fear retaliation. I'm in charge now. I will not allow it. Now go, before I change
my mind."

Tristan, recognizing a blessing when he heard one, motioned
for everyone to go. They all moved toward the door, but Josie
would not budge. Her eyes were glued to Monica's lifeless body.

"Josie, we've got to go," Tristan urged.

She nodded and gave in to his pulling.

"Thank you," Josie whispered to her friend as she was dragged
out into the night.

21. RILLE

GROOVES IN THE MOON'S SURFACE THAT
RESEMBLE CANALS OR CANYONS.

The sound of banging on the front door was almost lost in the
cadence of thrashing rain against the house. When Daniel Fallbrook opened the door, it only took seconds for him to assess the
situation.

"Bitsy! Get my bag!" Daniel yelled from the front porch.

He grabbed Tristan and pulled him inside, sitting him down
at the breakfast table. Bitsy's casual linens were swept aside as
Tristan placed his injured arm on top of the cool oak. Josie and
Alex filled the other two chairs and watched Daniel tend to his
wounded son.

"What happened?" he asked.

"Close range, twenty-two," Tristan answered.

Daniel removed the T-shirt tourniquet from Tristan's arm and cut off the sleeve of his shirt with kitchen scissors. Bitsy raced into the room carrying his medical bag, her silk gown fluttering behind her like wings.

"Tristan, sweetheart," she cried. "Are you okay?"

Her trembling hands made the sign of the cross as she hovered over the two most important men in her life.

"It went clean through," Daniel answered. "I'll just clean and suture it. You should be fine," Daniel said.

"Oh, thank God," Bitsy whispered.

It was then that she noticed the other two people in her kitchen. A large, shirtless Alex sat at her table. Water dripped down his muscled body in the most distracting way. Any other time, she would have reminded him of proper manners when it came to stages of nakedness at her breakfast table. But she figured she could overlook his indiscretions considering the circumstances. Next to him was a beautiful, sad girl. Her hair was slick and wet, fat tendrils sticking to the bare skin of her face and throat. Her arms circled around her body.

"My God in heaven! McKenzi Delaune, is that you?" Bitsy asked.

Josie glanced at Bitsy before her eyes immediately snapped back to Tristan. She didn't need to see the woman before her to know what she looked like. Josie knew the curve of her cheek and the way her smile fell to one side like her son's. She knew the sweep of her hair and her Cupid's bow lips.

"Bless her heart. She looks like she was eaten by gators and shit over a cliff," Bitsy muttered.

Daniel and Tristan both looked up, wearing matching expressions of shock.

"Oh, stop looking at me like that! Grandmother Ducote always said 'shit' was a lady's curse word."

Josie's body stiffened as she tried to take a breath. Though her lungs were burning, her body would not cooperate. Voices were murmurs of whirring sound mixed with the racing beat of her own pulse. She felt dizzy and weightless, numb and on fire at the same time. She wished the pounding in her head would stop. She wished that every time she closed her eyes she didn't see Monica's body lying at her feet like some kind of sacrifice. She wished it had all been a dream.

Finally Josie sucked in a deep breath, its elements giving her body just what it needed. With its exhale, the air left in a wailing sob, a scream that seemed silent in her own head. Bitsy embraced Josie. She ran her hands over the girl's hair and placed a kiss on her wet head.

"We didn't know, baby. We didn't know you were out there all alone," Bitsy said.

Tristan felt comforted knowing that his mother was looking after Josie. But he wished his father would hurry so that it could be his arms around her instead of Bitsy's frail and shaking limbs.

Daniel finished with Tristan and wrapped the wound with a bandage. Tristan bent his elbow and flexed his arm as if trying it out for the first time.

"Dad, check on Josie," Tristan said. "She may be in shock."

As Daniel took a seat next to Josie, Tristan followed. He knelt in front of her, the water from his jeans creating a new puddle on the tile floor. Daniel checked her vital signs and asked her simple questions, which she responded to robotically.

"She's responsive. Just needs some dry clothes and rest."

"Where is Monica?" Bitsy asked.

Josie's eyes snapped closed and she let out another cry.

"She's gone. She's dead," Josie said. "And it's my fault."

"No, it's not. She saved you," Tristan said.

Tristan slid Josie into his lap and he held her until their breaths became synchronized. One by one, Alex, Bitsy, and Daniel left the room. Alex said nothing as he passed. He simply squeezed Tristan's shoulder, letting the gesture say everything that he couldn't. *I'm sorry. I'm here.*

Tristan's legs were numb, his feet prickled with pins. The kitchen cabinet dug into his back, but he would not let Josie go. When she finally fell asleep, he carried her to his room and held her through new nightmares.

(

Two days later, Josie was finally feeling human again. Tristan's parents had been very sympathetic and accommodating. Bitsy seemed eager to cook for and entertain her houseguests. Josie felt cared for and safe in this place. She wanted to carry that feeling with her always.

Josie made her way down the curved wooden staircase and smiled at what she found there. Tristan and Alex were in an embrace. The two had grown closer through this ordeal and she was happy for it. They both meant the world to her.

"It's been proven relationships that begin with a shared traumatic event never last," Tristan said, smiling.

"Relationship? I don't wanna marry you. Not my type, *papito*," Alex answered, pinching Tristan's cheek until he was swatted away.

"You sure we can't take you to the airport, hon?" Bitsy asked.

"Nah, I got a cab," he said.

Josie cleared the bottom step and slid between the two men.

"Aye, *mami*. What am I gonna do now, huh?"

"You could stay here, you know," Josie hedged. "Start over."

As an adult, Alex had always been free to come and go as he

pleased, answering only to his mentors on the streets. The one day that wasn't his was Sunday. On the Lord's Day, his mother insisted that he attend church and visit with his brothers and their families. In the past, Alex had always loathed those days, feeling trapped by the traditions and customs of a dying generation. After this experience, he'd learned the importance of afternoon barbecues and quality time with loved ones. He would never take them for granted again.

He knew Josie didn't have any of that back in San Diego. So while he was going to miss her, he understood her wanting to stay here. This was the only family she had left.

"Nah, you know this city can't hold me."

Josie nodded and threw herself into his arms. Her feet hovered above the floor as he swayed back and forth before setting her back down to earth.

"Thank you, Alex, for everything. There's nothing I could ever say that wo—"

"No worries, Jo," he said, smiling. "Take care, *mocosa*."

A horn honked outside, and in an instant he was gone.

Josie sat on the end of Tristan's bed and eyed the designer bag at her feet. It seemed to stare up at her and demand attention. Inside were clothes, two pairs of shoes, toiletries, makeup, and this month's *Elle* magazine—probably purchased at the airport. It was all Josie had left of Monica Templeton.

She didn't know what to do with the bag, but after ignoring it for days, she couldn't take it anymore. Anger erupted from her.

"Why her?" she shouted to the empty room.

She stood and kicked the bag, watching it fly across the room and hit the door.

"She was good," she said.

She followed its path and kicked it again.

"It's not fair!" she shouted as she kicked the bag a third time.

This time shoes, the magazine, and a toothbrush came tumbling out of the bag. Josie dropped to the carpeted floor and sat staring at the items. She wanted to pick them up and put them away. But the thought of touching them made her nauseated.

"Josie?" Tristan called from the door. "What's wrong?"

"I'm pissed off," she said, pulling her knees up and placing her chin on top of them.

He appeared in front of her and sat down.

"I know. It's fine to be angry. It's the second stage of grief," he said.

Josie rolled her eyes and focused on the paint on her toenails. Purple. Pump Up the Jam.

"I know what'll make you feel better," Tristan said. He stood and retrieved her journal from his desk and lay down on his bed. "Come quiz me."

"That won't help," she said.

"Sure it will. Look, I'm a master of distractions. Come on," Tristan pleaded, patting the bed beside him.

Josie stood from her spot and lay on a stack of pillows, flipping through the pages of her purple journal. Tristan lay beside her in the opposite direction, his body pressed against hers at every possible point. He lazily traced patterns up and down her smooth legs.

"I'm going to give you a hard one this time," Josie said.

"Babe, they all have the same level of difficulty to me."

"Fine, page one twenty-two," she said, smiling up at him from behind the journal.

Tristan laughed and pressed a kiss against her calf.

"There's a new girl at school. Her name is Danielle Ryan. We met in English class and instantly became friends," Tristan recited in a high-pitched voice. "She's really pretty and her hair is this gorgeous red color that doesn't seem natural. I'd never ask. I found her sitting alone in the cafeteria and invited her to sit with us. Big mistake! Huge! All she did was smile and flirt with Tristan the whole time. Right in front of me. By the time I finished my sandwich, the girl was practically planning their wedding."

Josie laughed and closed the book.

"I didn't talk like that, ass."

"That's what it sounded like to me," he said, smiling. "There's also a doodle in the margin of a dog wearing a wedding dress on that page."

"You remember everything," she said. "That's amazing."

"You're amazing," he countered.

"As amazing as Danielle Ryan?"

Tristan raised his eyes to the ceiling, as if contemplating the answer.

"I guess. I mean, she had really nice hair. And killer boobs."

Josie threw the journal at him, hitting him in the chest with a thump.

"Ouch! You wound me, woman."

"That's nothing compared to what I'm going to do!"

Josie sprang to her knees and tackled Tristan. She was no match for his strength, but he surrendered. The feel of her body pressed against his sent his imagination running wild.

"You know I'll win this. Just give up," he teased.

"Say you're sorry."

"Never. Danielle's boobs would be hurt and offended if I retracted my statement now."

Josie leaned down, bringing her lips to his ear. Their chests pressed together, their hearts beating for each other.

"Do you care more about Danielle Ryan's tits or being inside me again?"

Tristan sat up quickly, knocking Josie back onto the pillows. He crawled over her and placed a kiss against her neck.

"I'm sorry. I'm sorry. I'm sorry," he whispered against her warm skin.

She smiled up at him and ran her fingers over his hair.

"That's better."

"I'll never mention Danielle and her stellar rack again."

Josie smacked his shoulder as a smirk slid across his face. It pulled the corner of his mouth higher on the left side. It was a smile that Josie knew well. It was teasing and joyous and something that she would never grow tired of.

Later that night, when Josie was sleeping in his bed, Tristan snuck out for a smoke. He sat on the back porch, in the dark, staring out at the trees. Like the last time he'd been there, Bitsy tiptoed across the porch and took a seat beside him.

"She's so different. So sad and hurt, but strong," Bitsy said.

Tristan nodded and exhaled his smoke. "She's everything," he answered.

Tristan felt disconnected from the moment. After everything he'd experienced, he wasn't sure if he would be able to go back to this straight life of family dinners and holiday visits. Not until the sound of his mother crying jarred him from his inner musings. Finally meeting her glassy eyes, his brick wall fell away and he pulled her into an embrace.

"You were gone for so long. I didn't know if we'd ever see you again, but I prayed every day that you were safe and happy. Were you happy, sweetheart?"

"'The reason people find it so hard to be happy is that they always see the past better than it was and the present worse than it is.'"

"Tell me in *your* words, Tristan," Bitsy begged.

"I was happy for a while. Fiona broke my heart, just like you warned she would. I don't think she ever really cared about me. But now I have Josie."

"And you've found your way home."

Tristan nodded and threw his inked arm around the back of the seat, resting his hand on her shoulder.

Daniel watched his wife and son's exchange through the plate-glass window at the back of the house. Even with the rift between them, he could sense that things were healing. The way their bodies leaned toward each other gave him a sense of relief. The warm light cast from the den painted the pair in scattered highlights and soft golden shadows. He smiled, content in the resurrection of that uniting force known as family.

22. NADIR

ON A CELESTIAL BODY, THE VERTICAL DIRECTION
BELOW THE OBSERVER'S FEET.

"I want your papers turned in by Friday. Make sure to really delve
into the underlying struggle between these two societies and cite
your sources, people," the instructor announced as the students
filed out of the classroom.

Alex slid his pen behind his ear and tucked his notebook beneath his arm. Taking a look around the room, he still couldn't
believe that he was here. Surrounded by off-white paint and fluorescent lighting, he found it humorous that he sat among these
young, impressionable kids four days a week. He'd once taken a
vow to never set foot inside another cinder-block institution. This,
however, would be his one exception.

It was the love and encouragement of Erin that had pushed him to do better, to be better. He wanted to be everything she needed and everything she deserved. Not to mention, for the first time in his adult life, he could be a role model. Her son, Parker, watched and mimicked his behavior. The boy looked at Alex like he was a superhero, making him accountable for his actions. Alex loved that Erin didn't try to change him; she embraced all of his bad and his good. It had been his idea to pursue a bachelor's degree in business management. Hell, he'd been managing some sort of business his entire life.

When Alex was younger, he had imagined what it would be like living the straight life. Punching in and out somewhere, paying taxes and collecting social security when he grew old. Though social acceptance appealed to most, it had never appealed to him. The thought alone had always felt suffocating. But when you have someone who holds you accountable, someone who isn't afraid to question you and desire more from you, it's all too easy to amend your aspirations.

In the past year, his relationship with Erin had been slow moving, but for the first time in his life he was okay with that. He loved her quick temper while she embraced his childlike personality. The sex was amazing, like nothing he'd ever experienced before. Erin had taught him to connect on every level, and as far as Alex was concerned, there was no other way to live. They were equals and opposites all at the same time. It was strange to have such a positive outlook on his future, to be so unsure yet unafraid of what was to come. He was free and he was loved, what more could a hoodlum from Logan Heights ask for?

He thought about Tristan and Josie often, marveling at their ability to survive such tragedy and tricky circumstance. He wondered where they were and what their lives were like, but he never wondered if they were together. That was a given.

Confined to the shadows of the streets of Prague, Rob Nettles pulled the gun from his waistband. His pulse thundered in his ears, making it nearly impossible to hear anything else. The index finger on his right hand twitched against the trigger, and he cursed his edginess. Bouncing his head off of the brick wall a few times, he fought to maintain control of his senses, focusing on the pain of the rough brick against his scalp. He wanted to remain entirely aware of what was about to go down. This was his destiny, his death.

In the year since he'd lost Monica, Rob had been focused on exterminating this bastard. He stumbled upon this ring of human trading and child enslavement. He'd heard about it through some punk rookie when he'd returned to Manhattan. Before Monica, the idea of this would have displeased him, but he would have sat back and done nothing. Now things were different. The idea of children being bought and sold and mistreated enraged him. He took it as a severe dishonor to everything Monica had ever worked for.

For months, Rob had been climbing his way through the organization, feigning indifference to the suffering of innocents. He endured so many pain-filled nights alone that he could not survive it any longer. If he thought the world was dark before he met Monica, it was downright abysmal now that she was gone.

Rob had been planning this suicide mission for a while, his resolve never faltering. Finally nailing down the leader's schedule, he waited in the most opportune place for an ambush. The man would be vulnerable for a few seconds, and with Rob's accuracy, a few seconds was all he needed. The only problem was that the man's guards would then descend upon him.

Echoing footsteps signaled their approach, and with self-loathing conviction, he stepped from the shadows and nailed his target before being perforated by their retaliation. He smiled at this, exhaling long and slow. He welcomed their punishments, each bullet bringing pain and absolution. He silently begged for forgiveness and pictured his Button's smiling face. Rob embraced his death and all that it offered him, peace and the end of heartache.

(

"What makes them glow?" Josie asked, leaning against the scratchy bark of the old tree and trying to follow the fireflies.

"'A type of chemical reaction called bioluminescence. The enzyme luciferase acts on the luciferin, in the presence of magnesium ions, ATP, and oxygen to produce light,'" Tristan answered, running his hands over her denim-covered thigh.

Josie rolled her eyes and smiled at him, showing that she loved his superior intellect just as much as she loved his handsome face. She watched him watching her and no longer feared judgment or rejection. She loved having his eyes on her, among other things.

"Do you think we'll ever be too old to climb this tree?" she asked, looking down at the ground.

"Yeah, one day," he answered. "But then we'll come and sit beneath it. We'll enjoy the shade and think about the days we spent up here."

"Hmm, that sounds promising," she whispered, leaning forward and capturing his lips.

There was no frenzied groping or sexual expectations, only chaste exchanges of love.

"Do you think I'll ever get my memory back?" Josie asked.

"Well, we've tried the reminder effect of reliving memories

through stories, and that didn't work. In most cases, memories only come back by spontaneous recovery. After this long, the odds are that your memories may never come back."

Josie sighed and watched the sun set behind the trees. Fiery gold and orange painted the sky.

"Are you okay with that?" Tristan asked, concern lacing his voice.

"Yeah, I'm fine. I accepted that a long time ago. As far as New York goes, I don't want to know those details. I've got you and your family to fill in the good stuff."

When Josie's skin chilled from the night air, they climbed down from the comforting branches and headed inside. Dinner was amazing, as always. Bitsy had been taking cooking classes and loved using the two as guinea pigs.

"Where's Dad?" Tristan asked, shoving another forkful of food into his mouth.

"He's on call and had to go in for a while. I guess you'll see him in the morning," she said, smiling sweetly.

"So, Tristan, how are classes going?"

"Great," he answered. "I tested out of the lower-level classes, and with my schedule I'll be graduating by this time next year."

Josie smiled at him, radiating so much pride. She didn't understand how Tristan had been led astray by Moloney, how he'd sacrificed so much. Then she reminded herself that it had been for the love of a girl that he'd done those things and suddenly it was much easier to comprehend.

"That's great, sweetie. And you, Josie?"

"I'm good. I'm doing a mural for this bank downtown. It's weird to be doing legit painting in the middle of the day. Art classes are a breeze, but the general ed classes are fucking killing me."

Josie slapped her hand over her mouth before mumbling an apology to Bitsy.

Bitsy nodded and they all went back to their dinner. When the food was finished and the dishes washed, the three of them sat in the den around the television.

"You two don't visit enough," Bitsy announced during a commercial break.

"Ma, not again," Tristan begged.

Josie giggled as Bitsy hit her son with the glare that only mothers possessed.

"Don't 'Ma' me, Tristan. I know school keeps you busy, but I expect at least one visit every month. You only live across the river. You could call more too."

"Okay, okay," he relented. "You heard from Dad?"

"Yes, he won't be home until around midnight," she answered.

Bitsy looked around, as if searching for onlookers, before rising from her chair. She sauntered toward the two, a devilish grin on her face.

"Can I tell you two a secret?" she whispered.

The pair looked on in curiosity as Bitsy began to unbutton her jeans.

"Mom! What the hell are you doing?" Tristan exclaimed, mortified by the thought of his mother undressing before him.

"Oh, calm down, Tristan. I just want to show you this."

Bitsy inched down her jeans to reveal a small red heart tattoo on her left hip. There was a white banner across the heart proudly displaying the name Daniel.

"Holy shit!" Tristan yelled.

"That is awesome!" Josie replied, inching forward to get a better look. "Damn, you're legit now!"

Bitsy laughed and refastened her jeans before settling back down into her chair, more than satisfied. Tristan sat motionless, just staring wordlessly at the space where his mother had been.

"Tristan? What the hell?" Josie asked, nudging his shoulder.

"Uh, what?" he asked, finally snapping out of his daze.

"Just don't say anything to your father, he hasn't seen it yet."

Tristan nodded, still reeling from seeing ink on his mother's skin. He wanted to pinch himself to make sure this wasn't a dream. Bitsy Ducote Fallbrook, daughter of Mr. and Mrs. Samuel Ducote III, winner of Miss Teen Louisiana and debutante of high-society clubs, had a tattoo.

"It looks like it's almost healed. How did you keep it from him?" Josie asked.

"Well, I've made excuse after excuse why we couldn't have sex. Usually, we have quite a healthy sexual—"

"Oh my God!" Tristan yelled, covering his ears and running from the room.

The two women burst into a fit of giggles over Tristan's theatrics. They laughed until sharp pains jabbed at their ribs and then laughed some more.

A few hours later, Tristan tucked himself into bed beside Josie's small warm body. The room was still unchanged since his high school years, though the scenery had improved greatly. The thin strap of her shirt had fallen down her shoulder and he praised the garment for framing her skin so beautifully.

Josie sighed contentedly and buried her face in his chest. She inhaled him as her fingers slid around his waist and up his arm. She lingered on the small scar on his biceps, pressing down on it before moving on. The feel of his bare skin beneath her hands made her hum in appreciation. Josie couldn't imagine existing in any place other than his arms.

"It's so bizarre to have you here in this bed," he said softly against her hair.

"You say that every time."

"I mean it every time."

Josie traced the curve of his forearm with her fingernail, before turning her face up to kiss his chin. She slid her leg up and over his hip.

"Have you ever had sex in this bed?"

Tristan laughed. "No."

A scheming smirk graced her pink lips as her hand continued its southward journey. She placed a kiss below his ear, her hot breath fanning over his skin.

"Do you want to?" she purred. "It could be a first we could share. One that I would remember."

Every reason that Tristan had concocted as to why this was a bad idea evaded him, and before either of them had a grasp on the situation, he had Josie's body pinned beneath him.

"Oh, you'll definitely remember it," he responded, smirking crookedly at her. Tristan ducked his head and ravished her mouth with kisses. The tiny moaning sounds coming from her throat drove him to devour her even more affectionately.

"I love you," she whimpered. "To the moon and back."

"Only 477,800 miles' worth of love? I love you that much times a googolplexian."

"That's not even real," she said, giggling.

"It is too. It's the largest number with a name."

Tristan placed kisses along her neck and collarbone before kissing her lips again.

Josie's hands flew to his grown-out hair, pulling and tugging at the coal-black mess. He hummed in approval and rocked his hips. Starting at her feet, Tristan bathed her entire body in kisses and tasteful benediction. He let his teeth scrape over her skin, trailed by his tongue, which refused to be left out. There wasn't one part of his anatomy that did not hunger for Josie.

"Stop teasing," she pleaded.

This was a new first, something they would share and equally recall. He wanted every detail of it to remain clear and unhurried. He wanted Josie to treasure it always.

After they'd exhausted every pleasure to be had, they settled beneath the cool sheets, curled together like woven ribbons. Tristan let his fingers roam Josie's satiated body. Just as his hand trailed from her knee up to her thigh, the clouds parted and the most beautiful moonlight bathed their bodies through the open window.

He was reminded of the lunar beams that had revealed Josie hiding among the iron railings of her fire escape not so long ago. Just as it did then, the light seemed to reveal and bind them to each other.

Josie sighed and pulled herself closer to Tristan. She ran her hand up over his hip, past his fingers, and around his biceps. She watched as his breaths became slow and steady as he drifted off to sleep. His face was perfection as far as she was concerned— hair that she loved to run her fingers through, eyes that always saw through her bullshit, and lips that spoke words of adoration. The feel of his body wrapped around hers was intoxicating and she couldn't remember ever wanting anything or anyone more than she wanted him. But what was most intriguing was what lay inside this amazing, complicated man. All of his memories, his intellect, his unwavering love and devotion for a girl like her is what made Tristan her perfect and beautiful addiction.